THE FIRE STONE

The "Stone Collection" Book 3

NICK HAWKES

Hawkesflight Media

The Fire Stone

First edition published in 2019 *(v.1.1)*
by Hawkesflight Media

ISBN 978-0-6481103-7-8

www.author-nick.com

Cover Design by Karri Klawiter

The Fire Stone

A novel

by
Nick Hawkes

Chapter 1

Spray shot up into his face as he hurtled through the water. He stamped on the footbrake and squeezed the front lever.

Perversely, the motorbike's rear tire skidded sideways.

Something whipped against his neck.

He had a momentary sensation of the bike flying out from under him—and everything going black.

A searing pain across his neck heralded his return to consciousness. It was a brutal way to learn he was still alive. The man gritted his teeth and attempted to look around to determine where the danger lay.

Blurry shadows blocked the light flickering through the tree canopy.

The biggest shadow moved.

Threat assessment? Unknown.

He moved his hands and explored the pain on his neck. No gaping wound. That was good. He flexed different sections of this body—arms, hands, legs, and feet.

Nothing broken.

The bigger shadow moved again. He blinked—trying to focus.

The shape began to resolve itself into a human being—still blurry.

Could he fight?

He tensioned his muscles. Probably.

He waited, willing his senses to return.

"Geese, mate, that's gotta hurt. You alright?"

Genuine concern.

The man exhaled. "Yeah, I think so."

Neither of them said anything for a while.

The stranger held out a hand. He was dressed in dirty jeans, scuffed Blundstone boots, and a sweat-soaked singlet. His hair was unkempt, and a beard hid most of his face.

Blood-shot eyes looked at him with concern.

The man took the proffered hand and allowed himself to be pulled to his feet.

The stranger looked him up and down. "You got a name?"

He didn't answer immediately. "Val," he said eventually. "You?"

"Waldo."

Val took off his helmet and began to explore the wounds across his neck and chest. There were no deep cuts, just bloody welts.

The stranger lent forward to inspect Val's wounds. "Locals know not to ride motorbikes through a lignin bush. Worth rememberin'."

Val turned and examined what it was that had unseated him. He'd never seen such a bush before. There were no leaves, just long stems that erupted from the ground. Val fingered one of them. It was tough and flexed like a fiberglass rod. The stems were hard, spare, and brutish. It was little wonder he'd been whipped off his bike.

Waldo walked over to the Yamaha, heaved it upright, and kicked down its stand. Val joined him as he began to check the bike for damage. The handlebar and forks looked straight. It seemed as if the bike had sustained little damage other than a scratch or two to add to the many it already sported. Waldo pointed to the gear lever. "Your gear lever is bent pretty bad. Everything else looks okay."

2

Val looked a the bike and grunted. "Dammit. It's not my bike."

"No worries, mate. I've got a vice bolted to the fender of the truck. You can take the lever off and straighten it." He stood up. "I'll get the toolbox."

Val turned and noticed a tired-looking Bedford truck partly loaded with timber posts. It was parked in a clearing forty meters off the track. A chainsaw and a can of petrol stood on the end of the truck-bed.

"Here you are, mate." Waldo dumped the toolbox down beside the bike with a jangling rattle. He grinned. "I'll let you do it. So if you bust it, it will be your fault."

Val nodded his thanks and began experimenting with a couple of spanners before selecting one that would unbolt the gear lever.

Waldo sat himself on a fallen tree trunk and began to roll himself a cigarette. "Wotcha doing out here, then?"

"Reminding myself how to ride a bike. It's been a few years." Val pried the gear lever off its spline. "The bike belongs to the farmer I'm working for. He lent it to me so I could get to work."

"Who you working for?"

"Shafers. I'm driving their dozer—carving out a dam for them."

Waldo picked a strand of lose tobacco from the tip of his tongue. "I know 'em. Done some work for 'em meself." He replaced the cigarette in his mouth.

Val glanced at him. He couldn't help but feel that the cigarette presented a significant fire hazard. The tip of it glowed amid a graying tangle of whiskers.

"You picked a remote place to learn to ride."

"I live pretty close."

"Yeah. Where?"

Val regretted giving a clue as to where he lived. How much should he say? He inspected Waldo briefly, came to a decision and said, "I live on Shafer's old houseboat. It's moored on the river opposite their property."

Waldo nodded and lapsed into silence. The only noise came from the forest—notably from querulous minor birds harassing a kookaburra.

3

Waldo finished his cigarette and wandered over to the truck. He hefted the chainsaw from the tray, sketched a wave, and set off into the forest leaving Val to his own devices.

Val locked the gear lever into the vice on the front of the truck and rummaged in the toolbox for something that would straighten it. He could hit it with a hammer but instead chose to use a length of two-inch water pipe. It would allow more precision and cause less stress. Val slipped it over the end of the lever and pulled hard.

Ten minutes later, he was satisfied the lever was straight. After bolting it back into place, he sat astride the bike and booted the kick-start. The engine fired into life, startling a sulphur-crested cockatoo on a nearby branch. Its ear-piercing screech caused Val to duck involuntarily as it flapped away.

What now?

Val glanced at the truck. It was partly loaded with posts. Each was a hand-span in diameter and a little over two meters in length. He could hear Waldo's chainsaw howling in the distance. Cutting and loading the posts would have to be hard work for one person. Unsure whether he was doing a wise thing, he dismounted and walked toward the sound.

He had chosen the banks of the Murray River as a place of concealment: a place from where he could watch. The mighty river snaked its way through the dry mallee scrub, bringing a ribbon of stately red gums and dark, flood-irrigated farmland. Vineyards and citrus orchards flourished under its beneficence. But some of the river's wooded floodplain remained wild and untamed—and it was in this wildness that he'd chosen to hide.

At first he'd seen nothing of his surroundings other than places of concealment, fields of fire, risk factors, and escape-routes. But as the days passed, he began to notice the ducks, ibis, and egrets. He watched the majestically plumed nankeen heron, the ring-tailed possums, and the long-necked turtle—and, collectively, they had stilled him. Whilst there was plenty of death in nature, there was seldom malice. And that was so shockingly different from his experiences in life that he'd seized upon its innocence as something salvational.

Away from the river's flood plain, the soil changed color to a rust red, and the vegetation featured the iconic mallee tree. These low, multi-trunked trees thrived with minimal rain. Sadly, too many of them had been cleared to make soldier-settlement blocks—farms that were barely viable. The Shafers, for whom he worked, had told him that they budgeted for drought one year in three. Fortunately, their property also straddled some black soil that could be flood-irrigated.

As Val crunched through the leaf litter, he reflected on the two weeks he'd lived along the river in secret, among the whispers of another people—an ancient people—still telling their stories in the long, elliptical scars on the side of dead trees. Canoe trees could still be seen standing like sentinels among the red gum and sheoak.

Up ahead, he could see Waldo stepping back from the tree he was cutting as it fell to the ground.

The man noticed Val and switched off the chainsaw. "Problem?" he asked, removing his earmuffs.

"Nah. I thought you could use a hand."

Waldo wiped his brow. "That I could, mate."

"How about you cut 'em and I carry 'em back to the truck."

"Serious?"

"Yeah."

Waldo nodded. "Works for me."

Val heaved a newly cut post onto his shoulder and was surprised by its weight. "Geesh, they're heavier than you think."

"Yeah. Sheoak is dense. Termites avoid it. That's why the vine blockies love 'em."[1] He looked at Val speculatively. "But you carry 'em a lot easier than I do. And you ain't no spring chicken. Do you work out?"

Val ignored the question. "Is that what these are for?" Vines?

Waldo nodded. "Yeah. They use 'em for trellising."

Three hours later, a healthy load of posts had been roped down and the truck was bumping its way down the overgrown track through the forest. Waldo had asked Val to ride with him part of the way in order to help if the truck got bogged. Val's bike had been lifted onto the tray top and secured behind the load.

The truck lurched and bucked its way along, giving little evidence of the synchromesh contributing much to progress.

Although the track was beginning to dry out, it was still covered in water in places. It was early July, and the mighty River Murray that cut off the south eastern corner of the Australian continent had been in flood.

Surprisingly, Waldo elected to keep to the forest track rather than make his way to the Murray-Valley highway where the going would have been easy. Val made a comment to this affect.

Waldo crunched the truck into a lower gear. "Well, the problem is; I've a sort of…impediment."

"An impediment?"

"Yeah." He spat out the window. "I was driving a semi-trailer through Melbourne one day, and a tram got in my way."

"A tram?"

Waldo nodded. "I lost my cool and pushed the tram out of the way with my semi."

"You did what!"

Waldo grinned. "Yeah. The passengers weren't too happy. I've been banned from driving for life."

"Gee. How do you get on, then?"

"Oh, I live by myself where I can't do no damage to anyone and drive tractors for the local farmers. I'm currently working on breaking my record for the longest time I can drive without sleep."

Val shook his head. "How do you manage that?"

"I take 'uppers'[2] and listen to dirty stories on CDs."

Val couldn't think of much to say after that.

Waldo finished the conversation for him. "So I've got to take the back roads." He shrugged. "I haven't got no license."

Val nodded. He didn't admit that he too had no license. It was impossible to have one if you wanted to stay anonymous.

Chapter 2

"Gert; move your arse." Sebastian banged the garden gate into the rump of the pig that lay across it. Water from the recent rains had collected on the dirt path making it a favorite place for Gertrude to wallow.

The pig grunted and heaved itself to its feet.

Sebastian waited for it to move off. Six years laboring on a Mallee farm had taught him not to rush. He gazed across to the sheds behind him. The ute was gone.[1] That meant his boss, Geoff Walsh, was not yet back from Swan Hill. He'd gone in to get a new pinion bearing for a wind pump.

Rusted farm implements, trucks, and cars stood beside the shed —their glory days long gone. Weeds grew up through them and tumbleweeds blown by summer winds lay trapped beside them. Behind the shed lay a giant windrow of mallee roots. They'd been collected from the land clearances. The piles of roots formed a protective windbreak on two sides of the farmyard. They also provided a fuel store for Mrs. Walsh's range cooker. She was in a race to burn the wood before the termites ate it. The race was leisurely; it had been going on for decades.

Sebastian stretched his back and breathed in the winter air. The morning frost had given way to a perfect sunny day.

Gert lumbered over the farmhouse lawn and settled in the puddle beside the rainwater tank.

Sebastian made his way to the veranda, removed his boots, and pushed past the screen door into the kitchen. He was hungry. He'd been on the tractor pulling the scarifier since sun up. A slight hangover had resulted in him skipping breakfast. He sniffed the air appreciatively. Lottie always provided a midday meal for anyone working on the farm. It was the main meal of the day. On other occasions Sebastian catered for himself in the shearer's quarters.

"G'day, Lottie. What's cooking?"

Lottie stood up from the range cooker. "Wash your hands."

"Yes, mother." He made his way to the laundry.

"Don't be cheeky," she yelled after him.

He glanced at the mirror above the sink. A young man with long unkempt hair and a sandy-colored goatee stared back—his brown eyes at odds with his sun-bleached eyebrows. His arms could be seen —tanned and well muscled. He wore nothing above his waist other than a green work-shirt with its arms ripped out. Sebastian rubbed at the stubble on his chin. His image seemed to accuse him. He'd turned twenty-four and had precious little to show for it.

Wash your hands: such an innocent comment. A wave of anguish swept over him. He closed his eyes and braced himself against the edge of the sink. When he opened his eyes, he could see the bandage that still protected the stump where his little finger had once been. Sebastian remembered very little of the night he'd lost it —just the pain. It had pierced his drunken haze and caused him to scream into the gag pressed against his mouth. The shocking brutality of the attack and senselessness of it had left him feeling vulnerable and… Tears began welling up in his eyes. *What the hell was going on?* He screwed his eyes shut and quashed his emotions brutally. *Stupid, stupid, stupid!*

He hadn't been able to tell the Swan Hill police very much.

"Did you know your attackers?"

"No."

"Do you do drugs?"

"No."

"Do you owe anyone money?"

"No."

"What did you see of your attackers?"

"Two men, both big, with scarves wrapped around their faces. Dark clothing."

"Age?"

"Young enough to be strong. Otherwise, no idea."

"Where had you been that night?"

"Drinking in the Commercial Hotel."

"Do the people in the pub know you?"

"Yeah. I drink there most weekends."

"And you were planning to drive home—even in your drunken state?"

"No. I sleep in my swag in the back of the ute."

Sebastian pulled himself back to the present, set a carefully neutral facial expression, and walked back into the kitchen. He bent down by the range cooker and scratched the chin of a white and tan Jack Russell.

"G'day Mitch."

The dog had backed itself into its favorite winter hidey-hole— the plate-warming alcove of the cooker. Some time in the past, its door had fallen off. Mitch gave what passed as a wag of the tail—his clouded eyes looking up at Sebastian even though he could barely see.

Lottie was an inveterate carer. Sebastian suspected that she was in crisis now her two sons had left the farm. Evidently, neither of them was very keen to take on such demanding work for so little return. One son had joined the navy, and the other was an apprentice diesel mechanic in Mildura. Being a person who needed to be needed, Lottie had compensated by collecting an assortment of animals to care for. Her menagerie currently consisted of Getrude, who was more pet than pork, Mitch, and Scat. Scat was an orphan kangaroo joey. Lottie had nursed it for many weeks carrying it in the pocket of her apron. The joey was now too big for the pocket, not that it stopped her trying to get into it. That's how it had earned its name. Lottie had always needed to yell, 'scat.' The young kangaroo was currently sporting a red waistcoat. Evidently, young joeys were susceptible to chill. Goodness knows where Lottie had got that information.

As he settled himself at the table, Lottie ladled dollops of lamb stew onto a plate and placed it before him. She sat opposite him with a portion half the size.

"Geoff called," she said. He's going to be late. He's asked if you could move the sheep from the forty-acre and bring them down to the home paddock. He wants to load them first thing in the morning."

Sebastian blew on the potato at the end of his fork. "Okay."

Lottie tilted her head sideways. "You're looking a bit seedy. What time did you get in last night?"

"Late."

"Sebastian McKenzie, it's high time you got yourself a good woman and settled down."

He glanced up at her. "There's only so many clichés I'll let you get away with, Lottie."

"Seriously."

He sighed. "There's no such thing as a good woman any more, Lottie. You were the last of them."

She rolled her eyes and leaned forward to place two slices of bread into the toast rack. Sebastian had made the rack out of fencing wire for her some years ago. She'd used it ever since.

He reflected with some bitterness that he had a very poor track record when it came to relating to women. The brief relationships he'd experienced had relied on him being drunk enough to strut his bravado in front of a girl, and the girl being drunk enough to respond and acquiesce. None of them were too keen next morning when they discovered he was just a farm hand.

Just a farm hand? Sebastian chewed on his piece of bread pondering the unfairness of that comment. He felt its injustice, not so much for himself—he was a relative newcomer to the Mallee—but for others who had worked here for generations. The farm hands he knew could read a sheep's condition just by looking at it, knowing when it was right to sell. They could fix a tractor, diagnose crop pests and diseases, handle heavy machinery, shear a sheep, wire a shed, and get themselves to work before most bankers and solicitors had woken up in the morning. On top of that, they had the unique privilege of being able to 'feel' the land. Those who worked it saw soft mornings when the dew glistened like jewels on a newly emerged crop. And they knew the seasons and movements of migratory birds such as the rainbow bee-eater. The bird's return from the north heralded the start of summer. Farm workers knew the land in all its beauty and harshness.

"Sebastian!" Lottie shouted. "Where have you gone in that head of yours."

He smiled apologetically. "Sorry Lottie; a lot on my mind."

"Humf!" I suppose you're too caught up with your thinking to be interested in some rhubarb pie."

"Your rhubarb pie is why I still choose to live."

"Oh spare me." She got up to fetch the pie. "And while I've got your attention, can you mend the lid on the header tank on top of the house. Geoff's always promising to do it but never gets round to it. I saw two galahs having a right old time splashing about in it yesterday. Goodness knows what bird-shit's coming through the hot water."

"I'll take a look at it after I've brought the sheep down."

"Thanks, Dear." She poured custard over Sebastian's serve of pie. "As you'll be leaving us soon, I have to make good use of you while I can." She sniffed. Lottie's sniffs were always eloquent. "Oh, I nearly forgot," she continued. "A parcel arrived for you this morning. It came by courier from Swan Hill. Must be important." She pointed to it. "It's on top of the meat safe."

After lunch, Sebastian fetched the quad bike from the shed and drove over to the kennels under the pepper tree. Both kelpies, Jackson and Millie, began barking with excitement.

He released the dogs from their pens.

Jackson immediately attacked Millie, and the two kelpies tumbled together in a brief fight to celebrate the joy of their freedom. Jackson then broke away to pee on the back wheel of the quad bike. Millie leaped up onto the front carrier rack, turned, and licked Sebastian's face.

"Gerroff!" he sputtered, wiping his mouth. Millie cocked her head trying to read what Sebastian wanted her to do next—impatient for work.

He looked round for Jackson and saw him exploring the smells coming from the bitch's box.

"Jackson. Git behind!" he yelled.

The dog bounded over to the quad and jumped onto the rear tray.

Sebastian kicked the quad into gear, and the three of them set off down the track.

———

Sebastian stuck his head through the kitchen door. "All done, Lottie. There shouldn't be any more bird shit in your coffee."

Lottie had flour up to her elbows and was rolling dough on a marble slab. She blew away a strand of hair that fell across her face. "Thanks, Dear. I could hear you clomping around on the roof. Thought you'd come through it."

Sebastian turned to go. She called after him, "Don't forget your parcel."

"What? Oh yeah…Right-oh."

"And take one of those muffins with you."

Back in his quarters, Sebastian sat on his bunk and turned the parcel over in his hands. He saw from the labeling that the parcel was from Norseman. Did he want to open it?

He laid the parcel on his chest and gazed at the ceiling. It was lined with hessian that had come away in several places. A huntsman sat half way up the wall, behind his head. The spider was almost as big as his hand—grown fat, no doubt, on the insects attracted to the light.

Mr. Norseman was a link to his father—now deceased, and remembering his father was not something he liked to do. But

Norseman had shown extraordinary generosity over the years and never required anything from Sebastian in terms of personal engagement. The man had held a short-term commission in the army before working for a mining firm as a geologist. He'd then struck out on his own, prospecting for minerals and diatomaceous earths in central Australia. Whenever he found them, he put together a company to mine them—and then sold the company off. Sebastian had learned all this from emails he'd received over the years. One of them explained how Norseman had met Sebastian's father.

I became friends with your dad in the army. He helped fund my first start-up company and asked nothing in return other than to look out for you if ever there was need.

After the death of Sebastian's father in prison, Norseman was true to his word and provided funds for Sebastian to do his high school education at Pulteney Grammar in Adelaide. After leaving school, Norseman had asked Sebastian to contact him if he ever needed help with higher education costs.

I've done very well—thanks, in part, to your father. And as expensive as it is to live in Sydney, I have little enough to spend it on.

Sebastian suspected Norseman did not have a family of his own.

Although emails from Norseman were infrequent, the two of them kept contact via chess. They'd been playing each other for years via the Internet. Sebastian had lost consistently in the early years but now won as often as not.

The huntsman lifted a leg, and then put it down again —delicately.

Sebastian weighed the parcel in his hands and then opened it.

Inside was a letter and a small package protected by bubble plastic. He read the letter.

Sebastian,

You tell me that you hope to pick up the Engineering, Planning, and Design course you were offered six years ago.

Sell this to cover your education costs. It's worth about $200,000, so you'll have a bit to put toward a house. It's a Koroit nut opal—one of the best specimens I've seen.

Contact this mining company (see below) and organize for them to put it with their stock going to the next gem auction in Dubai. They'll courier it there and organize its sale for a commission. It will cost you twenty percent. Don't let them charge you more.

The contact details of the mining company were written below. Norseman had signed off with typical brevity: *Norseman.* He'd written a P.S. on the bottom.

Look at the opal...and you will know why I call it 'The Fire Stone.'

Chapter 3

Pip was not sure she was ready for Adelaide. Eight weeks of buses, trains, and trekking through the most northern state of India, the Middle Kingdom of Himachal Pradesh, had ruined her taste for the West.

She chained her pushbike to the bike-rack and stood for a while, looking at the busyness of Rundle Street. Its pavement cafes were already filling up with people seeking breakfast and coffee.

What was it that bothered her about it? Was it the loudness of the adverts extolling things of no consequence? Was it the mannequins in the stores making fashion statements that were absurd? She thought ruefully that it was probably the sheer abundance of provisions. The options on display in the supermarkets seemed obscene after days spent in villages where there were only a few tiny shops built of stone and rusted tin. For all their humble simplicity, you could nonetheless sit at a trestle table and eat a delicious meal of *dham* served with *mash daal*—even if it was served on a plate made from leaves.

She'd loved the people of India—so friendly. They chatted happily with each other and were deeply engaged in each other's affairs—in marked contrast to the behavior of relationally anxious Westerners staring into their smartphones.

She was being unkind, and she knew it. Part of her brain told her that her feeling of displacement, grief, and anger would pass. The siren calls of Western comforts, conveniences, and conventions would soon become normal to her again.

But for now, she missed the beauty and grandeur of Himachal Pradesh and its scenic mountain villages. She recalled how the morning light would bathe the snowy peaks above the Spiti Valley in gold. The land had entranced her.

Pip sighed, squared her shoulders, and walked into the café behind her—*Little Sister*.

A few patrons were already sitting at tables savoring their coffee and biting into their pastries.

Mario, the café owner, had his back to her and was stretching up to pour coffee beans from a bucket into the chrome hopper of the roasting oven.

"*Ciao, Mario*," she called.

Mario turned, put the bucket on top of a sack of unroasted beans, and held out his arms. "*Ciao bella*," he cried and embraced her with a hug. "Welcome back. This place runs better with you here." He held her by the shoulders at arms length. "But you look thin. You need to eat."

Pip patted Mario's stomach. "And you need to go easy on Nonna's cooking."

He shuddered. "No one says no to Nonna's cooking. Ah, but look at you—skinny." He let her go and wagged a finger. "And you still don't look the part. Why won't you dress like a waitress, eh?"

Pip made her way behind the counter to check there were no outstanding drink orders clipped above the coffee machine. "I'll dress like a waitress on the day you commit to ethically sourced coffee beans."

"*Mia bella*," he protested, "my priority is the best, wherever it comes from."

Mario routinely complained about Pip's dress code. It was a long-standing argument, comforting in its predictability. Pip had sought to explain that the café was only two-hundred meters from the front gates of Adelaide University, and that students were looking for a café with individuality and character. Today, Pip had chosen to wear a black tee-shirt and jeans held up by braces. The bottoms of the jeans were rolled up to reveal her suntanned calves and Doc Marten boots. She'd pulled her hair back into an untidy knot, which meant that her tattoo would be showing. It sat high on her back at the base of her neck. It was a simple red rose. Her mother had died two years earlier of cancer, and it was her way of remembering.

Mario muttered something inaudible as he made his way back to the roasting machine.

There came a squeal behind her and a shout. "Pippy: you're back!" Pip turned to see Tiffany advancing on her with arms out wide. "Daahhling, I've so missed you. It's been hell without you."

Pip was not at all sure she wanted to know the hell Tiffany was currently in. She usually had several to choose from at any one time.

Tiffany's mercurial mind suddenly changed tack. "And are you okay for this Saturday? They want the Mendelssohn. Honestly! So passé."

"Yes, I'll be there…" began Pip but she was interrupted.

"Oh, I've so needed you here." Tiffany dropped her voice to a whisper. "I've met this guy…"

Pip groaned inwardly.

Tiffany fell in love with any young man who came into the café on more than three occasions. She would usually herald her infatuation by choosing to draw a heart in the froth of the man's cappuccino, prior to serving it to him personally.

Pip was spared any more details by the arrival of customers. Soon, everyone was busy.

Little Sister was all about coffee. If anyone was in any doubt about this, all they had to do was view the coffee pots, grinders, and percolators of every conceivable shape and size displayed on the shelves around them. Sacks of coffee beans were also stacked against the wall beside the roasting oven. They were stamped with the names of the places they'd come from—Rwanda; Brazil, India;

Sumatra; Honduras; Panama; Costa Rica; Mexico; Zambia; Ethiopia; Kenya; El Salvador; Guatemala; Antigua; Brazil; Dominican Republic; Columbia; and Indonesia.

Mario roasted his own coffee beans. The roasting oven and cooling bin provided both ambience and theater in the café. Customers loved to watch—children particularly. The beans were fed into the oven from the hopper. Once they were roasted they dropped into the cooling bin where they were stirred with a mixing arm until they were cool enough to collect. Sadly, occupational health and safety strictures required the delicious smell of roasting beans to be vented via a metal chimney to the roof.

Mario boasted that his coffee blend was the best in Adelaide. Pip suspected he was right. Significantly, the café was popular with old Italian men. Pip glanced at her watch. They would begin arriving in half an hour. They'd greet each other effusively then settle down to argue over the events of the world and reminisce over the glory days of their youth. Pip loved them.

Over the course of the morning, Tiffany brought Pip up to date with the affairs of her heart and her music. Tiffany was beautiful to look at, with super-long blond hair that she showed off to good effect. She had modeled herself on Guinevere. Prints of paintings featuring the medieval queen in a diaphanous shift, with knights kneeling at her feet, adorned the walls of her apartment.

"He comes in at eleven. I'll point him out."

"Have you actually conversed?"

Tiffany bunched her fists and hissed, "No, of course not."

"Then guard your heart, Tiff. Go steady. The poor guy doesn't even know that you're making a play."

She scoffed, "Oh! You don't understand."

Pip was very much afraid she did. Tiffany inevitably frightened off any man who showed interest by her intensity and demands. She was the most insecure person Pip had ever met, and one of the most talented. Tiffany played the violin with fantastic verve and virtuosity. She and Pip were in their final year at the Elder Conservatorium, 'the Con,' as it was known. It was where the two of them had met. Pip's chosen instrument was the cello. She loved its warmth and dignity. It was dark honey drizzling from a spoon. She and Tiffany occasionally played in a quartet for weddings. It was a useful way of earning extra money. But Pip was under no illusions: the group would soon disband. The Adelaide orchestra was already showing interest in Tiffany. Pip sighed. No one showed any interest in her. It looked as if she would end up teaching—the fallback position of all frustrated performance artists.

"There he is," said Tiffany. She bounced up and down on her toes as she shook Pip's arm.

"Steady, girl," warned Pip. She had been heating up a tin jug of milk with the steam pipe.

"Oh, I can't bear it. He's fabulous."

Pip glanced up and saw a man with long, dark hair sit down at a table and remove a laptop computer from a shoulder bag.

Tiffany clutched Pip's arm harder. "Pippy, could you ask him if he's interested. You always know what to say to people. Please. Just for me?"

"Certainly not. It's your love life, Tiff. You sort it out."

"Please, please. I'll do one of your shifts next week."

Pip sighed, knowing that she was never going to hear the end of it. She looked at her friend with exasperation. "You take over here. I'll go and take his order. But I'm not promising anything."

Tiffany balled her hands into fists and shook them in triumph.

Pip approached the young man with a notepad. "If you're studying English lit, then I recommend the Columbian coffee. It has a mellow acidity and a strong caramel sweetness. If you're studying law, go for the Kenyan coffee, it's as aggressive as hell and will keep you up all night."

The young man smiled. "And what is the usual house coffee? I liked it last time."

"It is a blend that Mario keeps secret, even from his wife."

"I'll have a long black of the er...house coffee."

"Right-ho. Anything to eat? The almond croissants are fabulous."

"Okay, I'll try one."

Pip nodded, and then said as casually as she could, "A girl in here thinks you're pretty hot. I've been sent to check you out."

The man blinked, leaned back, and regarded her with a smile. "My, my, this is an interesting morning. Who is she?"

"The blond behind the counter."

He tilted his head to look past Pip. "Hmm, she's very...striking."

"Well?"

"What's she like?"

"Honestly?"

"Hmm."

"She's intense and talented...and the sort of girl who gives pet names to her car."

The man nodded slowly. "I'm not sure I've got the energy for that."

Pip smiled. "You can thank me later for saving your life." She turned to go. "I'll let her down gently."

The man held up a hand to forestall her leaving. "But what about you? What's your name?"

Pip weighed him up and decided the man was harmless and basically nice. Nice people got more information. "Pepita Albright. They call me Pip."

The man drummed his fingers on the table and looked at her speculatively. "Well, Pepita Albright, I don't suppose you'd...?"

Pip patted his arm. "Don't even go there. I've got to live with her."

He smiled. "A pity."

"Well?" demanded Tiffany as Pip stepped behind the counter.

"He's gay," she said.

Chapter 4

The houseboat was moored front-on to the bank, held secure
by two bow lines and two stern lines. The vessel was small and
scruffy. There was little evidence of anything being spent on main-
taining her over the last few decades. However, the little Evinrude
on the back still worked. This allowed Val to motor across the river
and moor the houseboat away from Shafer's land under the trees of
the forest that grew on the river's southern floodplain. Val pottered
across the one-hundred meters of river every morning to get to
work; and every night he returned again to the forest's isolation.

The boat's remote location was not without its benefits. The
surroundings were magnificent. Trees framed the languid river as it
meandered through the flatlands of the Mid Murray. The river was
now retreating after the floods and was once again confined
between its banks. Plenty of water remained, however, in the creeks
and hollows of the forest making the tracks within it all but
impassable.

Val had finished early on the bulldozer, as the dam was now
complete. His boss, Mr. Shafer, could now only offer employment
on a part-time basis. He'd advised Val to find extra work elsewhere.

The wind was still. The trees were perfectly reflected on the river's surface. Val sat down on the deck and dangled his feet over the edge of the pontoon. Forty meters away a spoonbill was working the shallows, moving its beak back and forth in search of shrimp. A few meters further on, a straw-necked ibis stood above its reflection, perfectly still. Waiting. *A bit like me.*

Val leaned forward and pulled at a chord dangling over the side. Presently, a galvanized dip tin broke the surface. Water streamed out of the perforated holes in the tin to reveal three yabbies. The small lobster-like crustacea snapped and flicked their tails as Val tipped them into a bucket. They would form the basis for his dinner tonight. He moved the dip tin further aft and lowered it back into the water. The chop bone in the bottom of it had not yet been picked clean and would attract yet more yabbies. If he didn't get any more of them he could almost guarantee some shrimp—useful as bait when fishing for carp.

Val stood up and removed his jacket. With the whole afternoon at his disposal, he could begin his daily exercise routine early. He walked down the gangplank to the fire pit on the riverbank. The plowshare he'd been using as a cooking plate sat on a heap of ashes. He picked it up, held it above his head, and bent from side to side. Once he was warm, he began his routine of twists, kicks, and punches. *Krav maga* was a no-holds-barred mixture of martial arts developed by the Israeli military. He'd chosen it because it was not a discipline aimed at self-defense. It taught people to kill, and to do so without thought—as a reflex—a reflex he'd practiced over and over again. He remembered the words of his instructor: 'Your aim is to neutralize your opponent. Dead is safest.'

Forty minutes later, he'd finished. He knelt down on the edge of the river and splashed his face with water.

What next? It was a perfect afternoon. He put his hand in his pocket and pulled out a frayed white handkerchief. Cupping it in both hands he whispered, "Tell me what to do," before putting it to his cheek. He remained motionless for many minutes. After a while, Val leaned back and blinked away a tear. As he did he noticed the canoe that had been lashed down on the roof of the houseboat. The sun had bleached its green gel-coat, and he suspected it hadn't been used for years. He returned the handkerchief to his pocket, unfastened the canoe, and hefted it down to the foredeck. Val inspected inside the hull with a torch to check it was free of spiders and snakes. The brown snake was the second-most venomous snake in the world, but they were usually shy. The same could not be said of the tiger snake.

Soon, he was on the water paddling upstream close to the shoreline. The trees along the edge had been partially undercut by the water exposing a convoluted tangle of roots of giant red gums. Occasionally he passed a tiny shed housing an irrigation pump. Most had mud swallow nests attached under their eaves. There were similar nests under the houseboat between the pontoons. He'd found them when hiding a long parcel he needed to keep safe.

Val paddled upstream, pushing himself hard—seeking the exercise it gave. After thirty minutes of paddling, an old hump-backed caravan came into view on the northern bank. He decided to use that as his turning point. But as he got closer, he spotted a familiar figure sitting in front of it on a trunk by the water's edge.

Val angled across the river to say hello.

"G'day, Waldo. So this is where you live."

Waldo put down a plastic bottle he was fiddling with and grinned. "Yeah, mate. This is my hacienda."

"Nicely simple, and a great view."

"It's bloody ramshackle—deliberately so. Waldo spat into the river."

"Deliberately so?"

"Yeah." Waldo rubbed the back of his neck. "I says to myself one day: Waldo, you're a mean drunk. You'd better sort yourself out."

"So you've stopped drinking?"

"Hell no! I choose to live 'ere by meself where I don't do no one no harm. I just smash up my own place."

"Oh, right." Val tried to think what to say next.

Waldo spared him the need. "Look mate, do me a favor: paddle over to that snag over there and tell me if me drum nets is showing."

"Snag?"

"Snag—it's what we calls them bloody great tree trunks that fall into the river. Them and the reefs—the mud banks in the river—were a pain in the arse for the early paddle-steamers. One of 'em's wrecked over there." Waldo pointed to the southern bank. "You can still see some of its timbers when the water level is low. The Captain's swearwords are legendary, even to this day."

Val paddled over to the snag Waldo had pointed to. Sure enough, he could see the humped arches of two drum nets in the crook of its largest tree branches. Val made his way back to Waldo.

"Yeah, mate. They're showing."

"Bugger. The fisheries officer might see 'em. I'll have to move 'em."

"How will you do that? You've got no boat."

"I swim."

"I'll move 'em for you if you tell me what to do."

"Nah, mate. I'll do it later. S'gotta be done right."

Val decided that Waldo might be a good person from whom to learn the finer arts of fishing in the Murray. He was a little weary of eating only carp. "I've dropped a line in a few time and can't get anything to take the bait except carp. I'd hoped to bag a Murray cod. Got any tips?"

Waldo laughed. "Mate, ninety percent of the fish in this river are carp. Bloody pests. That's why the bloody river looks so brown: they stir up the bottom."

"Doesn't anyone catch anything else?"

"Oh yeah. There's redfin, yellow-belly, and catfish. But the best is cod." He kissed his fingertips. "S'beautiful."

"How do I catch 'em?"

Waldo pulled his hat down onto his head and stood up. "If you come in, I'll show ya."

Val beached the canoe, pulled it up the bank, and walked over to where Waldo was standing near the trunk of a tree. He was holding a spade. Val watched as Waldo scraped the bark and leaves from the base of the tree. He then cut away the top inch of soil.

"Come 'ere," he said. "Do you see them holes in the ground?"

Val leaned over. He could see that Waldo had exposed three holes in the soil, measuring about three-quarters of an inch in diameter. They appeared to be lined with a gray cardboard-like material. "That's not a trapdoor spider hole is it?" he asked.

"Nah, mate. That's a bardi grub. They're the larvae of the rainmoth. It's a bit like a witchetty grub. Cod love 'em." Waldo picked up what looked to be a length of brake cable. A partly unwound metal spring had been braised onto one end. He dropped the spring end into the hole until it could go no further, twisted it and pulled it out. Hooked on the end was a large fleshy grub."

"Here ya go, mate," said Waldo showing it Val. "Get some of these guys, an' go fishin'. It'll improve your odds."

Val nodded his thanks.

"D'you wanna beer? I owe you for the other day."

"Yeah. That would be good." Mindful of what he'd learned of Waldo's drinking habits. He added. "One would go down well."

With a beer in hand, Val made himself comfortable on the log by the water's edge while Waldo tended to a small fire burning in front of the van. After placing a billie-tin onto the coals, he joined Val on the log.

Val gazed across the river, appreciating its stillness. "It's not a bad place, this, eh?"

"Nup. S'good."

Silence.

"The bird life's fantastic."

Waldo nodded. "S'all right. Have you seen the sea eagle?"

"No."

"There's a pair nesting in a dead tree in the lake back behind here. You can see 'em any time of the year."

The two of them lapsed into silence again.

Eventually Waldo asked. "How come you're not working?"

"We finished digging out the dam. Shafers can only give me part-time work. So I need to find more work. I don't suppose you've got any ideas?"

"What sort of work?"

"Any, as long as it pays in cash."

Waldo laughed. "People only ever get paid in cash around here. No one could get anyone to work for 'em otherwise." He took another pull at his beer. "The local farms sometimes need a bit of a hand. Valencia oranges are being picked, and the vine blockies are still pruning. You'll always find work with them at this time of year."

"Yeah? What's the work like?"

"Repetitive. You'll be cutting up, pulling out, and wrapping down—and doing it hundreds of times over. You'll be knackered at the end of your first day."

"You don't do it?"

"I got arthritis in me hands. Can't go more than a few days when I have to stop."

The sound of a high revving engine could be heard in the distance.

Waldo looked up. "Someone's coming."

Val picked up his sunglasses and hat from behind him. He'd placed them beside Waldo's collection of bottles behind the log. For some reason, Waldo had taped a stone onto the bottom of each of the plastic bottles with gaffer tape. Val put on his sunglasses and pulled the rim of his hat well down at the front. He nodded toward the bottles. "What are those for?"

Waldo was watching a speedboat come creaming round the bend of the river. "Eh?"

Val pointed to the bottles.

"Oh, them. I'm fishing."

The speedboat throttled back and was now coasting into the bank in front of them. Wash from its wake started to surge against the riverbank.

Waldo lifted his feet to avoid getting them wet. "Bloody holidaymakers."

Val was not at all sure they were holidaymakers. The three men in the boat were all very large, and nothing about them suggested they were holidaying. There were no water skis, fishing rods or eskies of beer. One of the men had a camera with a telephoto lens.

As the boat nosed into the shore, the man at the wheel said, "Who are you guys?"

"Who's asking?" said Waldo, ignoring the rope that had been thrown to pull them ashore.

The man gunned the engine and ran the bow of the boat up the mud.

The cameraman in the back of the boat started taking pictures of both Waldo and Val.

"Put that bloody camera down, you bastard," shouted Waldo. "You don't photograph anyone without their say-so, and you don't come to a bloke's fire without permission. Bugger off."

The man at the wheel held up both hands placatingly. "Sorry, mate. It's just that we've been asked to find a bloke who lives around here—a loner. We need to tell him one of his relatives has died. The post office reckons he could be around 'ere. You wouldn't know of such a bloke, would ya?"

"I'm born and bred 'ere mate, and I seen no one." He cocked a thumb toward Val.

Val held his breath.

"...and me mate 'ere is from Shafer's farm." Waldo turned to Val. "You seen anyone new?"

Val shook his head.

Waldo continued. "If we find your bloke, where can he find you?"

The big man appeared nonplussed by the question. Eventually he said, "Swan Hill—at the Riverside Caravan Park."

"Right-oh."

"Do you mind if we have a look around," persisted the big man."

"Yes, I bloody do," said Waldo. He picked up one of his empty soft drink bottles and began filling it from a white plastic container.

The man at the wheel stood up. "Look, mate; I've tried to be polite. Get out of our way, or I'll squash you like a bug."

Waldo directed a stream of invectives toward him, and began shaking the bottle.

All three men were now on their feet beginning to get out of the boat.

Waldo lobbed the bottle into the water under the boat's stern.

The explosion, when it came, was so powerful that it knocked Val off the log.

He shook his head and groped toward the log for support.

Once he'd regained control of his senses, he spun round in a crouching position ready to fight. But there was no need. One of the men had been thrown into the water, and the boat was half swamped. The other two were trying to pull their friend back into the boat whilst clutching their throats and coughing.

As the man was hauled on board, one of his helpers turned and spluttered hoarsely, "We'll be back for you, you bastard."

By this stage, Waldo had scampered back to the van and reappeared with a shotgun. He discharged two shots into the branches overhanging the boat, causing twigs and leaves to rain down on its occupants. "Piss off," he yelled. "And don't come back."

The men ducked for cover and backed the boat off the shore. A moment later, it was scything round in an arc and speeding back along the river.

Val removed his sunglasses and rubbed his eyes. "Geese, mate. What the hell was that?"

Waldo lent the shotgun against the log. "That, my friend, was calcium hypochlorite. It's used for sterilizing swimming pools. I had the stuff in the bottom of the bottles. I just added some brake fluid, screwed the cap on, and dropped it into the water." He sounded pleased with himself. "It will explode, typically, in twenty-five seconds—depending on the temperature."

"You nearly killed them."

He waved a hand dismissively. "Nah. They'll be all right... although their lungs might be a bit sore for a few weeks." He sat down. "You've got to be careful not to breathe in the phosgene gas afterward."

Val raised a questioning eyebrow.

"It was used as poison gas in the trench warfare of World War I. Killed eighty-five thousand people, evidently."

Val whistled. "And you just happened to have this stuff ready to hand?"

Waldo grinned. "You're not the only one who has trouble

getting a fish to take a bait." He pointed to three fish lying belly up on the surface of the water. "Like I told you, I was getting ready to go fishing."

Val couldn't suppress a laugh. "You'll have to teach me to do that some day."

Waldo shook his head. "No way."

"No? Why?"

"It will kill you or maim you if you play with it. That's not a probability: that's a guarantee. Don't mess with it if you value your life."

"But you do it."

"As I say, no one does it if they value their life."

Val expressed his breath slowly.

The birds that had been startled by the explosion began to return to their roosts, and peace, of a sort, returned to the river.

Val reflected on the disturbing words of his host. Eventually, he cleared his throat. "I could come next Saturday with some roo to barbecue, if you'd like some company. It's top of the tail—the best."

Waldo scratched his crotch. "I usually get dunk on Saturday if no one's around, so yeah. I'd like that. Better not bring any beer. It wouldn't do me no good."

Val nodded.

The two of them watched as the shadows lengthened and the light began to fail.

Val got to his feet. "Better get back, mate. Thanks for the beer."

Waldo held the canoe steady as Val got into it. As Val slid into his seat, Waldo said quietly, "Those bastards weren't looking for me; and you'd better hope they weren't looking for you. They don't look too friendly."

Chapter 5

Clat. The screen door banged shut behind Sebastian as he padded through the laundry into the kitchen in his socks. "Morning Lottie."

Lottie was arranging storage jars on the kitchen table.

"Put the kettle on Dear. Geoff said to wait for him here. You might as well have a brew."

"Oh yeah? Where's he gone?"

Lottie wiped her forehead with her sleeve. "He got so riled up at seeing a mob of the neighbor's sheep in his top paddock again that he's finally doing something about the fencing. So he's picking up a bloke from Shafers' who is looking for some work." She placed a mug in front of him. "Geoff reckons there's about a week's worth of work for the two of you. He wants the fencing overhauled over the whole farm."

"Geoff and I could have done it."

"Normally, yes. But he's getting his foot done this afternoon. The doc's told him he'll need to keep off it for a while." She reached for the kettle. "And I told Geoff it wouldn't be good for you to do it on your own. Fencing is tough on hands."

He looked dumbly at his left hand, hating its deformity, hating the memory.

Twenty minutes later, Sebastian heard the dogs barking as the ute rattled through the yard and headed up toward the shearers' quarters. He got up from the table, put on his boots, and made his way after it. He felt ambivalent about sharing his sleeping quarters with a stranger. Having company was a good thing, but it was always a bit of a lottery as to what type of character you ended up sharing your bunkhouse with. Now that he was in possession of a two-hundred thousand dollar opal, he could not suppress a pang of anxiety. He'd wrapped it up in bubble plastic and put it in a leather travel pouch on his belt. The pouch would be under his pillow at night.

The Fire Stone—Sebastian had spent a long time looking at it. The gem was mesmerizing. Flickers of flame leaped out from a background of blues and turquoise as if a primal sea was on fire. It seemed to draw him into a world of secrets. The stone was the size of a large quail's egg and had been polished so that it was perfectly smooth. Could an opal really be worth so much? Its value opened up a world of possibilities, and yet the thought of selling it, of parting with something so extraordinary, so beautiful, was unthinkable. What minerals, and what ancient seas had been trapped within it millions of years ago? What was its story?

Sebastian brought his thoughts back to the present and climbed up the worn wooden steps into the corrugated iron shearer's quarters. He could hear Geoff speaking.

"The water is rainwater, so go steady with it. And the dunny is outside, round the back." Geoff turned as Sebastian came in. "Sebastian will tell you where everything else is."

The stranger was bent over his rucksack, removing his wash-kit. He paused for a second before he clipped shut a small padlock that secured the zip on his rucksack. As he stood up, Sebastian held out his hand. "G'day. I'm Sebastian. We'll be working together this week."

The man held out his hand. "I'm Val," he said in a gravelly voice.

Sebastian felt the stranger's eyes run over him, pausing briefly at the sight of Sebastian's left hand. Sebastian moved it out of sight and continued to speak. "The kitchen's got a fridge. There's fresh eggs from the farm and some mutton chops—not much else."

The stranger nodded.

Geoff broke in. "Pick up your sheets and blankets from Lottie tonight, and give her any washing you have."

"I've brought a sleeping bag," the man said.

Geoff waved his hand. "Lottie wouldn't hear of it. Let her look after you." He glanced at his watch. "I have to clean up and get into Swan Hill." Geoff turned to Sebastian. "There's a new roll of eight gauge fencing wire in the back of the ute. You know where the rest of the gear is, so I'll leave you to it."

Sebastian nodded and turned back to the stranger. Val was of average height and looked to be about fifty years of age. Gray flecks could be seen in his close-cropped beard and over-length hair. His face was deeply tanned. Perhaps it was this that caused his gray eyes to appear so surprising. Although the stranger's face looked benign enough, the rest of him did not. A half-length oiled coat failed to hide his heavily muscled frame. The sheer physicality of the man was disturbing.

Val looked around the bunk room. "Nice and simple."

Sebastian nodded. "Yeah. No TV."

"So what do you do in the evenings?"

"I read." Sebastian pointed to the Kindle lying on his pillow. "I can fit a thousand books on that."

"What do you read?"

"Anything and everything. I find most fiction pretty pointless, so I tend to read biographies—sometimes a bit of philosophy."

Val raised an eyebrow.

Sebastian shrugged. "Just trying to make sense of things." He switched the conversation to a safer subject. "Have you done any fencing before?"

"No."

"There's not much to it. You'll pick it up pretty quick." Sebastian hoped he didn't sound as patronizing to Val as he did to himself. He cleared his throat and continued. "We'll head down to the shed. We'll need fencing pliers and the chain wire strainer. And I'll find you a pair of gloves. You'll need 'em."

Soon they were barreling along the dirt track up to the top paddock, the ute juddering across the dirt corrugations. They came to their first gate. Sebastian never failed to wonder at the creative variety of farm gates in the Mallee. The first one they came to was simply a loose section of fence that had been pulled across the gateway. It was levered into place with the length of pipe hanging on the gate-post. Val managed to work out how it functioned without help.

It wasn't long before they came across their first broken fencing wire. Sebastian guided Val through the steps of making a repair.

"Make a loop on the end of the broken wire, then feed the new wire through the loop bending it round so you make a figure of eight knot. The knot will become tighter the harder you pull."

Val did as he was instructed.

Sebastian nodded his approval. Val had strong hands and managed to twist the wire easily without using the pliers.

"Now grab the wire strainer; clamp the end of the broken wire into the tail unit of the strainer; then put the end of the new wire into the ratchet end." Sebastian reached for the ratchet lever on the strainer. "All we do now is operate the lever until the wire is tensioned. Then we tie the end of the new wire to it. Simple."

It may have been simple, but it was not easy work. Wire had the habit of behaving perversely when not under control. Sebastian waited for Val to show signs of tiring, but he worked steadily, doing the lion's share of the physical work without demur.

"What causes the fences to break?" asked Val.

"Panicked stock, a big roo; quite often an emu."

"An emu?"

"Yeah. A one-hundred-and-twenty pound emu running at forty miles an hour can do a bit of damage. And they're really stupid. I once saw a bird bounce off a fence, then get up and run into it again, and again—like a yo-yo. I reckon he'd still be there if I hadn't moved him on." Sebastian found himself wanting to impress this strange man—and wasn't sure why. He knew he was speaking too much. "There's a big male emu that's often around. He's a grumpy old sod and can frighten you to death when he comes pounding up. We call him Oigle. One of these days I'll shoot the bastard."

"So you do some shooting?"

"A bit. Rabbits mostly. They'll get away from you if you slack off. We use a bit of 1080 poison; shoot a few; and hope like hell that the latest Department of Agriculture biological control virus still works."

"What gun do you have?"

"I use Geoff's. It's a Savage .22." Sebastian pointed over the fence to a dillon bush. "The rabbits build their burrows under thorny bushes like that. Makes 'em hard to get to. Soon as they hear a shot, they all run under 'em." He scratched his stubble. "What I really need is a silencer—a suppressor."

"They're illegal."

"Not many policemen out 'ere, and the Savage is threaded to take one."

Val said nothing.

"A guy in the pub said you could make your own suppressor with a series of plastic drink bottles."

Val paused from twisting the new wire into place. "Don't do that."

Sebastian was slightly irked by Val's assumption of authority. "Why?"

"Just don't. A bullet can do odd things if it hits anything—even quite small—just after leaving the muzzle."

Val's words disturbed Sebastian. The man had been content to sit under Sebastian's tutelage, but had stepped out from the shadows briefly to assert himself. It changed the feel of the relationship he was trying to establish.

Unsure of what to say, he turned his attention to a flock of ibis flying east toward the salt lakes.

The two men continued to patrol the fences together, stopping now and then to effect a repair. Where possible, Sebastian drove on the edge of a paddock that was fallow where there was less chance of being bogged. He glanced across the fields as he drove. The farm always looked good at this time of year. Everything was green. He was glad to see that the birds hadn't done too much damage, and the wheat was tillering nicely.

When everything looked this good, it was hard to think of leaving the farm. He grunted. It was a darn sight easier to contemplate during the brutal months of summer when the paddocks contained nothing but dust and sun-bleached stubble. It was a cycle —a senseless cycle—a demanding one that totally controlled his life. He wondered for the umpteenth time what the point of it was. Everything seemed meaningless—a waste of time. You plant a crop; and have to do the same thing next year. Alternatively, you could go to uni—get on the treadmill, but why? He banged the steering wheel irritably. Get drunk. Wave your fist in the face of it all.

The other part of his brain continued to work on the matter at hand. Sebastian looked out at a distant fence that ran between two paddocks sown to wheat. The land dipped at that point and there was standing water along the fence-line. He pointed. "We're going to have a tough time getting to that section of fence."

Val raised a questioning eyebrow.

"We'll walk there with the gear if we have to, but first let's find out if we need to."

"How are you going to do that?"

Sebastian grinned. "I have a little trick." He reached behind the seats and pulled a box from the parcel shelf.

Moments later, he'd set up a quadcopter drone on the tail-gate of the ute.

Val turned one of the drone's four rotors round with a finger. "What sort of range does this have?"

"About two kilometers. It has brushless motors, so it's pretty efficient. But you haven't got long. The lithium batteries only give me about five minutes. That's why I carry a few of 'em."

Sebastian fitted the display goggles over his eyes. "This lets me view what the camera sees—to see what a pilot on board would see." He picked up the control unit, and seconds later the little drone was zipping down the hill to the far fence.

"Gee, it's quick," said Val.

Sebastian ignored him and concentrated on the liquid crystal display. He decelerated the drone and began side-slipping it along the fence so he could see the wires. Two minutes later, he piloted the drone back and landed it in behind the ute.

"No busted wires," he said as he pulled off his goggles.

Val nodded. "Impressive."

They got back into the ute and continued to patrol along the farm's fences.

A few minutes later, Val interrupted Sebastian's reverie. "What sort of training do you need to work a farm like this?"

"You need a frontal lobotomy."

"Seriously."

Sebastian thought for a moment. "Not the sort of training you get at college, that's for sure."

Val raised an eyebrow.

Sebastian marshaled his thoughts. "You've got to know how to dong a brown snake with a long-handled shovel, and how to treat a sandy rise so it doesn't blow away in a dust storm."

"That's it?"

"And a few other things."

"Maybe you could teach me a few of 'em."

Sebastian had the feeling Val was deliberately deferring to him. He decided to take advantage of it. "Farming here is no picnic. Summer is hot as hell, and we have to cope with droughts."

"But you still manage to grow stuff."

"Yeah. Just. We work a three-year rotation—wheat, barley, and peas. Sometimes we grow medic instead of peas or leave the field fallow for sheep. It's all about balancing water, soil nutrients, and weed management."

"Do you see your future in farming?"

Sebastian shook his head. "Nah. Farm workers like me are a dying breed. Not many farms can afford us any more. Farmers would rather rely on sons to work the farm for minimal pay knowing that they will inherit some day. And there are fewer farms now. They're being amalgamated to increase profitability through economy of scale. Geoff will be selling this one in the next five years."

"That bother you?"

"A bit. Someone's got to stop the place becoming a weed-infested rabbit warren, someone who understands the land."

They drove back to the farmhouse for lunch.

Scat, dressed in her red waistcoat, watched them enter the kitchen from the doorway to the lounge. Whilst the little kangaroo loved Lottie, it had always been wary of men. Sebastian was not surprised to see her hop away into the lounge when they appeared.

Fortified by Lottie's shepherd's pie, they set off to work once more, picking up the routine they'd established in the morning.

"What will you do when you leave the farm?" asked Val.

"I deferred my uni course, but you can only do that for two years before you have to re-apply. I've been told to make an appointment to see them." Sebastian stood up, stretched his back and gazed over the farm. He loved its stillness—particularly in winter. The only sound came from the wind and the warbling of magpies in the trees. Winter brought a few months of welcome respite from the flies that normally crowded at the corner of his eyes and mouth desperately seeking moisture.

They also loved wounds.

Sebastian fingered the stub on his left hand.

He shivered, knowing that he needed to leave this place, this place he'd called home for so long. It was a place where strangers attacked and mutilated.

"You all right?" asked Val.

"What? Oh, yeah. Fine."

They worked together without saying anything for some time.

Eventually, Val broke the silence. "So where do you come from originally?"

"Adelaide."

"So your dad wasn't on the land."

"No. I'm not sure where he was from."

"You're joking."

"He died when I was young." Sebastian did not want to say anything more. Most kids could boast about their father. He never could. How could you tell anyone that your father had been sent to prison for murder, and had died there. Sebastian hated the shame of it—and hated being alone. His mother had died a year before his father was imprisoned, so the bastard had deserted him at the time of his greatest need. Sebastian was shocked to hear himself say, "He abandoned me to the world of men when I was six."

"The world of men?"

"I was abused by my first foster father."

There was a long silence.

Sebastian tried to understand why he'd shared that information. It was the first time he'd ever done so. He held a fist to his forehead. *You idiot.* He'd allowed his anger at his father to spill out?

Val cleared his throat. "I'm sorry to hear that."

Sebastian breathed out slowly. "Nah. She's right. The second foster-carer was better, and the third one was great. Stood by me even when I got into trouble."

Silence.

The magpies continued to warble.

"And how are they treating you here?"

"What? Geoff and Lottie?"

"Yeah."

"They're great. Geoff's tough but fair. He's the brother of my last foster carer. That's how I came to be here." He snorted. "The hope was that it would straighten me out. And Lottie has a heart of gold. She's a Mallee girl through and through. She once tied a knot in the tail of a brown snake as it went through a hole in a fence paling of her chicken coop. She left it there for Geoff to kill when he got home.

Val lay on his bunk with his hands behind his head mulling over the events of the day. He was on his own. Sebastian had decided to go with Lottie into Swan Hill to visit Geoff who was recovering from the operation on his foot.

Outside, the wind moaned and sighed around the chimney stack. He glanced at his watch. Sebastian wouldn't be back for at least three hours—plenty of time. He got up and fed some broken bits of mallee root into the pot-bellied stove. Smoke occasionally puffed out from the edge of its steel door when the wind gusted.

Val lifted his rucksack onto the trestle table and removed a long bundle wrapped in toweling. He laid it on the table and undid it to reveal the rifle.

The Barrett 98B was chambered to accept the 300 Winchester Magnum round. The gun was rugged, easy to operate, and accurate for over a mile. Equally important, it could be stripped down so that it would fit into a rucksack. Val had left the Schmidt and Bender 3–27 scope on top of the Picatinny rail but the stock had been folded forward; and the rifle's barrel removed.

He squeezed the take-down clip to remove the bolt assembly. A moment later, the trigger assembly was dismantled.

When he'd finished cleaning and lubricating the parts, Val replaced the bolt and trigger unit. Next, he slid the barrel into place, fixing it into position with the two locking screws.

Val examined the gun critically as it sat on its bipod rest. It was a good gun. Its oversized bolt handle made it easy to operate—essential when he needed to get a number of rounds off quickly. It slid easily in its polymer guide.

Val had set the trigger weight at two pounds so it required only the lightest of touches to set off a round. He'd fired scores of rounds to zero the rifle. A 'dope card' stuck onto the side of the gun now told him the number of clicks he needed to hear as he turned the elevation knob on the scope for various distances.

It was nearly ready for use.

He reached into the rucksack, pulled out the rifle's suppressor and screwed it onto the muzzle. The gun now looked menacing—but it was not yet deadly.

Bullets.

Val picked up a box of match grade Black Hills ammunition and loaded the magazine. *Click, click, click, click, click.*

He pushed the magazine into place.

Now it was deadly.

Chapter 6

Pip wheeled the trolley of chattering tea-cups from the kitchen and positioned it beside the coffee machine. She looked around to check that everything was ready for the next day. Satisfied, she yelled, "I'm off, Mario. See you later."

Addio, mia cara Pepita, he called from the kitchen.

Moments later, she was riding her bike down Rundle Street, dodging the traffic as she headed home. The winter filigree of the oaks and London plane trees lined the road. Some of the skeletal trees still held on to a few of their leaves as if reluctant to part with the past, holding on like the lingering fingers of departing lovers.

Lovers. She reflected with some bitterness that her love life was non-existent. She told herself that she found young men shallow and two-dimensional. Their thinking seemed to orientate solely around sex and pleasure. Pip assembled a familiar list of complaints against them: They were IT savvy, but didn't know who they were. They were idealistic—but not prepared to forego a caffè latte to put anything right. They wanted to change the world but sabotaged these ideals by having the resilience of a snowflake. Their idealism swam in a soup of sentimentality that was uninformed and ungrounded.

Once she'd finished eviscerating the Y chromosome, she discovered that she didn't feel any better.

The truth was; the major impediment to a serious relationship was the sheer pace of life she led. What with her studies at the Conservatorium, her work at *Little Sister*, and playing at weddings, there was little time left to invest in long-term relationships. Young men who expressed interest soon tired of being low on her list of priorities—which was a pity because, by and large, boys were intriguing things, and sometimes interesting.

She made her way to her home suburb of Norwood, ducked down a tiny service lane, and entered the rear of the house via the garage.

The house was one in a terrace of bluestone cottages, each sporting a bull-nosed veranda. They'd been built in the 1880s. The hallway and the front three bedrooms all had high ceilings and solid timber floorboards. A modern extension had added a kitchen/dining/family area at the rear.

Pip's father used the front bedroom as a study. Bookshelves lined the walls either side of the fireplace, and a desk stood against one wall. A wing-back chair sat in front of the lantern window overlooking a narrow strip of garden.

Pip knew that the walls of any home were porous; they absorbed the character and culture of its occupants, and metered it out in their absence. And she loved the feel of the study. She even derived comfort from the noise of the floorboards creaking under the carpet. It was the sound of a building that had stood the test of time. It called to mind tweed jackets, pipe smoke, and dry sherry— and there was nothing she enjoyed more than to fill the room with the sounds of Bach and Beethoven. Pip practiced her cello in the study whenever her father was not using it. His only protest was to hang his felt trilby on top of the cello's scrolled end whenever she forgot to take her instrument from the room.

Her father was in the kitchen when she arrived. He had washing-up gloves on but was perched on a kitchen stool reading a journal.

"Hi Dad."

"Ah. Hello Lovely One." He looked around him. "I'd hoped to have the washing up done before you got home. Left it a bit late. Sorry."

"Did you eat lunch?"

"Um... Thought I'd have a late one. Then it got later, and I thought I'd wait for tea."

Pip recognized the plates from breakfast. She sighed. "What are you reading now?"

He brightened. "Rather interesting, actually. It's an account of an archaeological find made by Professor Eleazer Sukenick and his assistant, Nahman Avigad."

"Hmm," she said, as she made her way to the sink. The water was cold.

"They were excavating the tombs of the Kidron Valley on the eastern edge of the temple mount in Jerusalem, and discovered a tomb that had been blocked by a large closing stone." He pushed his glasses further up onto his nose. "Inside it, were eleven ossuary boxes containing bones." Her father peered down at the article and started reading.

Pip began running hot water into the sink. "And..." she prompted.

"Aah yes. Bones. Yes. Well one of the boxes was inscribed in Greek with 'Simon Alexander of Cyrene'...with slight misspelling of Cyrene." He smiled. "Nice to know our progenitors struggled with spelling too. Anyway, archaeologists think that it is highly likely that these were the bones of the son of the chap forced to carry the crossbeam of Jesus' cross. The man's name is mentioned in Mark, chapter fifteen, verse twenty one."

"Had you planned anything for tea?"

"Um. No. Is there any of your lasagna left?"

"No. We finished that two days ago, the evening I got home."

"Aah, sorry."

Pip kissed her father on the top of his head. Doesn't matter. "I'll rustle up something. Let me have the washing-up gloves." If she was going to practice her cello afterward, she didn't want soft, water-soaked fingers. She was looking forward to playing one of her favorite pieces, Bach's Cello Suite No. 1. The work had a plaintive tranquility, and she felt in need of that tranquility now.

"It's nice to have you back."

"Thanks, Dad."

She reflected on her father with fondness. David Albright was tall, slightly stooped, and thin as a rake. His hair was prematurely gray, and he dressed in clothes that would not have been out of place in the nineteen forties. He was the rector of St. Georges in Magill, the neighboring suburb. Although he was in his mid fifties, this was his first placement in a conventional Anglican parish. Prior to that he'd been a missionary for ten years in Vanuatu. The years of mission work overseas had thrown Pip and her parents together so that they'd enjoyed an unusually close relationship. She'd hated having to part from them for boarding school during term time. Pip sighed. The death of her mother two years ago had been devastating for both her and her father.

After tea, Pip began her cello practice in the study. Having settled her emotions with Bach, she progressed to Brahms—the master melodist. His music would keep her in that gentle place where it was impossible to think much could be wrong with the world.

It had been dark for many hours, but she hadn't drawn the binds across the window. Only the net curtain stood between her and the darkness. She finished the closing chords and sat still, allowing the soul of the music to play with her emotions until it laid her gently on a pillow of clouds.

Beautiful.

She sighed, leaned her cello against the wing-backed chair, and made her way to the kitchen to reward herself with a hot chocolate.

Her father was buried in an armchair—still reading. He looked up as she came in. "Finished?"

"Yes, Dad." She smiled. "You can have your room back."

He got up and wandered down the hallway. A few moments later he was back, clutching another book.

"Would you like a hot chocolate?" she asked.

"Hmm. Thanks."

Moments later, Pip cupped a mug between her hands and made her way back to the study.

She'd almost reached the door when all hell exploded around her. The brutal stutter of a machine gun could be heard above the splintering of glass and the thuds and smashing of destruction. It seemed to go on forever.

Pip dived for the floor, dashing hot chocolate over the hall runner. She put her hands over her ears, curled into a fetal position, and screamed.

Then everything stopped. There was the sound of tires screeching...and she was left in silence.

Only her ears were ringing.

Chapter 7

Val nodded to Sebastian as he climbed out of the ute. "Thanks, mate." It was Saturday morning, and Sebastian had volunteered to drop Val off at Shaffer's farm so he could keep his appointment with Waldo. Sebastian had also agreed to pick him up next morning—a generous gesture as it entailed a forty minute round trip.

"Say g'day to Waldo for me," said Sebastian. "I knew him briefly before he got banned from the pub."

Val sketched a wave and was thoughtful as he watched the ute disappear back down the farm track. Sebastian's ute had two spotlights mounted on the bull-bar and sported a long high frequency radio antenna. He could see it swaying to and fro as the car bounced over the potholes. It made the ute fairly conspicuous. *A pity.*

Val lifted his rucksack onto his shoulders and walked over to the farmhouse.

A few minutes later, he was having a cup of tea with George and Wendy Shaffer. They were having a lazy morning, and George was still in his slippers. "How's the work over at Geoff's?" George asked.

"Going well," said Val. "We're nearly done."

"So what brings you back then?"

"I promised to bring the makings of a barbecue for a bloke I met a few days ago. He seemed lonely. I've come to collect some of the roo you gave me from your freezer, if that's still okay."

"That's fine. Who's the guy?"

"Don't know his surname. He lives in a caravan by the river. Called himself Waldo."

George Shafer froze, and then he folded up the paper he was holding. He looked grim.

"What's the matter?"

"You've obviously not heard."

"What?"

"Waldo is dead. He was found in the water two days ago, not far from his camp—drowned apparently."

Val closed his eyes and rubbed his forehead. "Dammit."

"Are you all right?"

Val was not all right. He was appalled at the news, and very angry with himself. He should have foreseen the possibility, and urged Waldo to be more careful. Guilt stabbed at his heart. He was the one who had brought the killers to Waldo's door. Val knew with absolute certainty that Waldo's death was not accidental.

"What are the police saying?" he asked.

"Still making inquiries. They're keeping an open mind, evidently."

Val drew in a deep breath and said, "I'm very sorry."

The farmer nodded.

"George, after I've finished working for Geoff and Lottie, I think I'll head off, probably to Kerang, and look for work there. So, tonight will be my last night on the houseboat." He leaned back in his chair. "I've enjoyed living on board. Thanks a lot."

George nodded. "Can't say I'm very surprised. I wish I could offer you more work, but..." he shrugged.

As they finished tidying up some financial loose ends, George's wife, Wendy, came into the kitchen carrying an ice-cream container of eggs. "I'm going in to Swan Hill in an hour. Do you need anything Val?"

He thought quickly. "May I cadge a lift and come with you?"

"Sure. But it'll be about two hours before I'll be coming back."

"That's fine." Val turned to George. "Can I use the bike to get down to the houseboat?"

"Of course. Just leave it in the shed tomorrow before you go."

Twenty minutes later, Val stepped back on the houseboat. He looked through the side window to the doormat inside the cabin door. He'd used a piece of string to pull up a corner of the mat so that it rested against the inside of the door.

The mat was now lying flat. Someone had been on board in his absence. He wasn't surprised. Val nodded to himself. The ball was now in play.

Let the game begin.

Wendy drove Val through the flat irrigation land into town. One part of Val's brain noted the long, tin roofed racks used for drying sultanas, the market gardens, vineyards, and orchards. The other part was working on a plan.

When they arrived in town, they agreed on a rendezvous time and parted company. Val walked down toward the river. There, he attached himself to a knot of people wandering along the path that led to the Riverside Caravan Park. He nodded and smiled at strangers—*be a local*—and kept his eyes everywhere.

Val bought an ice-cream from a kiosk and surveyed the caravan park. The speedboat was immediately visible. It was moored in front of some cabins on the foreshore. He sat on a bench behind a family group with children and watched covertly.

Val discovered that there was only so long you could play at eating an ice-cream before it melted over your fingers. He was thinking he might have to supplement it with a coffee when the door of one of the cabins opened and a man in a black jacket stepped out and walked toward the outside bin with a plastic bag of rubbish.

Got you.

Two hours later, Wendy and Val returned to the farm. Val retrieved the motorbike and took it down to the riverbank where he began untying the mooring ropes of the houseboat. Moments later, the little Evinrude was pushing the boat across the river to his sanctuary among the trees. Once he was moored, he set about removing any evidence of ever having camped there. He filled in the latrine and fire pit, and then covered the disturbed soil with leaves. When he came back on board, he took out his phone.

The weather app told him the wind would rise in strength during the evening ahead of a storm front that was expected to bring heavy rain.

Google maps told him that the river was eighty-five meters wide opposite the caravan park.

Once evening had fallen, Val dressed in black jeans and jacket. He transferred the small white handkerchief into his pocket and pulled on some black leather gloves. He motored the houseboat back to the northern bank, shrugged a rucksack onto his shoulders, and walked down the gangplank to the motorbike.

Val motored down the farm track. Occasionally, his headlight picked up the silver reflection from huntsman spiders. To take his mind off what he must shortly do, he did a mental inventory. The light reflected by the eye of a fox was yellow. A rabbit; red. A roo was also red. A sheep was green. Never shoot at a green eye.

The track eventually disgorged him onto the bitumen road where it was easier driving. He forced himself to relax and motored on into the darkness.

Half an hour later, Val turned off the Swan Hill Road onto the dirt track behind Pickering Transport yards. The track led to an open space dotted with occasional clumps of trees. Beyond the open space lay a thick belt of trees that marked the banks of the Murray. He hid the bike inside the tree line and made his way through to the riverbank. It was a deserted place. Just as well, he thought. The eucalypt twigs and leaves he was walking on were brittle, and this made it impossible for him to move without making a noise. He pressed on.

Soon, he could see the lights of Swan Hill reflecting on the surface of the river. He settled down beneath the trees at the river's edge and waited, listening for anything that might alert him to the fact he was not alone.

In front of him, the River Murray turned ninety degrees from the south-east to the north-west, making the river bank on which he stood a headland.

After twenty minutes, Val removed the Barrett from his rucksack and began assembling it—first the stock, then the barrel, and finally the suppressor. He'd practiced doing it blindfolded for hours.

He glanced at the sky. It was still mostly clear. The brilliance of the Milky Way, smudged with its Magellanic Clouds, was clearly evident. The Milky Way, he mused: Scorpius, the scorpion—very appropriate tonight. There were also signs the storm front was getting closer. Clouds were beginning to scud across the sky. He would have to expect the wind to rise.

Val folded down the bipod and peered into the Schmidt and Bender scope. Its fifty-six millimeter objective lens gave him excellent clarity of vision. And he was pleased to note that there was more than enough light coming from the caravan park.

The range was one-hundred meters; much closer than he was used to shooting—almost ridiculously so. He settled down to wait. Patience was everything. You out-wait those you hunt; then visit hell upon them in seconds.

In the event, he didn't have long to wait. Three men came out of the cabin. One of them busied himself at the barbecue whilst the other two sat on bench seats at the nearby picnic table. Val could read the patch on the cut-off denim jacket—'Saracens.' It was hard to kill someone you know, and he didn't know these men personally. However, he was very familiar with the group to which they belonged—and he had no compunction about killing them.

The man nearest to the water's edge leaned back and gripped the edge of the bench with both hands.

Perfect.

The cold shot, the first shot with a cold barrel, would be the most accurate, not that it mattered at this range.

Val centered the cross hairs on the left hand, on the finger, and calmed his heartbeat down. He felt the first pressure on the trigger, then held his breath as he squeezed slowly, feeling for the second pressure. His chest was still, but his heart was still beating. He waited for the split second between the beats, and fired.

Bang! The Barrett kicked viciously. The sound was appalling. It was never as quiet with a suppressor as most people believed it should be.

The man with the shattered finger yelped. It caused his colleague at the barbecue to spin round.

Val worked the bolt instantly and centered the crosshairs on the heart of the man holding the barbecue tongs.

The Barrett kicked again. A second bullet crossed the river at three-thousand feet per second.

Val didn't bother to check the hit. It was a certain kill. He picked up the two spent cartridges, put them in a plastic bag, and pushed them into his top pocket. Calmly, he dismantled the rifle and stowed it away.

Four minutes later, he puttered across the open ground to the track alongside the transport yards.

Val kept to the speed limit, grateful that he only met one oncoming truck on the Swan Hill road. He turned left, and then left again onto Speewa Road without encountering any more traffic. This gave him the confidence to veer off the road occasionally into the water lying in the spoon-drains in order to wash the dust from the killing site off the bike.

Once he arrived back at the houseboat, he threw the spent cartridges into the river and motored across to hide once more under the black fringe on the southern bank.

The rain began to fall as he secured the last mooring line—the rain that would erase all footprints—and cry for the dead.

Chapter 8

Sebastian was a few minutes early driving down the dirt road to Shafer's farm. For some reason, he felt it was important for him to be on time to pick up Val. He wasn't sure why. Val was an enigmatic character who didn't say much, but he found himself drawn to him.

He rubbed the stubble on his chin and yawned. He'd have given quite a lot to be able to be late. The hangover from Friday night had got no better after Saturday night, and his body craved sleep.

Val was standing at the farm gate waiting for him. The man lifted his hand in salute and swung his rucksack into the back of the ute, where he took the unusual precaution of tying it down. As he climbed into the cab he glanced at Sebastian. "Hard night?" he inquired.

Curse him.

Sebastian put the ute into gear, backed the car round, then spun the tires as he took off.

For a long while, his passenger remained silent. The man's lips were compressed and he tapped a forefinger absent-mindedly on the dash.

They drove south through the black lands out into the sand

country. The winter sun was still low and so the mallee trees beside the road were casting lancing shadows across the track. Long strands of bark hung from the trunks revealing the new wood, shining like bronze in the morning sun. It should have been a magical morning—if his head didn't hurt so much.

Sebastian swerved to avoid a shingleback lizard making a perilous journey across the road.

The move seemed to wake Val up from his thoughts. The man took a deep breath and said, "Sebastian, do you mind if we have a bit of a talk?" He pointed to a farm gate up ahead. "Perhaps you could pull in there."

Unsure of what to expect, Sebastian did so.

Val got out of the ute, pulled at a stalk of grass and leaned on the farm gate.

Sebastian joined him.

Some galahs started to squabble and shriek in the trees beside them. One slipped and half somersaulted on its perch, screeching indignantly—careless of the two men nearby.

Nothing was said for a while. Then Val removed the grass stem he was chewing and said, "I'm afraid I have two fairly big surprises for you, Sebastian, and I wish there was an easier way of telling you."

Sebastian stood up from lounging on the gate. "What?"

"Have you lost anything recently?"

"What on earth?" A faint suspicion began to dawn. Sebastian felt for the leather pouch on his belt, opened the flap, and removed the small parcel inside it. Sebastian turned away from Val as he undid it. When he did, he did not uncover the brilliant splendor of The Fire Stone, but a piece of ordinary stone. He swung round to Val. "What the hell? What have you done? Did you steal…?"

Val held up a hand to forestall the torrent of outrage, put his hand into his top pocket, and removed The Fire Stone. He held it up to the morning sun, causing the flames inside the stone to flicker and dance.

Sebastian reached for the opal, but Val pulled his hand away and closed his fist around it. "You were pretty drunk on Friday night, so it wasn't hard to remove it."

Silence.

Val continued. "The Fire Stone deserves a better owner than a drunken farm hand whose life is going nowhere." He lifted the stone up again to the sun. "This stone could change your life, but I very much fear you will simply piss it against a wall. So, tell me: do you think you are, and will be, a worthy owner of this stone?"

Sebastian's mind was in a whirl. "How do you know this..." he pointed to the stone. "How do you know it is called 'The Fire Stone?'"

Val said nothing.

Then realization dawned. "It's because you're...."

Val nodded. "Yes, I'm Mr. Norseman."

"You're kidding me."

"Our chess game: you took my rook last Thursday, but you'd better look out, because I'm about to take your bishop...and that will be 'check.'"

"But, but...you've been in contact with me for years...providing for me. I, I..." Sebastian couldn't find the right words to say.

Val held out the stone to Sebastian. "Take good care of it, and let it change your life."

Sebastian nodded dumbly as he took it.

The galahs continued to shriek and squabble.

Val turned back to the farm gate and continued to chew on his piece of grass.

Sebastian leaned back on the gate. He wished he could look as nonchalant as his companion. What was coming next?

"I have something else to give you, and this might be another big surprise."

Sebastian stiffened. What could possibly be a bigger surprise than the one he'd already had?

Val again fished in his top pocket and produced a small plastic vial with a screw lid. Floating in the faintly yellow liquid, was the end of a finger.

Sebastian's mouth dropped open in shock.

Val took his foot off the bottom rung of the gate and faced him. His voice faltered. He cleared his throat and said. "Your little finger was mailed to a post-office box at Yowah—that's a tiny opal-mining town in central southern Queensland. I used to visit the town once a fortnight to get supplies."

"That's where The Fire Stone came from?"

Val nodded. "The thing is…" he cleared his throat. "They sent it to me to flush me out of hiding."

Sebastian furrowed his brow. "Why would you be hiding? And why would my finger…" he trailed off.

"I wish there was an easy way to break this to you, Sebastian." Val drew in a deep breath. "They sent it to me, knowing that I would respond…because I am your father."

Sebastian demanded explanations. He ranted. He said it was not true. He said Val was playing a sick and cruel joke. He yelled, he threatened, and finally he sobbed. "How could you say such a thing. My father is a murderer. He was imprisoned when I was six, and died three years later." He clenched his fist and screamed, "He's dead, and I've hated him for years."

Val didn't try to stop him. He just stood there, ashen faced, looking grim.

When Sebastian's tirade finished and he'd run out of the energy to say anything more, Val lowered his head and said quietly, "I don't blame you for hating me. It's understandable."

"Understandable," screamed Sebastian. "How dare you patronize me with that sort of crap! It's bullshit. That's what it is."

Silence.

Eventually, Val began to speak. "I was there at your graduation ceremony at school, when you won dux of the class, and another prize for physics." Val shrugged. "I had to be there, even though I was meant to be dead.

"You were there?" Sebastian asked incredulously.

"You had grown a rat's tail—which I'm surprised the school let you wear—and you had a look of defiance about you when you held your prize for being dux aloft. Do you remember?"

He did. Sebastian had wanted to show the nerds who couldn't believe he was in their class, that he'd beaten them. He remembered only too clearly.

Val nodded. "There's a whole lot that needs to be explained, and I promise I'll do so, but I'm afraid that we have to move pretty smartly right now and get away somewhere safe."

"Why's that?" demanded Sebastian.

"Because the people who want to kill me have successfully flushed me out of hiding, and they will get to you in order to get to me." He compressed his lips. "I'm afraid this is serious, and we have to leave—today. In an hour, if possible."

"What?"

"Afraid so."

"Where shall we go?"

"What's the status of your university application?"

Scarcely believing he was taking anything Val said seriously, he found himself saying, "They said I need to go for an interview. They are interviewing this coming week, and again in two months time. I'd planned to go in two months."

"Can you ring up the uni and make an appointment for this week?"

"I can try."

"And how long will it take you to pack your things and square things with Lottie?"

Sebastian pushed his hat back and rubbed is forehead. "About an hour, I suppose."

Val banged a hand down on the top of the gate. "Then let's get going. I'll talk on the way."

Chapter 9

Pip trundled the wheelie bin into the ruined front room. The police forensic team had finished their work the previous afternoon but neither Pip nor her father had the heart to tackle the mess until this morning. They reasoned that it would be a time when their energy level, if not their optimism, was higher.

Cleaning up was dispiriting work. Her father periodically retreated to the desk chair and put his head in his hands. His books had helped minimize the damage done to the room. No bullets had pock-marked the wall. It was a small mercy. Her father tried to smile. "I've only lost about a dozen books," he'd said. "Most were on Reformation church history. It was never my favorite subject."

The biggest loss was her cello. It had been completely shot to pieces. Nothing was salvageable, not even the strings. She picked up a fragment of the end scroll. Whilst it was not a particularly good quality instrument, it was hers. It had taught her to play, and she understood its idiosyncrasies. In truth, she had been thinking of buying a new one but had postponed doing so until she knew what direction her music career would take—if it would go anywhere at all.

She began to sob. It was the first decent cry she'd allowed

herself. With one hand on her forehead and the other on her chest, she bent over and sobbed. She wept for the bewildering shock of it all. She wept because she didn't understand. She wept because she'd been violated. The attack had been brutal, life threatening, and senseless. She, who had once prided herself on being so worldly wise, now felt she didn't understand the world at all.

Pip felt her father's arms around her. She turned and buried her head in his chest.

"Why, why, why?" she cried.

He held her to himself, smoothed the top of her hair, then kissed it. "I don't know, my darling. I don't know."

She clenched her fists against his chest. "It's so senseless. And why you? You've never hurt anyone in your life."

"Hmm. There are a few on Parish Council who might disagree."

Pip pushed her fists angrily into his chest. "Seriously! And what if whoever did this comes back? We don't know what their purpose was."

Her father grunted. "The police gave me a good grilling as to possible drug connections. They made me feel quite, er…exotic." He took her head between his hands and looked into her eyes. "We will get through this. We've been through worse together, haven't we?"

She nodded dumbly.

"What will you do about your cello?" he asked. "You've got your performance exam next week."

She wiped her nose. "I can hire one from the Con. They've already offered me one." She wiped the tears from her cheek. "It will be a horrible, hard mouthed thing with no volume at all, but it will have to do."

"There, there; life will go on," he cooed. "Some very unpleasant people will have realized by now that they have shot up the wrong place—and will probably be feeling a little foolish. Please don't let this ruin your preparation for your exam."

Pip blew her nose noisily and turned away. Part of her brain was trying to make sense of what she saw, and she didn't like the place the evidence was taking her. She glanced at what was left of the armchair. One wing of the chair and much of its back had been shot to pieces. The police had said that the shooting was probably designed to frighten and intimidate. It was not uncommon for there to be a drive-by shooting—usually just a few pistol shots into the garage or front door. The occupants of the house invariably said it was a case of mistaken identity and claimed to be bewildered as to why it happened. The reality was that such behavior was the warning biker gangs gave to those who were behind in payment.

She looked at the devastation around her. This was no warning. The shots had been concentrated in one spot—the chair, and her cello. That suggested focused intent. The police had said that the weapon used was probably a machine pistol. A machine pistol, for goodness sake! The police estimated that twenty shots had been fired. "A complete magazine," they'd said. She'd never heard of anyone being warned off by a machine gun. That was the stuff of Chicago gangsters.

Her father started sweeping the wooden floor of debris. Once he'd cleared a space, he began taking books from the ruined bookshelf and stacking them against the wall. His declared aim was to get things back to normal as soon as possible. Carpenters were coming that afternoon—even though it was Saturday, to begin repairs to the window casement. Glaziers would follow. Fortunately, the bulk of the repairs would be covered by insurance. Pip sighed. She wished that human emotions could be as easily repaired.

They'd put the overhead light on in the room as the window was boarded up with plywood. As she moved to help her father, Pip noticed her father's felt trilby at the base of the bookcase. She picked it up and examined it. With horror, she discovered four small holes through its crown.

"Dad," she said. "Where was this hat when you last had it?"

He gave a rueful smile. "I'd just put it on top of your cello."

A nasty suspicion began forming in her mind. She stepped back over to the window and tried to imagine the scene before the attack. The wing-backed chair was angled slightly away from the window to allow her father to read with natural light. Her cello had leaned against it, with her father's hat on top. She pictured what it would have looked like from the curbside six or seven meters away. Pip found it impossible to repress a shiver. It would look as if someone was sitting in the chair. And the hat would have identified that person as her father.

Someone wanted her father dead.

Val was not sure how to begin the conversation with his son. He sat in silence for the first half hour, making occasional small talk, feeling his way. It was a surreal feeling to finally be known by your son after all these years—although he suspected Sebastian didn't yet believe it. It would be a long time before they could have anything like a father-son relationship—if they ever would.

"How did it go with Lottie?" he asked.

Sebastian rested two hands on top of the wheel as he piloted the ute along the Murray Valley Highway. He kept his gaze to the front.

"There were tears."

"I can imagine."

"No," said Sebastian. "You probably can't." He sniffed, almost in contempt. "She's probably been the nearest thing I've had to a mother in my life."

It was a riposte that was designed to hurt, to keep Val at bay. Val kept quiet and waited for Sebastian to be ready to talk, to set the agenda.

Sebastian turned off onto the Mallee Highway at Piangil. "So, you really are my father," he said.

"Yes."

"And, obviously, quite alive?"

"Yes."

"And…" Sebastian's voice was slightly hesitant, "you're not really a murderer, are you?

"Yes, I'm afraid I am. That bit's quite right."

There was a long silence.

The giant wheat silos of Piangil passed by.

Val cleared his throat. "Would it be helpful if I told you about your mother—about what happened?"

Sebastian shrugged.

Val fought down a wave of irritation at his son's lack of enthusiasm. He breathed deeply a few times to calm himself. It wasn't Sebastian's fault. He would have no idea what it would cost him emotionally to talk about his wife, even after all these years. Val tried to order his thoughts. How did he begin to talk about his road to hell?

"She had blonde hair like you. You've inherited more of her features than mine."

Silence.

Val began again. "We met in Townsville. I was up there with the Third battalion, Royal Australian Regiment. We were doing an information thing at a school when we met. She'd just started as a special education teacher there." He glanced at Sebastian. "Do you know what a special ed. teacher does?"

"They work with kids who have disabilities." The words seemed to come reluctantly from Sebastian.

"And that was your mum all over. She was beautiful on the outside and on the inside." Val felt the familiar pain of loss well up inside him. "Some day, I'll tell you more about her." He drew in another deep breath. "When you were born, she gave up teaching instantly and devoted herself to you. She didn't have an easy time with your birth. There were complications that meant that she couldn't have any more children. So she doted on you." He smiled. "She played with you like a kid, and sang. She sang a lot."

Val noticed that he'd opened his fingers—reaching. He balled them into a fist. "Anyway, we moved to Adelaide when I was seconded there as an instructor. We were only meant to be there for a year, but it ended up being longer. You'd started school by then, but your mum refused to work full time. She wanted to be there when you came back from school. But just occasionally, she'd do some relief teaching, or do an assessment of a child.

"One night she was returning from doing an assessment at Balaclava when her car broke down on a road that was…" he worked his lips, willing the words to come out, "pretty desolate."

Part of Val's mind noted that the road they were driving on was now threading its way through some salt-pans. *Salt. Tears.* He closed his eyes and tried to sound matter-of-fact. "Your mother's body was found next day by a farmer. She'd been raped and murdered."

"What!" exclaimed Sebastian.

"Yeah."

Silence.

Val stared at the road ahead. "As it transpired, there was a witness who saw some of the incident that evening—a farm hand who was up to no good with his girlfriend in a car under some nearby trees. He said that three men got out of a car ostensibly to help your mother. The bloke managed to see the shape of the patch that one of them was wearing in the headlights."

"Patch?"

"The identifying patch worn by members of a motorbike gang on the back of their cutaway jackets."

"Who were they?"

"The Saracens." Val drew in a deep breath. "The bloke told the police enough for them to arrest two of the three men. The trouble was, the witness withdrew his evidence before the trial started and so the case collapsed."

The tendons of Val's forearms were standing out as he clenched his fist. He slowly undid his fingers and stared at his hands. Did these hands really belong to him? he wondered fleetingly. Had they really done what he'd been accused of?

Sebastian broke into his thoughts. "What happened next?"

"I, er…I executed them."

"You did what?"

"I shot them." He shrugged. "It's what landed me in prison."

Silence.

Val sighed. He felt utterly spent. "So now you know."

Sebastian pushed irritably at the steering wheel. "But how come you escaped, when you were meant to be dead?"

"That's a story for another day. Now I'm going to sleep. Keep an eye on the rear-view mirror. If a car tails you for more than ten minutes, wake me up." *Leave me with my demons and let me fight them alone.*

"Okay. Just one thing…"

"What?"

"What were you an instructor for in the army?"

"Hand to hand combat."

"So that was your specialty?"

Val nodded. "That, and sniper training."

Chapter 10

David Albright sat in a chair in the late afternoon sun. He'd positioned it beside the front porch of the church. He liked this part of the building. It was built with round, river-washed stones by the early settlers, and there was a comforting integrity about it. He glanced at the lychgate that stood at the end of the path. It too had been built by those seeking to transplant the certainties of their English culture to the other side of the world.

To his right was the columbarium, the place for storing cinerary urns. It detracted a little from the ambience, as it was a modern thing made of bricks, quite at odds with the rambling headstones that stood between him and Church Street. The headstones seemed to sit gently with the stones of the church, as if sitting with friends.

Insects buzzed around in the warm winter sun. David, like them, was keen to feel its warmth—for the thoughts whirling round his head were disturbing. He sat forward on the chair, giving a fair imitation of Rodin's 'Thinker,' and tried to analyze the significance of his conversation with Pip.

She'd insisted that his life was in danger and laid out the evidence for it in a way that almost convinced him. There were two reasons why he hadn't reacted to her convictions by promising to take extra care regarding his safety. The first was that he could think of no one, outside a couple of witch doctors in Vanuatu, who would wish him dead. There had been a couple of tricky situations way back in his early missionary days, but that was ten years ago.

The second reason for being more sanguine about his situation than Pip thought he'd any right to be, came from a theological conviction. It was a conviction that was hard to explain. In part, it was a reluctance to give evil the power to determine how he would live his life. But beyond this was another conviction. It was the knowledge that he was under God's management. As such, he could rest back into God's love and get on with life. This didn't give him a mandate to take stupid risks, nor did it mean his life would be free of trauma. It was just that he was able to see beyond the trauma to something more certain.

This was not to say he didn't grieve at life. Grief always seemed to be present in the background, like tinnitus—a nasty background noise that ate away at joy. It was a grief at people not knowing their sacredness. It was a grief at the hurtful place Australia was being led to by strident people who were careless with truth. He very much feared that children would pay a heavy price for society cutting itself free from godly principles that had stood the test of centuries. A values-free society that had nothing to say about identity and purpose was an unkind burden to lay on any child. He sighed. Perhaps Professor Arnold Toynbee was right: civilizations are never destroyed by attacks from the outside, they self-destruct from the inside.

Certainly, he was bewildered by the modern world. He felt as if he was passing through a strange land that was a little disappointing —like an unripe cherry. Yet he knew that God had reserved him for this particular period of history, so his ministry must have some sort of significance. He shook his head. For the life of him, he couldn't imagine what it was.

Thoughts of children led him to think again of Pip. Would she ever be a mother? Would he have grandchildren? He smiled. He very much hoped so. At the moment, however, things didn't look promising. In the evenings, Pip would confide her angst to him.

"Dad, where can I find a man with character? I despair, I honestly do. Will I have to settle for some self-obsessed idiot with no spiritual fiber and no moral compass?"

He'd tried to reassure her. "Darling, things may look impossible now, but trust me, they have a way of working out." His assurances always sounded like weak platitudes—even though he knew the truth of what he was saying.

His ruminations were brought to an abrupt halt by the appearance of Mrs. Troubridge who came bustling around the corner of the porch. She was holding a rag stained black from cleaning brassware.

"Aah, there you are Vicar. There's someone to see you."

David raised an eyebrow. "Oh. Who?"

"A stranger. He didn't give a name."

As the front door on the porch was locked, he followed Mrs. Troubridge around to the vestry entrance into the church. He moved through it into the coolness of the building. Shafts of light from the window dispelled any sense of gloom. He hoped it was a parable.

A man was sitting in a pew about halfway down the church. He was wearing dark glasses despite being inside.

David made his way down the aisle until he came level with him.

"Hello. My name is David. I'm the vicar here."

The man said nothing.

David persisted. "Can I help you?"

The man nodded. "I want you to hear my confession." The stranger's voice rasped like a muffler trailing over a tarmac road.

"I'm happy to do so, but you do know this is not a Catholic church, don't you?"

"I do."

David sat down next to the man. "Was there any particular reason you came here to me?"

The stranger removed his sunglasses. "Yes. I came because you signed my death certificate fourteen years ago."

David Albright did not react with shock. During his time in ministry, he'd had to deal with a number of delusional people. He took off his glasses and polished them with his handkerchief. "You look remarkably well for someone who is dead."

The man appeared unruffled by the rebuff. "And you look remarkably like a priest for someone who was once a prison doctor."

A seed of uncertainty began to play in David's mind. "I trained for the mission field, so I studied both theology and medicine." He paused. "May I ask your name?"

The man coughed a brief laugh. "That rather depends on who you ask. At the mine site, I'm Val Norseman. To my parents, I was Jack McKenzie. To the governor of the prison you worked in…" the man paused, "well, he gave me his own nickname."

David waited for him to say more.

"He called me 'The Valkyrie.'"

"After the mythical Norse angels of death?"

The man nodded.

"What would you like me to call you?"

"Val, is fine."

"Okay Val, tell me your story."

There was a long pause.

"I was in prison for killing two members of the Saracens bikie gang." The man drew in a sharp breath. "They raped and murdered my wife."

The sanctuary lamp above the altar continued to glow a peaceful red, unruffled by the terrible disclosure.

The man continued. "Some of the Saracens were in the prison. They organized most of the drug supplies for the inmates." He sighed. "The warders did a pretty good job of keeping them separate from me. They only slipped up once. But on that occasion, one of the Saracens had a knife."

Silence.

"What happened?" prompted David.

Val shrugged. "I stabbed the man with his own knife, pulled the windpipe out of another and broke the neck of the third."

It was the dreadful matter-of-fact way it was said that shocked David. "You did what?"

"But I didn't quite get off scot-free. One of them damaged my windpipe. It's why I sound a bit hoarse."

David shook his head in disbelief.

Val continued. "Well, that quietened things down a bit, but one day, I was taken to see the prison governor, Geoffrey Stoddard." He looked up. "Do you remember him?"

"Um, Slightly."

"Well, he had a problem. The Saracens were leaning on him to turn a blind eye to certain activities that allowed drugs to get into the prison. They actually threatened to attack his daughter." Val put his hand to his throat and coughed.

David had the impression that speaking for long periods of time was not something his visitor found comfortable.

"Would you like a drink of water?"

Val waved the offer away. "Evidently, the three guys I'd taken out were the linchpins for the Saracens' drug trade in the prison, and the Saracens were eager to get the trade back." Val coughed another laugh—a derisive laugh. Unpleasant. "As I had a certain track record when it came to the Saracens, we made a deal."

"And what was that?"

"Stoddard would organize my escape from prison, and I would remove the two key players in the Saracens who were leaning on Stoddard."

"And just how did you manage to escape from prison?"

"I was found hanging in my cell."

David raised an eyebrow.

"Yeah. Just a few prisoners saw me before Stoddard shut the cell door and called for help." Val smiled. "I was actually hanging using one of those harnesses they use to stage hangings in films and theaters. Anyway, I was taken down to the clinic and left there." He glanced at David. "This is where you were duped, I'm afraid."

"How so?"

"A doctor had just left the clinic after visiting a dead prisoner and writing his death certificate. You were invited in to write another one for the same bloke half an hour later, except with my name. Stoddard had swapped photos on my prison records and personally identified the body as being me." Val shrugged. "It wasn't hard."

David expostulated. "You couldn't have got away with that. What about the funeral, and all the rest that goes with it?"

"There was no funeral, just a death certificate. I was the son of Scottish immigrants who stayed in Australia long enough to dislike it and return home. I was a rebellious teenager who decided to stay and join the Australian army." Val paused. "No one was looking to attend my funeral."

"I don't believe it." David glared at Val.

Cool eyes looked back at him levelly. "I think you probably should, because someone is trying to kill you, very probably for your part in springing me from jail." Val leaned back in the pew. "The Saracens are not a forgiving lot."

"What?" David frowned. "Don't tell me… You didn't, um…you didn't actually…fulfill your contract with Stoddard?"

Val didn't respond. He just continued to look at him.

"Good God!" David put his head in his hands. A moment later he sat bolt upright. "Is my daughter safe?"

"Probably not."

David closed his eyes and groaned.

The light coming through the windows had dimmed. Twilight was overtaking the optimism of the day.

"How did you find out about us being attacked?" demanded David.

"The car radio; you were on the news. It took me a moment to link your name with the events that have been happening to us. But when I did, I thought I'd better come round and warn you."

"Who is 'us'?"

"My, er…son, Sebastian. He was attacked in order to flush me out of hiding."

"Attacked?"

"They cut off one of his fingers and sent it to me."

68

David narrowed his eyes. "If no one knew you were alive; how did the Saracens know where to send...the finger?"

"I think they pressured Stoddard."

"Oh. And what makes you say that?"

"They tracked me down to the opal fields in South-West Queensland, but they didn't know exactly where I was. They sent it to the post office at Yowah. Suspecting that I wouldn't be using my real name, they addressed it to 'The Valkyrie.'" He wiped a hand over his face. "Someone at the post office remembered hearing my name, 'Val,' and thought it could be me. There was a note in the parcel telling me to contact them." He paused. "They didn't feel the need to tell me who they were."

David struggled to make sense of all that he was hearing.

Outside, he could hear a pair of magpie larks squabbling on one of the windowsills. He could see their shadows bouncing up and down through the colored glass. It was the sound of a carefree life, one that was careless of the machinations of violent men.

"And where is your son now?" he asked.

"He's hopefully concluding a deal—trading in his ute for a second-hand car." Val looked at his watch. "He'll pick me up from here any time now."

"How much of this story does your son know?"

Val grunted. "He doesn't know much. In fact, he didn't even know I was alive until yesterday."

David was at a loss for words. Eventually, he said, "I think we'd better go to the police."

The man tapped a forefinger on top of the pew back. "The police will not be able to protect you for the rest of your life. I'm sorry, but you need a better, more lasting solution."

Silence.

Val, continued. "What sort of protection are the police currently giving you?"

"They send a patrol past at night, and I get a phone call each day."

The finger kept tapping. "That's not much."

It was now quite dark in the church. The light from outside had almost gone. The only light in the church came from the red glow of the sanctuary light—blood red.

David drew a deep breath. "I think we need to get everyone who is involved together and try and work out what to do."

Val nodded.

David took out his phone and rang his daughter.

Chapter 11

Pip leaned her bike against the wall as the automatic garage door slid down behind her. She glanced at the door at the other end. What lay beyond it? Would she want to know? Her father had only told her that two visitors had come who might be able to shed light on why they had been attacked. If that wasn't alarming enough, he let slip that he'd met one of the men years ago when he was an inmate of the prison he was working in.

Pip's hair had been gradually escaping the bun on top of her head all day. She pulled the remaining locks free and shook her hair over her shoulders. Taking a deep breath, she picked up her shoulder-bag and opened the door.

The view into the family room from the darkness of the courtyard outside presented a diorama of three people. Her father was in an armchair, seemingly lost in thought. A square-shouldered man with a stubbly beard sat behind the kitchen bench well back from the light of the standard lamp, as if seeking out the shadows. The man noticed her as soon as she'd walked through the garage door. His hooded eyes followed her movements as she crossed over to the glass doors of the family room.

She paused before opening the sliding door to inspect the third person in the room. He was, she felt, particularly contributing to the silence inside. His arms were folded across his chest, and he looked so obviously out of place, it was comical. He wore a work-shirt with its arms ripped out, jeans and stockinged feet. She could see his boots beside the back door. Having spent a large part of the day mentally railing against the privileged excesses of Western city-dwellers, to be faced with a young man who was palpably not one of them, was disturbing.

Shaggy hair and beard kept much of his face a secret. He looked a mess—an overdone caricature of a country hayseed—except for those long, tanned arms...*uh-oh, he's seen me.*

As she stepped inside, her father took charge and made introductions.

"Aah, Pip. Good to see you. May I introduce Mr. McKenzie..."

The older man nodded. He didn't offer a handshake. Pip was glad. She was wary of his sheer physicality, his history—and of the information that he might soon give.

Pip interrogated her father's face for any signs of distress he might be feeling in the company of his two visitors.

She could see none.

Her father gestured toward the younger man—the hayseed.

"And this is..."

The young man lurched to his feet, knocking over the magazine rack beside him. It held her music scores. Some of them spilled over the floor. He stammered his apology and bent to pick up the music. She instinctively went to do the same, causing them to bump heads. He apologized again.

When all was tidy, Pip straightened up and put her hands on her hips.

The young man's eyes never left her. Brown, she noticed.

"And you must be Farmer Joe," she said with a touch of exasperation.

"And you must be..." the man glanced at the music score he was holding. It was Mendelssohn's 'Song without Words' in D. "You must be one of Odyssey's sirens, whose songs enticed men..."

"To the rocks," she finished.

How on earth does a hayseed know about the Odyssey? She mentally tried to recalibrate—but failed.

Her father came to the rescue. "This is Sebastian, Mr. McKenzie's son."

The young man held out his hand—firm and work-hardened. "Hello."

It was a truce, of sorts.

Moments later, she was helping her father organize mugs of tea for them all.

"Dad," she hissed. "Can these people be trusted?"

Her father looked surprised. "Yes, of course. Well, it rather depends..."You know, it didn't really occur to me...that they couldn't be."

She rolled her eyes but felt somewhat reassured. Pip knew David had an unerring instinct when it came to people. It was as if he could see into their souls.

Her father nodded toward the older man. "I feel quite safe with him. He was driven to violence by the most extreme of circumstances."

Violence. Great!

When everyone was settled, David cleared his throat. "Pip, Mr. McKenzie is going to tell you a story, and I must warn you, it will shock you. It is both tragic and brutal, and it is one that may explain what happened to us the other night."

Icy fingers of fear gripped Pip's heart. She squeezed the sides of her chair and waited.

The deep rasp of the man's voice surprised her, as did his opening comments for he did not direct them to her, but to his son.

"Sebastian, you're finally going to hear the full story that explains why I've needed to be anonymous to you for so long. Believe me, I wish it could have been otherwise. Being cut off from you for the last seventeen years has caused me more grief than I can say." He looked up to the ceiling briefly, and continued. "It all began when I met...your mother."

When he finished telling the story, no one said a thing. Silence hung in the room, open-mouthed in shock and shrieking its questions. Only the kitchen clock remained unruffled. *Tick, tick, tick.*

Pip was the first to speak.

"Mr. McKenzie, your story is…tragic…and I'm so sorry for all that you've suffered; but are you really a…"

"A killer?" he volunteered.

"Er, yes. I'm wondering how safe you are—for my father and me right now."

Her question seemed to stir Sebastian into life. "Oh, no. He would…"

McKenzie interrupted. "I would never hurt you." He rubbed his forehead with a knuckled finger. "I don't like it when innocent people—good people like yourselves—are threatened. That's why I'm here. I feel responsible. My intention is only to help."

Pip pressed further. "So if I phoned the police right now, what would you do?"

McKenzie smiled wearily. "I would thank you for my mug of tea, and leave pretty smartly."

Pip pointed to Sebastian. "What about him?"

"Sebastian has nothing to fear from the police and has his own future to live. He'll probably be based here in Adelaide, at least for a while. I only want to ensure that Sebastian, and now also you, remain safe."

Sebastian turned to his father. "You'd really leave? Just like that?"

McKenzie nodded. "If it's for the best."

The young man shook his head slowly and stared at the floor.

If ever there was a picture of a tortured soul, McKenzie's son epitomized it.

Tick, tick, tick, tick.

Pip broke the silence. "How does this end? How can there be a resolution?"

"With me, it won't end. Not until…" McKenzie didn't finish the sentence. "But for you and your father—possibly. I need to talk with the Saracens to find out why you're a problem to them." He shrugged. "If attacking you is simply another way of flushing me out, then I'll do my best to make it clear there is nothing to be gained from targeting you, and then I'll get out of your way."

"You'll direct fire away from my father?"

"Yes."

"And from Pip?" asked Sebastian.

McKenzie nodded.

"What happens in the meantime?" she demanded.

"It will take a while to organize a conversation with the Saracens. It won't be…a straightforward thing."

David expostulated. "Hardly surprising, given that you've killed…what is it—seven of them?"

"Mmm. Eight, actually."

David groaned and dropped his head into his hands. "This is getting ridiculous."

Pip cleared her throat. "The big question is: do we go to the police with this information?" She turned to McKenzie. "We'd obviously give you time to get well out of the way. It's the least we can do as you came here to warn us."

McKenzie nodded. "That would be…" he paused, "a sensible thing to do."

Pip looked at him quizzically. "I'm getting the feeling that you're not giving my idea a ringing endorsement."

Sebastian turned to his father. "What's the problem? I…we… don't want to bring any problems down on these people." He'd got up from his seat and was standing next to her. She could smell him —the odor of a male body that had worked hard. Not unpleasant.

Pip hauled her mind back to the matter in hand. She very much feared she understood the problem only too well.

"The problem is already here, isn't it," she said. "It won't go away…until something happens."

McKenzie nodded. "Unfortunately yes. I need to find out the threat level against you."

David, still with his head in his hands, spoke through his fingers. "Which will involve you talking to the Saracens."

"Yes."

"Who know you have killed eight of their members."

Val didn't answer.

Silence.

Pip leaned back, pushed her hands into her pockets, and bunched them into fists. "Mr. McKenzie, Is my father safer with you here, or will your presence put him in more danger?"

"You are already in danger. You've been machine-gunned."

Sebastian made to interrupt, but Pip took a hand out of her pocket and held it up to forestall him. "Please be frank." She worked her lips—forcing the words out. "Do you have the capacity…" she paused, then continued, "the capacity to keep us safe?"

The clock in the kitchen ticked. *Tick, tick, tick, tick.*

McKenzie turned to Pip. His gray eyes disturbing, unblinking. "I have a certain, capability. But I can't be on watch all the time."

Pip pressed on. "But if they know you are here, will they be reluctant to come near us."

Val nodded slowly. "I think I can guarantee that."

"But how will you let them know?" asked Sebastian. "This is crazy."

"I can let them know in the next fifteen minutes if you'd like."

David sat bolt upright. "How?" he demanded.

Pip frowned, trying to comprehend what was being said.

"I notice that you have a wooden ladder fixed to the corrugated iron on the roof."

"You mean the ladder going up to the air conditioning unit," she said.

"Yes."

"May I use it to get to the top of your roof?"

"Why?" demanded Pip.

"Did you notice a black Commodore a hundred and fifty meters down the street when you came in?"

Pip froze. "No. Are we being watched?"

"He was there an hour ago. If he's still there, I can let him know that I'm watching over this place." Val shrugged. "It's your call."

"No, no, no," protested David.

Pip interrupted. "Will anyone get hurt?"

"Not on this occasion."

"You can guarantee it?"

"Yes. I'll just take out one of his headlights."

Sebastian turned to his father. "You can do that from a hundred and fifty meters?"

"Yes."

"But the noise…" Sebastian shook his head.

"I'll use a subsonic round and a suppressor. You won't hear it, even in here."

David lowered his head back into his hands. "I don't believe I'm hearing this."

Pip glanced at both Sebastian and Val. "You realize that this would mean you have to stay here, at least for the time being, at least until you have your talk. Where are you staying at the moment?"

Val shrugged. "Nowhere particularly. We spent last night in a caravan park."

Sebastian stared at Pip. "Is staying here even possible?"

"No," her father said.

"Yes," she countered. Pip turned to her father. "There's the loft above the garage. We never finished the loft conversion after mum died. But the basics are there. A shower and toilet."

"But nothing else. There is no furniture, no floor covering. One wall doesn't even have any Gyprock," protested David.[1]

McKenzie interrupted. "We don't need beds."

Pip rushed on. "We've got camping stretchers. Will they do?"

"Are you inviting us to stay for a while?"

She turned to her father. "Dad, are we?"

Her father slumped back in his chair and stared at McKenzie, then at Sebastian. The young man had rested a hand on the back of his chair. Artistic fingers, Pip noted.

David glanced at her briefly. Eventually, he nodded.

McKenzie got to his feet. "Will all of you please stay in here until I get back. Don't go into the front room or come outside to watch. It is best if you see nothing."

David and Pip nodded dumbly.

"Perhaps play some music," he added, then lifted his rucksack onto a shoulder.

———————

The stereo was half way through the haunting sweetness of Mozart's Clarinet Concerto, the Adagio, when there was the sound of something bouncing on the roof and sliding down the corrugated iron.

Pip shivered. It would have to be a spent bullet cartridge.

Chapter 12

Moonlight slanted across them from the window of the loft. It fell across the barrel of the Barrett causing it to gleam dull blue. Val had set it up beside his camp bed. There was no possibility of hiding it from Sebastian any more as he needed the gun ready to hand. Although Sebastian had made no comment about it, Val knew the gun must present a disturbing sight. He sighed and wished it could be otherwise.

The camp bed squeaked as he sought to make himself comfortable. Sleep was a two-edged sword, and Val had learned to seek it with caution. When it gave him the gift of oblivion, it was wonderful. When it thrust gruesome images and accusations at him, he woke exhausted, drenched with sweat.

He listened to Sebastian's breathing. It was not yet the slow measured breathing of sleep. So he was not surprised when Sebastian spoke.

"Was all the information about you being a mining geologist compete bullshit?"

Val knew the questions would come eventually. He took a deep breath. "Most of it. I had to invent a plausible back-story—one that came closest to what I was actually doing."

"And what were you doing?"

"Well, as you know, I did actually join the army."

"And the mining stuff?"

"Not entirely fiction. I didn't live in Sydney, but I did work at a mine—an opal mine."

"What, for all that time? For twelve years, or whatever?"

"Hmm, for most of it, certainly for the summers. For those months, I was the only person at the mine site. I was the caretaker."

"Caretaker?"

"Yeah. The guy who owned the mine lost over a million dollars worth of heavy machinery to thieves once. They took the lot away one summer." Val shrugged. "Nothing was insured. No company will insure machinery that's left for months unattended in the bush. So, the boss bought me a rifle to guard the place and gave me permission to do a bit of digging on my own—provided I didn't use any of the heavy machinery."

"You didn't actually…use the rifle, did you?"

"I took out the front headlights of a low loader that came snooping around one night."

"You didn't."

"Hmm. It probably wasn't a good move. I reckon that's how the Saracens got the idea I might be living in the area."

Sebastian's bed creaked as he turned over. "How so?"

"It's the only reason I can think of. The links between motorbike gangs and the trucking industry are well established—particularly with truckies engaged in illegal activities. If the word was out to keep your ears open for a sniper calling himself 'The Valkyrie'… and discrete inquires about some mad bastard shooting the lights out of trucks turned up the name 'Val,' you'd be suspicious, wouldn't you?"

"I suppose so."

Silence.

"So, The Fire Stone; you actually found it?"

"Yes. It was my best find in ten years. It was in the heart of an ironstone rock about the size of a fist. That's what we mined for, the rocks. They call them Yowah nuts. About one in a thousand contain good opal." He paused. "I've always dreamed of the day I could pass it on to you. And now you have it."

Sebastian levered himself to a sitting position and rummaged under the pile of clothing by his bed. Val watched him take The Fire Stone out of his leather pouch and unwrap it. A moment later, he was inspecting it in the torchlight of his phone.

"It's…fabulous."

Val smiled. From where he lay, he could see the dancing fire tease and mesmerize. The stone's beauty and sheer aliveness was breathtaking.

Sebastian turned the stone in the light. "So, this came from Yowah."

"Yeah: near Yowah. It actually came from the Koroit opal field, which is about eighty kilometers northwest of Cunnamulla. There's no town—just mines."

"Sounds remote."

"It is. The roads are pretty basic and often treacherous. Visitors are not encouraged. Sensitivities are acute around mines."

Val thought back to the place that had hidden him for so many years—Koroit. It seems such an innocent name, faintly suggestive of something exotic. It was, in fact, a brutal hammer waiting to crush the hopes of men foolish enough to dream. The fractured, rugged landscape was devoid of pity—particularly in summer. Then, the foul breath of Hades blew among the ranges and dry creek valleys, sucking up all comfort, all hope. Only stunted gidgee and mulga survived. The heat kept out all who were sane…and all who were good. Only the desperate lived there.

Sebastian seemed to read his thoughts. "Didn't you go mad, being alone for so long?"

"Nah. It suited me. And the rest of the mining crew turned up in the autumn, so it wasn't so bad."

"But what did you actually do?"

"I did my own mining during the day, and, like you, I read at night."

"So you never left the mining site, for…what would it have been, twelve years?"

"No. I got away for three or four months each year. The boss of the mining site and I went halves on a sailing boat. He sailed it in the summer, and I sailed it in winter and spring."

"You went sailing?"

"Yeah. It's a good way of keeping out of people's way."

"So, you can live on board? It's a big boat?"

"Fairly."

Sebastian put the stone away and lay back down.

Silence.

Val again listened to his son's breathing. He was still not ready for sleep.

"Val, these are good people. I don't want us to put them in danger."

Val was shocked at Sebastian using his name, 'Val.' He'd obviously decided he was most comfortable with it. It wasn't yet 'Dad' but at least it was something.

"Us? You talk about 'us' putting them in danger?"

"Well, I'm not sure about the legal side of things, but I'm pretty sure I'm the wrong side of the law for keeping information about you from police."

"Umm, yeah: you're right. If you are not a spouse, then you're obliged to testify against a family member if subpoenaed."

"So it's us." Sebastian paused, and then hurried on. "It's not a father-son thing, you understand. It's just that we are both in this together—on the wrong side of the law."

"Then we better make sure you never have to be subpoenaed."

Silence.

"Val."

"Yes."

"Do you really have subsonic bullets?"

"They're handy if you want to be quiet. Subsonic is good for heavier bullets. They retain a lot of energy."

"You didn't answer my question." He paused. "You didn't really shoot out the headlights of a car tonight, did you."

"What do you think?"

"No."

Val sighed. "You're right. It would just inflame things. You can't be doing that sort of thing in the streets of Adelaide without risk."

"Then why…the pantomime?"

"I did it so that David and Pip would believe they were a bit safer." It wasn't the whole truth, but Val hoped it was enough for the moment.

"But they're not safe."

"No."

After a while, Sebastian broke the silence again.

"How do I keep Pip safe? I'm not trained. And I'm certainly not armed."

"You'd be an extra set of ears and eyes. Just your presence is enough in most situations. It takes a lot more courage to tackle two people—and it's certainly a lot harder to get away with."

"I really want to keep her safe."

"Then stay alert."

"But for how long?"

Val didn't answer. He couldn't. He rolled over and begged for sleep—a sleep where there were no more questions and no self-recriminations. But it was at night that the demons attacked him. Images of stricken faces, uncomprehending at the shock of dying, would materialize in the darkness. These were the ones he'd killed face to face. There were others that he'd seen just for seconds through a telescopic sight who were almost anonymous. He'd tried to dismiss them, telling himself they were of no account. And yet the nagging thought persisted that someone had given birth to them —someone who cared. Most nights, the faces of the dead emerged from the walls of the room, ballooning in front of him, pushing into his face, leering, before contorting in agony. He would lash out to fend their ruined faces away, but they just laughed and lunged back at him.

And behind them all, standing in the distance, was his wife—the one he'd failed to protect.

Chapter 13

Pip was perched on a stool in the kitchen stirring her muesli when Sebastian and Val came through the glass doors to join her for breakfast. They were tangible evidence that what she'd experienced the night before was no dream.

She sighed. "How did you sleep, Mr. McKenzie?"

"Well enough," he rumbled. His eyes appraised her for a moment. What she saw in them disturbed her. It was so completely unexpected. She saw both wistfulness and sadness. It was fleeting, but it was there.

He continued. "Would you feel more comfortable if you called me Val?"

"Would you?"

"Yes."

Pip nodded.

"And how did you sleep?" asked Sebastian. "You didn't have any nightmares as a result of…?" he trailed off.

In truth, she had not slept well. "Fine," she said.

"Your father not around?" asked Val.

"He's in the study. He gets up early for his quiet time. He'll be through in a minute."

Sebastian raised an eyebrow. "Quiet time?"

"He hangs out with God—reads the Bible and prays."

"Oh."

Val and Sebastian remained standing.

"Is anything the matter?" she asked.

Sebastian gave a self-abashed smile. "I'm sorry. It's just that I…I don't know the rules."

"Rules?"

"What I'm allowed to do."

She looked at him quizzically.

He shrugged. "In the families I lived with, there were always…rules."

At that moment, David came in from the hallway clutching a newspaper still wrapped in its cling film. "What you are allowed to do," he said unwrapping the paper, "is make this place your home." He turned to his daughter. "Pip, have you given them a key?"

"Not yet, but I will."

Pip glanced back at Sebastian. "Oh for goodness sake, sit down and make yourself breakfast."

The two men set about the task.

Val filled the kettle. "It does raise the issue of what is and is not expected domestically."

David grunted. "Treat the garage loft as your own space and the family room as shared space. Have your meals in here, but leave the study to me and Pip."

Val nodded.

Pip was anxious to address her own particular concern. "But what about during the day, Mr, er…Val? Will you be looking after my father? How do you see that working out?"

"I would like to tag along with you, David—particularly when you're walking around in public."

"What about Pip?" Asked Sebastian.

"Pip is probably not in any danger. But the thing is, we can't be sure. I'm reluctant to take the risk."

"Can I help?" asked Sebastian.

Val looked at his son. "I thought you wanted to go to the university today to check it out before your interview."

Pip was alarmed to hear her father say, "Pip goes to the Conservatorium there and works at a café nearby. Sebastian could keep an eye on her."

"No way!" she protested.

Val gave no indication that he'd heard her. "You are too recognizable, Sebastian. The Saracens know what you look like."

David interrupted. "That's a pity because I'd feel more comfortable if someone could keep an eye on Pip, particularly during those times she's in public."

"Oh for goodness sake. I'm in public most of the time. No way do I want a…" *hayseed*, she thought uncharitably, "a bodyguard who looks like…" she broke off and turned to Sebastian. "Have you really got an interview at the University tomorrow?"

"Yeah." He thrust his hands into his pockets. "Can't say it fills me with wild enthusiasm."

"Why?"

He shrugged. "Can't see much point in it, really."

"What!" objected Pip. "You can't see any point in going to uni?"

"Not really. You do exams, get qualified, strut your stuff, then die." He shrugged his shoulders. "It all seems pretty meaningless."

David lowered his paper and looked at Sebastian over the top of his glasses. "So what should you do?"

Sebastian hunched his shoulders and gave an unconvincing grin. "Drink beer."

"Drink beer?"

The young man held a hand up in apology. "Don't take me seriously."

Pip glanced at her father and smiled to herself. Sebastian had no idea what was coming.

David folded up the paper and put it down beside him. "Well, the thing is: I do take you seriously, Sebastian. I take you very seriously indeed."

Sebastian looked embarrassed. "I didn't mean to…"

David interrupted. "The observable universe is ninety-three

billion light years wide and filled with unimaginable wonders. Its laws of physics are finely tuned to a ridiculous degree to allow intelligent life to exist on at least one planet. So, unless you have a theory that explains how everything came from nothing as a result of a mechanism for which there is no precedent, you have to take very seriously the possibility that life was intended." David paused. "You may, in fact, be very sacred indeed. So live your life well, Sebastian."

Go Dad.

There was an awkward silence.

Pip allowed the seconds of quiet to do their work before coming to Sebastian's rescue. "So you're going for an interview. Which department?"

"Engineering, Planning, and Design."

She nodded, then put a hand in front of her mouth to hide her smile.

"What?" he demanded.

"You'd go to an interview looking like that?" she waved a hand at him.

Sebastian looked affronted. "I'd change my shirt. I've got a good shirt."

Pip burst out laughing.

Val glanced at her. "And what would you suggest he look like for the interview?"

Pip was unsure she liked the direction the conversation was now heading, but she rose to the challenge. "Cut off the beard; get a decent haircut; get some good trousers, and a shirt." She pointed to his boots by the doorstep. "And get rid of those." She ran her eyes over him. His tanned skin would look great in a white shirt. But it was winter. He'd need to keep warm. "Do you like jumpers...pullovers?"

"Hate them."

She was pleased. His shoulders would show off better in a jacket. "Then he needs a jacket—a good one."

"Ridiculous," protested Sebastian. "Conformist, bourgeois absurdity."

Val shrugged. "If you want to keep an eye on Pip, you have to change your appearance."

Pip scoffed. "Blow that. If you want anyone to take you seriously at the interview, you need to change your appearance."

"So it's up to you," said Val.

Sebastian looked at Pip.

She tilted her head sideways, giving him as much sass as possible for daring to size her up.

"Okay," he said.

"No way," Pip protested again.

Val growled. "Pip, if I gave you some money, could you supervise Sebastian's new look? It sounds as if he might need a bit of help."

Every instinct in Pip screamed against having to play nursemaid to a helpless male—and then have him intrude on everything she did through the day. But the idea of taking this man on, of finding out a little more of what lay behind those eyes, of learning why he knew about Homer's *Odyssey*, was intriguing.

Sebastian rubbed his forehead wearily. "I can pay my own way, thanks very much—if I have to."

Pip spared him no mercy. "Oh, believe me: You have to. I shall enjoy spending a large amount of your money."

David smiled. "Splendid. I'm very grateful, Sebastian."

Pip shot her father a suspicious glance. He was looking altogether too pleased.

Val lifted the teapot and raised a questioning eyebrow.

She nodded.

As Val topped up her mug, she felt emboldened to ask. "What are you going to do for lunch?"

"Why do you ask?" he rumbled.

"David usually forgets to eat it."

"So you'd like me to make sure he does."

"Yes."

He nodded. "No problem. I'll be responsible for his lunch."

Pip picked up her mug of tea and tried to make sense of the absurdities of life. She'd negotiated with a convicted killer to ensure her father would eat lunch. Yet somehow, it didn't feel wrong.

Pip glanced at Sebastian. Having him around definitely *was* wrong.

Chapter 14

Val was alone in the kitchen deep in thought, trying to work out what he should do. He was acutely aware that whatever happened next would be critical for Sebastian and David's safety.

Sleep—he'd give a lot for a good night's sleep. The emotional toll of being with his son after seventeen years of separation was a great deal more than he'd anticipated. It was a storm of emotions— a seething mess of delight, disappointment, curiosity, hope, unreality, anger, and intense longing.

Sebastian was feckless, irresponsible and adrift, and yet, he caught glimpses of—what? Val shook his head. Perhaps it was just that he had his mother's eyes. Whatever it was, he was determined that nothing on God's earth would ever harm his son again.

Val reached into his pocket and pulled out the frayed white handkerchief. He caressed it and held it to his mouth in what might have been a kiss. "I will look after him, my love. I will." He reiterated the familiar promise.

But Val was under no illusions. The threat posed by the Saracens was very real. He was only too familiar with their violence. It was a gratuitous, merciless violence calculated to demean, extort, and intimidate. As he pondered it, the smoldering monster deep within him—that thing of which he was most afraid—began to waken. He gripped the edge of the breakfast bar and closed his eyes. It was violence; terrible, merciless violence. The monster came, promising redemption, but only delivered screams in the night. And it was incessant in its demands.

He was rescued from its foulness by the washing machine.

The machine, located in a cupboard off the kitchen, came to a shuddering halt and started to beep.

Val got off his stool and switched it off.

Pip and Sebastian had left for the day—goodness only knew how they would get along. Only he and David were in the house.

Val wandered down the hallway to the study and knocked on the door.

"Come in."

He put his head around the door. "The washing's finished. Would you like me to hang it out?"

David dropped the book he was reading onto his lap. "What? Ah, washing. Of course. Yes. Thank you."

Val retreated back to the kitchen. Moments later, he was hanging out the washing on the extendable line in the courtyard. He thought ruefully, that David had probably not the least idea what was in the washing machine. Pip had switched it on before she left. Some of the washing contained her clothes—including her under-garments. He felt slightly uncomfortable pulling them out of the machine into the basket.

Val pegged out the clothes steadily. Some of his and Sebastian's clothes were among them. All went well until he picked up one of Pip's bras. As he held it in his hands—memories of him doing a similar task eighteen years ago came flooding back to him. On that occasion, he'd held a bra briefly, and smiled, before pegging it onto the Hills hoist in their back garden. It was such an innocent, inti-mate thing—so feminine, so her.

Val put his hand out to steady himself against the wall, bowed his head and, appallingly, began to weep. He cursed himself for his weakness and railed against his stupidity, but the grief within him would not be denied. He wept in a way he'd not wept for years. He wept his longing and confusion. He wept his memories and love. He wept his loneliness and despair. Still holding Pip's bra, he put his head against the wall and sobbed.

When the paroxysms of grief finally eased their grip, Val was startled to hear David behind him. The cleric calmly reached into the washing basket and began to peg out the clothes.

Val looked at the bra he was still holding.

"I'm guessing you've not held one of those for a long time," said David.

He cleared his throat. "Eighteen years."

"Hmm. Why don't you get us both a cup of coffee and let me finish here?"

Val nodded, and made his way to the kitchen.

Minutes later, they were both seated in David's study. Although the room had suffered huge violence, David had moved quickly to put it back to rights. Despite the new chair and the smell of paint, the room's ornate ceilings, lantern window, and creaking floors now looked benignly on them, unruffled by the madness of history.

A vase of flowers was on the desk. Pip's work, no doubt.

Val said gruffly, "Sorry about...that."

David waved his apology away. "Quite understandable."

Val sought the comfort of his coffee.

David leaned back in his office chair. "I've wept a few times out there myself. My wife died of cancer two years ago."

Val nodded. "I'm sorry to hear that."

"What was the name of your wife?" asked David.

"Mandy."

"The big difference, of course, is: your Mandy died suddenly; horribly, and you never had a chance to say goodbye."

Val stared at the floor. "I was one of the best trained men in the army, and I couldn't protect her."

"But you couldn't have known what was going to happen."

"She died alone, on some waste ground beside a country road."

David said nothing.

"She was doused in petrol and burned—probably while she was still alive—after she'd been..."

Silence.

David nodded slowly, "That's a heavy burden to bear."

Val tilted his head back and blinked. "Yeah, it is." Emotion began to well up in him again. It was high time to change the subject. "So don't underestimate the violence we're facing. We're up against serious brutality."

"You're concerned?"

"Of course I'm concerned, particularly for Sebastian. He's vulnerable enough in life, and now he's a lot more vulnerable because of me."

"Vulnerable enough in life?"

Val was vaguely surprised to have heard himself say the phrase. He marshaled his thoughts. "It's just that I don't think Sebastian is handling life too well at the moment, and I'm not sure what to do. I've tried to steer him…from a distance over the years but…"

Val wasn't sure he wanted to say any more, but David's silence was insistent. He sighed. "The single most common factor associated with male delinquency is the absence of a father figure." He looked at David. "You learn that in prison. And that fact has haunted me every day of my life."

David nodded.

"Sebastian believes that I chose to absent myself from him for all those years. I suspect that he'll now choose to absent himself from me in retaliation."

"And that bothers you?"

"Yes. That, and his drinking."

"His drinking?"

"Yeah."

Magpies sitting in the Manchurian pear tree outside warbled musically at each other, careless of his angst.

"I've been an absent father. And I reckon there's a sense in which Sebastian desperately wants to find acceptance—to belong."

"You think he drinks in order to socialize, to feel he belongs?"

"Maybe. I dunno." He shrugged. "Maybe he's just trying to buy some fun."

"Do you think he is an alcoholic?"

Val grunted. "I wouldn't leave him alone with a bottle I hoped to see again."

"Well, if it's any consolation, I don't see much that would concern me in him. And I have a feeling that a lot of things are about to change."

Val directed a bleak gaze at David. "Why do you say that?"

"You think it's impossible?"

Val shrugged.

"I'm comfortable with impossibilities. I've learned to change what I can, and trust God for the rest."

The magpies continued to warble.

David leaned back in his chair. "So how are you going to get in contact with the Saracens? Personally, I can't think of anything more dangerous."

Val was glad of the reprieve. He pointed to the computer on David's desk. "I think we should begin there. If we are to regain any control of the situation, we need information."

David swung round on his chair. "What am I looking for?"

"Do an online search for 'Saracens; outlaw; Adelaide.'"

The search yielded immediate results. David pushed his glasses up his nose. "Wow, there's quite a lot." He peered at the screen. "There are press reports about an ongoing stoush between the Saracens and the local council about their headquarters in the North-Western suburbs. The council are calling it a fortress, which is illegal."

"Does it give the address?"

"It gives the street name." David read it out.

Val nodded. He wasn't surprised. The street was seared into his memory. It was where he'd shot Greg Vossik and Tony Sharpov when they were getting out of their car. "I know it," he said gruffly.

"There's a picture of a whole bunch of them riding without helmets at a funeral."

"Type in, 'Saracens; president Adelaide.'"

Val peered over his shoulder and looked at the matrix of images that came up on the screen. He pointed to one of them. "Click on that one."

When the image came up in full size, it was a picture of a big man with a shaved head and tattooed neck. He was standing next to a brutal-looking red and black car. "Who is he?"

David clicked back to the page the website image came from and peered closely at the screen. "He's the president of the Adelaide chapter. His name is Carlo Vossik."

Vossik! Val stared at the man, fixing the face into his memory. He looked to be about thirty years of age, which would mean... Val did the math, and nodded. In all probability Carlo Vossik was the son of the man he'd assassinated. *Well, well: he'd risen to the rank of president—just like his father.* Val rubbed his forehead. Their situation suddenly looked a whole lot bleaker. The motives behind all that had happened were personal, very personal indeed. He pointed to the picture. "What sort of car is that?"

"No idea," said David. "I'm not much good with cars. But I'll find out."

After searching for a few minutes on the web, they got their answer. David read out the name. "It's a nineteen-seventies Chrysler Valiant Pacer—quite a rare car, evidently."

Val turned away from the computer and stared at the Manchurian pear tree outside. He watched its petals fall, like tears, weighted by the grief of life.

Chapter 15

Pip stepped off the bus acutely aware of Sebastian behind her. He looked a fright. His hair gave no indication of having been brushed, and he was wearing his trademark dark green shirt without the sleeves. He had, however, assured her it was a new one—clean.

"How many shirts do you have?" she'd asked.

"Three."

"Three!"

"Two work shirts and one good shirt."

She'd been appalled.

They walked from North Terrace to Rundle Mall. Moments later, they arrived at *Little Sister*.

Pip wasn't sure she was ready to explain who Sebastian was, so she suggested he sit at one of the tables on the pavement while she went inside to see if she could have the morning off work.

In the event, things did not go according to plan—and she only had herself to blame for it. Mario demurred at giving her the morning off. "*Mia bella*, I always need you. You know that."

"But Mario, I need to help my…friend…find his way around and get himself sorted for his University course. He's not used to the city."

"We will be busy in an hour, and the boys always want to see you."

At that point, Tiffany pushed between them holding a tray of coffee cups. "Who is that weird-looking man you came with?" She hissed. "He looks like one of the 'big, bad Banksia men.'"

Pip thought quickly. "Distant cousin."

Tiffany tossed her head. "You have strange cousins," and continued on with her coffee cups.

Pip turned back to her boss. "Be kind to me, Mario. It could all turn out to your advantage. Sebastian is studying design. He could probably give you some tips on how to smarten this place up."

"Really?"

Pip instantly regretted what she'd just said. "Yes, but…" However, it was too late.

Mario marched out of the front door and sat himself down opposite Sebastian. "I hear you are studying design and might be able to tell me how to improve the look of the café."

Sebastian looked startled. Pip, standing behind Mario, gesticulated silently imploring him to go along with it.

He nodded slowly. "Perhaps, Mr…"

Mario offered his hand. "Mario. Call me Mario." He stood up. "Come inside. I make you the best coffee."

Pip protested. "Mario, we haven't got time. We need to get to the hairdresser's."

"But have a look. Tell me what you think." He ushered Sebastian inside.

Mario waved his hands around the cafe. "What you think?"

Pip clenched her hands into fists and closed her eyes.

Silence.

Sebastian cleared his throat. "Hmm. I like that." He pointed to the coffee-roasting machine. "And the hessian sacks look good. So does the display of coffee percolators. But it's quite dark at the back. The room is long and your only natural light comes from the front windows."

"So, what would you do?" demanded Mario.

"I'd go to a builder's salvage yard…"

"You'd do what?" interrupted Pip, not really believing what she was hearing.

Sebastian nodded. "Get some old wooden window frames, well aged, distressed and with lots of character."

"And…" she prompted.

"Glaze them with mirrors and hang them on the walls."

Mario pursed his lips and glanced around the café. After a moment, he turned back to her. "You have the morning off. But I need you here tomorrow." Mario yelled for his son who was working in the kitchen. "Nikko, Nikko…I have a job for you."

Pip didn't wait. She grabbed Sebastian and towed him out of the café.

"How did you do that?" she hissed.

"What?"

She grunted in exasperation and led him along the footpath to the hairdressing salon four doors down. It was an upmarket affair full of chrome, black tiles, and brutal minimalism. Two clients were already being attended to, but Andrio, the owner, was free. He smiled when he saw Pip and came over to embrace her. "Aah, Pepita."

"Hi Andrio," she said kissing him on both cheeks. "May I present a victim for your ministrations." She waved her hand at Sebastian who was trailing behind her. "But I don't have a booking. I was hoping we might get in if we came early."

"Victim! Pepita, you are cruel." Andrio turned to Sebastian. "My, my, what a fine, young man." He smiled. "For him, you need no booking."

Sebastian rolled his eyes and looked as if he wanted the earth to swallow him.

"What should I do with him, *ma cherie?*"

"Medium length, textured, and tapered, I think."

Andrio threw his hands up. "Oh, no, no, no, no. With his curly hair, I should do a high fade with a long fringe." He shepherded Sebastian to a chair and pushed him down into it.

"No, Andrio. He has to break girls' hearts, not boys' hearts."

"But he would look," he kissed his finger tips, "*superbe.*"

"Andrio, hear me. Think George Clooney in his prime."

Andrio ran his hands through Sebastian's hair and shook his head, mournfully. "Ah ya, ya, yah." He walked to the side and studied Sebastian. "And the beard?" he asked. "I could do…"

Pip interrupted. "Cut it off. I want no hint of Ned Kelly." She looked at Sebastian. *I want to see what you look like, my good man.*

She watched in fascination for the next half hour as the transformation took place. It was as well it took place gradually, for she would never have believed how different Sebastian could look. In truth, she was in shock and trying to overcome a sense of…what? Was it shyness? She couldn't believe herself. *Get a grip, girl.*

Sebastian's aquiline nose was now framed by the strong planes of his face—a very handsome face, she decided. His brown eyes were made all the more compelling by the pale eyebrows and his now stylish blond hair. He could be a model for a country fashion label. The thought caused her to look forward to seeing what he would look like in some decent clothes.

During the morning, she found out.

––––––––––––

Sebastian stood with Pip in front of the Conservatorium. He'd spent the entire morning with her. He wasn't sure he'd spent daylight hours with any girl before, at least in his adult life. And if being with a girl wasn't heady enough; being with Pip was…he shook his head…something else. It was terrifying, bewildering, and strangely compelling.

He caught sight of himself in the reflection from one of the windows. It was extraordinary. He wouldn't have recognized himself. Smart jacket, open-necked shirt, good trousers, and stylish shoes. If the clothes weren't different enough, their combined effect on his sense of identity was profound. It was as if the new pieces of clothing were conspiring together to re-engineer his very soul.

Pip turned to face him. "Right. I'll leave you here."

Sebastian dragged himself back to reality. "When do you finish?"

She looked at her watch. "In two and a half hours."

"I'll wait for you in the foyer."

Pip sighed. "Is that really necessary? We could meet back at *Little Sister*."

"I'll see you here."

"Hmph." She pulled a face. "What are you going to do in the mean time?"

"I'll check out where I have to go for the interview tomorrow."

"What department?"

"The interview is at Engineering North—wherever that is."

"That's over the Eastern side of the uni, near the Maths Lawns." She gave him instructions on how to get there.

Sebastian found the School of Civil, Environmental, and Mining Engineering easily enough. But it was surreal walking through the university. He felt like a fraud, as if he didn't belong—could never belong.

He mounted the steps to the Engineering building and made his way along the corridor. No one challenged him. Various rooms led off the hallway. Some were lecture rooms; others seemed to be engineering laboratories. The door of one of them was open. He stepped into the doorway.

A young man with long hair was at a bench making a statue of a horse from strands of copper wire. It was an impressive looking thing that stood about two feet tall.

Sebastian nodded appreciatively. "Looks good."

"Thanks." The young man looked Sebastian over. "You a student here?"

"Nah. But I've got an interview tomorrow."

"Yeah. Who with?"

"Engineering, Planning, and Design. Thought I'd better check out where to come and get some idea of what the place is like. I deferred six years ago, and now I have to reapply."

"Oh yeah. Why Engineering, Planning, and Design? It's not the easiest course."

Sebastian shrugged. "Making things is what I do. It's my safe place when I can't make sense of anything else."

"Yeah?"

The coil of copper wire buckled up in front of the young man as he sought to feed it through the wire matrix in front of him. "Damn it."

"Here, let me give you a hand." Sebastian put down the shopping bags containing his old clothes and took the coil of wire from him. He untwisted the buckle and fed it back through the wire armature to the young man.

The conversation drifted on.

"Why wait six years?"

"Waiting for my balls to drop, I suppose."

The young man laughed. "Seriously, why now?"

Sebastian sighed. "I was told this morning to make the most of my life. Thought I'd better give it a go." He picked up a piece of the copper wire. "Can I take a bit of this?"

"What for?"

"I've got two hours to kill. Thought I'd make a bracelet for a friend of mine."

The young man turned around. "The lab tech's not around. How much do you need?"

"About two yards."

"Go your hardest." He handed Sebastian a pair of pliers. "Use the vice over there."

Sebastian nodded his thanks and took off his jacket.

"Have you done any engineering?" the man asked.

"No. I've been working on a farm for the last six years."

The man laughed. "So you're used to working with wire."

"Yeah, suppose I am."

"Done anything technical?"

"Nup. Although I did rewire a shearing shed."

"But nothing mechanical?"

"Fiddled with a quadcopter and hotted up a car." He grinned. "Doubt that's going to count for much."

"But fun."

"Yeah."

"Anything with computers?"

"Had to fix the boss's a few times."

"Don't tell me: your boss was a baby-boomer."

Sebastian nodded.

"How are you going to make your bracelet?"

"I'll weave it from eight wires. There's one central wire; one wrapping wire and six woven wires."

"Hmm."

The two of them worked on in silence.

Sebastian anchored the central wire in place and began to plait and wrap the others around it. "What's it like being a student here? Is it as boring as hell or do you actually get to be creative?"

The young man brushed some strands of hair from his face. "It's up to you really. You can be as creative as you like."

"And the staff. What are they like?"

"The staff are pretty good—except for the deputy head of department. He's a bastard."

A pall of dread came over Sebastian. "Right. I guess there's a chance he'll be interviewing me tomorrow. What's he look like?"

"He looks like me."

Realization dawned. "Oh no!"

The young man held out his hand. "Professor Jim Dakin. "Don't worry, mate. I'm pretty confident you've just passed your interview."

───────────

Sebastian felt less self-conscious than he expected to as he lounged against the wall of the foyer, waiting for Pip. Students filed past him, in and out of the Con, carrying music cases of every conceivable shape. He would never admit it to Pip, but he was glad he was wearing his new clothes. He would have felt appallingly conspicuous and out of place in his old work-shirt and boots.

Pip came into the foyer. A small smile played on her lips. "Hmm," she said. "You don't look too bad for a bogan."[1]

"But a bogan I remain at heart."

She cocked her head sideways. "You don't have to be, you know."

"Yeah, I do. I don't get how you can like this la-di-da, poncy classical rubbish?"

She glared at him. "Poncy classical rubbish?"

He nodded.

Pip grabbed him by the arm. "Come with me, you ignorant, red-necked, peasant."

Sebastian allowed himself to be propelled along the corridor and pushed into a small room. Inside it was a piano, a music stand, and an armchair.

She pointed to the armchair.

"Sit," she ordered.

He sat.

Pip pulled a pair of headphones out of her shoulder bag. She plugged them into her phone, fiddled with it for a few moments and then stood in front of him with one hand on a hip.

"You are about to hear *The Swan*, the 13th and penultimate movement of 'The Carnival of the Animals' by Camille Saint-Saëns." She took off her woolen cap and shook her hair free. "Put this on," she ordered, "and pull it over your eyes. Leave your ears free."

He did as he was ordered. The perfume from the cap teased him —lavender.

She fitted the earphones to his ears.

"I've turned the music up quite loud. Keep your eyes shut and listen."

The music began with the tinkling of a piano. It was pleasant, but nothing special. And then the cello came in with gentle, sweeping stateliness. Instantly he was there: he could see the sunlight glittering on the water—and the swan, tall and stately, gliding like a galleon through it.

The work was very short, and it left him in a state of profound peace. He wished he could stay a bit longer—with the lavender on the riverbank.

He removed the headphones and the cap—kneading the wool between his fingers.

"Well?" she demanded.

He shrugged. "It was all right."

Her mouth fell open. "All right!" she expostulated.

He laughed. "Actually, it was pretty amazing."

"Hmph." She took the headphones and cap back from him and said tartly, "Well, Mr. Bogan. That's what I want to fill the world with."

Sebastian raised his hands in surrender. "Okay, okay. It's a…" he tried to find the right words. "It's a worthy goal."

There was a glint of triumph in Pip's eyes as she made for the door.

He scrambled to his feet to follow her. When he caught up with her he said, "One of these days, Pip, I will introduce you to my world."

She gave no indication of hearing him. "Let's get home," she said. "But first, I need to call in to *Little Sister* to pick up next week's roster."

He put out a hand to stop her moving off. "I…er, I have something to give you."

"What?" she demanded.

Sebastian pulled out the woven copper bracelet and handed it to her.

Pip picked it up and looked at him quizzically. "Nice. Where did you get it?"

"I made it."

"You made it!"

He nodded. "In one of the labs in the engineering block."

Pip turned it over in her hands. "Wow. That's…" she paused, "beautiful." She slipped it over her wrist…and then rummaged in her shoulder bag. "And I've got something for you."

"Really?"

"Yes." She grinned and handed him a hairbrush.

When they arrived at the café, Pip suggested that Sebastian wait for her outside at a table on the pavement.

Moments later, she was negotiating her roster with Mario. He always wanted her to work more hours than her music studies allowed. As she argued her way to some sort of compromise, Tiffany came up to her bouncing up and down excitedly. "Pippy, I've just seen this divine man. He's sitting outside."

Pip glanced up. "Where?"

"There," Tiffany pointed.

It took a moment for Pip to understand. She was pointing to Sebastian.

Pip tried not to laugh. "Forget it, Tiff," she said eventually. "He's…" *what?* She thought wildly…"family property," she finished lamely. *Family property! Couldn't I think of anything better than that?* She hurried on. "And he doesn't like classical music."

Tiffany furrowed her brow. "Oh. Really?"

"He's not for you, Tiff—seriously." Pip patted her arm. "But don't worry: another man will turn up tomorrow."

Chapter 16

Val held the handkerchief in his hands as he stared out of the dormer window. Darkening clouds were bringing a frown to the end of the day, and the light was fading fast. He'd turned to the window to prevent himself from staring at his son. Seeing Sebastian clean-shaven and dressed smartly had been a shock—the more so because his features reflected the eyes and mouth of his wife. Sebastian presented a picture that was both troubling and wonderful.

His son had caught him staring at him. Sebastian had shrugged awkwardly and grinned. He was obviously self-conscious in his new skin. But Val had seen something else in his son's demeanor that he could not yet place. He had energy about him. As he didn't feel he had the right words to inquire about it, he let it be.

Seeking to break the silence, he said, "We need to talk." He glanced at his watch. "We've got an hour before tea, so let's try and work out the two issues that are most pressing."

Sebastian raised an eyebrow. "Which are?"

"Getting enough intelligence about the Saracens to let us know what we're dealing with."

"And?"

"Organizing how to meet with them in a way that avoids a blood bath."

Sebastian stretched himself out on the camp bed and put his hands behind his head. "Nothing serious, then."

Val cut off his rebuke before he could utter it. Sebastian couldn't yet appreciate the full brutality of the world he'd been led into. He closed his eyes and tried to think of what he'd need to do to keep his son alive. Whatever it was, he'd have to move quickly if he had any chance of siezing the initiative and setting the agenda. If the Saracens ever succeeded in wresting that from him, Sebastian and the Albrights would be running and hiding all their lives. And that was no life at all. He sighed. He'd need to act—tomorrow, if possible.

Reconnaissance: that was what was needed, and for that, he needed a car. Surveillance work was tedious and dangerous. There was also the risk of being discovered, so he wanted to do it alone.

Val cleared his throat. "Can I borrow the car tomorrow?" Sebastian had, on his instructions, bought a nondescript second-hand Ford sedan. It was an inconspicuous, common make of car, and one that had lots of space.

"You don't have a license. Do you want me to drive you?"

"No. I'll risk it."

"What are you going to do?"

"I know where the Saracens' headquarters are. I'm going to watch it to see who's about, and perhaps follow them to see where they live."

Sebastian sat himself up. "Will it be dangerous?"

"I'll take the Barrett."

Sebastian nodded slowly. "I take it that means, 'yes.'" He paused. "What can I do?"

"Just keep an eye on Pip."

"You also need a safe place to meet with the Saracens."

"Yes."

"I might be able to help with that."

"I don't want you to get involved."

Sebastian laughed—not an altogether pleasant sound. "Bit late for that, isn't it?"

"I'm serious."

Sebastian got to his feet. "Well, so am I. You forget. I spent the first eighteen years of my life in this city, and ran a bit wild in it for a while. I know my way around pretty well." He put his hands on his hips. "So tell me, what sort of place are you looking for?"

"You'll take no risks?"

"No risks."

Val nodded. "I need a place where the Saracens can only come through one entrance. But somehow, I've got to be able to get there ahead of time by another way, one that's not obvious. I'll need it as an escape route."

"Anything else?"

"It needs to be away from the general public."

"You don't ask much."

"That's not the worst of it."

"What else?"

"I need some sort of screen between them and me which will stop the bastards shooting me—but through which I can be heard."

Sebastian rubbed the back of his neck.

Val sympathized. "Yeah. It won't be easy." He turned away and stared out of the window. It was dark now. He could see across the back alley into lighted windows, behind which peaceful domestic scenes were being played out. A woman pushed a cat off a kitchen bench and then bent down to talk to a child.

Distracted as he was, he was unprepared for Sebastian's next comment.

"I think I know a place which might suit."

He turned round. "Where?"

"In the city, on a rooftop."

"A what?"

Sebastian held up a hand. "Let me check it out first. Things could have changed over the last six years. It's not worth planning anything until I know what's possible."

"How will you do that?"

"Pip is playing at a music concert in Elder Hall tonight. Apparently it's her performance exam." He dropped his head. "I'd sort of hoped to attend. But I'll use the time she's at the performance to check the place out."

"It's an odd time of day to check things out."

"It's an odd place."

Val nodded.

Silence fell between them for some minutes.

Val cleared his throat. "Tell me about drones. What can your drone do? Do you have to be in line of sight for it to work?"

Sebastian rubbed a hand through his hair.

"My drone can operate on two frequencies. High frequencies give you better response and more immediate optics. Low frequencies give a greater range and an ability to penetrate objects standing between you and your drone. But I'd have to use a large antenna to operate in the low frequency range. It would be quite conspicuous."

"What range do you have on low frequency?"

"Two kilometers."

"Can the drone carry cargo—say, a small parcel?"

"Yes. I've added a couple of channels so it can do that." He grinned. "I delivered Lottie's birthday present with it once."

"What weight can it carry?"

"It'll carry seven ounces quite easily."

"Hmm."

"But there's a complication."

Val raised an eyebrow.

"If you don't fly 'line of sight,' you're no longer classed as a hobbyist and you need to be licensed by CASA."

"CASA?"

"Civil Aviation Safety Authority."

"I take it that you don't have a license from CASA."

"Correct."

Val drummed his fingers. "I don't want to lead you onto the wrong side of the law."

"As I said before; I think I'm already on the wrong side, don't you?"

"Not badly."

Sebastian pulled a wry face. "Then I'll do my best to remain in the 'not badly' bracket."

A cry came from the courtyard below them. It was Pip's voice.

"Dinner's ready, you guys. And Sebastian, I expect you to be dressed properly for it."

Val passed Sebastian his jacket.

Chapter 17

"You won't be late, Dad?" Pip leaned forward and kissed her father on the cheek.

"Your performance exam—after three years of hard work, I wouldn't dare."

She reached up and straightened his tie. "It's just that it's easier to play to a crowd. You don't notice the examiners so much."

David kissed the top of her head and gave her a gentle push toward the door. "You'll be fine, and I'll be there."

The front door was open, and Sebastian was waiting for her outside. He was standing beside the Manchurian pear tree. It was white with blossom, adorned like a bride for a wedding. The cheerful confetti lent an air of hope. In view of what faced her that evening, she was grateful for its optimism. Sebastian was dressed in stark contrast. He wore black jeans, sneakers, black tee-shirt, and a padded lightweight jacket. She sighed. At least he wasn't wearing his green work-shirt.

"Where are your new clothes? You've got your interview after lunch."

He lifted up the small haversack at his feet.

She grunted. "You look like an Italian waiter."

"You actually don't look so different."

Pip conceded that he had a point. She too was dressed in black. But she had an excuse: it was the expected uniform of musicians. Her only departure from tradition was to wear black slacks rather than a skirt. She told herself that it was less constricting when playing the cello. And the soft rubber-soled shoes—they were a concession to comfort. She'd be wearing them all day. A wave of self-doubt washed over her. Perhaps she should have dressed more formally.

"Come on, or we'll miss the bus."

Pip pulled her coat across her shoulders, picked up the music satchel, and hurried after Sebastian.

She was very conscious of his nearness as they sat together on the bus. As disturbing as it was, it paled in comparison with the challenge that awaited her that night. Her performance exam—finally. She shook her head. After all that had happened, the shooting, the very real danger to their lives, the intrusion of Sebastian into her life—it seemed laughable that she should worry about a music exam. But she did. Fortunately, she'd done lots of practice before her cello had been destroyed, but she'd done next to none in the last few days. She wrinkled her nose.

"What's the matter?"

Damn, he'd noticed. "Um, I've got my performance exam tonight in Elder Hall."

"I know. Is it very important?"

She nodded. "It's the culmination of all the tuition I've had over the last two-and-a-half years. I have to perform and show leadership of the group accompanying me."

"But you're not taking your cello."

"My tutor is lending me *The Lady*."

"*The Lady*?"

"It's what he calls his cello. It's a beautiful instrument, much better than the one I've borrowed from the Con—but it's not mine, so it's not what I'm used to."

"Is *The Lady* a better instrument than your old cello?"

"Yes."

Sebastian nodded slowly. "Then let it sing your praises."

What an odd thing to say.

She reflected on his comment. It had surprised her. Pip looked up at him, and wished she didn't feel so shy. "Will you be coming to the concert? It starts at 7:30."

"No."

Damn the man. She felt unaccountably angry. *Him and his bigoted dislike of classical music.* She thought briefly of arguing the case, but feared it would only sound pathetic. His 'no' had been emphatic. Pip slumped back into her seat. She'd have a better chance arguing with a lamppost—one with a broken light.

Sebastian turned to her. "I'd like to, but I need to check out some places tonight where Val can meet with the Saracens: somewhere safe—where he won't be killed."

Pip suddenly felt dreadful—ashamed. "Of course," she said weakly.

"But I'll be there to pick you up afterward."

She nodded.

They entered *Little Sister* twenty minutes later and were greeted by Mario. He threw up his hands. "Ah, ya, ya, yah. The only day you ever come like a waitress—you no work for me. Why is that, eh? You dress for music instead."

Pip kissed him on both cheeks. "It's one of the cruel ironies of life, Mario."

At that point, Tiffany arrived, carrying a shoulder bag and a violin case. Tiff looked at her aghast. "Are you dressed for the concert already! Uggh. I'll be going home to change first." She took Pip by the shoulders and looked her up and down. "Look at you. This is your performance exam!"

"We don't have to look like the Lady of Shalott in mourning, Tiff. I'm smart enough."

Tiffany rolled her eyes and turned to Sebastian. "Hello, I'm Tiffany. I hear you don't like…"

Pip interrupted her, "Sebastian: Tiff and I are going to spend an hour or so sorting the final details of tonight. Then we're going off to the Con to meet up with the rest of the quartet and my piano accompanist. As I'll be with Tiff, why don't you take the day off for yourself."

Sebastian nodded. "Okay. What time shall I pick you up?"

"About 9:30."

Mario bustled past them again. "I suppose you want coffee."

"Yes please," said Tiffany at his retreating back.

He continued to grumble on his way back to the coffee machine. "I'm losing two waitresses today. What am I gonna do?"

Pip was surprised to hear Sebastian call after him. "Can I help?"

Mario spun around. "What? You wanna work here? You make coffee?"

"No, but I can wait on tables—at least for the morning."

"Pepita: is he a good man?"

Pip felt lost for words. "I, err…yes. I suppose."

Mario turned back to Sebastian. "You want to be paid?"

"No, but I need a place to change for my interview after lunch— somewhere to leave my clothes."

Mario grinned. "You see, Pepita: God is good. He sends me a waiter who looks like a waiter."

Tiffany grabbed Pip by the arm, turned her around and steered her toward a table. "Are you two an item?" she whispered.

Pip's mind raced. What should she say? What would require the least explanation, and protect Sebastian?

"We might be…er, exploring the possibility."

Lord, forgive my lie.

Although the interview was brief, it left Sebastian emotionally exhausted. It wasn't because of the difficulty of the questions: in fact, a good part of the interview centered on a discussion of drone technology—a subject he was comfortable with. The issue was one of fear and self-doubt. He couldn't allow himself to believe that he could, or should, be at university. People like him didn't go to such places.

Professor Jim Dakin had sat between two other academics on

the other side of the table. At the end of the interview, Dakin said, "You look knackered. Don't tell me we were too hard on you."

Sebastian jerked himself upright. "No, no. Not at all. It was good. It's all just a bit…big."

"Too big?"

"No. I just need…" *a drink* he thought to himself, "to do something with my hands—to make something—so I can process it."

Dakin nodded. "Well, make sure you do process it. You'll hear officially in a few weeks, but I'd be planning to attend here at the start of next year, if I were you." He looked at Sebastian and smiled. "I can offer you a workshop if you want to make something."

"Seriously?"

"If you keep out of people's way and only use stuff from the scrap bin, yes."

"I'd like that."

"I'll ring down to the lab tech and tell her to expect you. Just make sure you stay under her supervision."

At this point, the academic sitting to his right lifted a cautionary hand and started to talk about risk and insurance.

Dakin slapped the table. "For goodness sake, Peter, we foster inquiry and creativity. Surely, that's our core business."

Sebastian left as soon as was decently possible.

A few minutes later, he was sitting at a workbench in the laboratory. Surreptitiously, he took out The Fire Stone, unwrapped it, and reached for a steel ruler. After measuring its length, he set to work.

Chapter 18

"I'm afraid you can't go in until the concert is finished." The attendant in the foyer of Elder Hall was polite but insistent. "It would be unfair on the exam candidate to be disturbed during a piece."

Sebastian nodded. "I understand. I'm actually here to pick her up and take her home."

He could hear the music through the door. It sounded good. The applause that followed certainly suggested it was. As it worked out, it was the final piece and people soon began to stream through the doors and out of the foyer. Sebastian held back and waited for Pip. Eventually she came out holding onto the arm of her father.

She grinned at him when she saw him.

"It sounded good from here," he said.

Pip gave a small bow. "Why thank you, kind sir."

David nodded. "Yes, she did well." He squeezed her shoulders. "Let's head home."

Pip pulled back. "No way. I'm far too wired to go home. I need to walk, I need a large ice cream—and I need to do something crazy."

Sebastian blinked. "An ice cream! It's winter."

She grinned. "The comfort of calories acknowledges no seasons."

David grunted. "Well, I need to get home. You and Sebastian can do your own thing. Just take care."

Pip kissed her father. "Thanks Dad. We won't be late."

"Here, let me carry your music satchel," added David. "And Sebastian, would you like me to take your haversack?"

"Thanks." Sebastian slipped it off his shoulder and handed it to him.

Pip and Sebastian made their way to Rundle Street where they bought ice creams—vanilla with warm butterscotch sauce. "The best," Pip assured him.

"So, you're pleased with how you went tonight," he said.

Pip licked her fingers where some of the butterscotch had dribbled. "Yep. It went pretty well. Although I had to fight Tiffany for leadership of the group now and again." She grinned. "The trouble is: she's actually pretty good and has a real instinct for knowing what's best." Pip licked her ice cream. "And what did you get up to today?" She suddenly stopped and slapped her forehead. "I'm sorry: I'm so full of my own agenda I forgot to ask. How did your interview go?"

"It went well. I'm in, unofficially."

"That's brilliant."

They continued walking.

Sebastian was wrestling with the novelty of spending an evening with a woman—an intoxicating woman. The fact that any young woman would show genuine interest in his affairs was bewildering. He fell into silence, unwilling to risk saying anything that might break the spell. Instead, he luxuriated in the waft of her perfume. It was subtle and teased like a distant memory.

Pip broke the spell. "And did you find...a place for Val?"

Sebastian heard a slight tremor in her voice.

"Um...I explored a stair well."

"A stair well?"

"And a roof."

"A roof! Where?"

Sebastian stopped and pointed to the top of a building on the southern side of the Mall. "That one."

Pip craned her neck back and looked incredulous. "You're joking!"

"Actually, I'm not."

"But that's...illegal, isn't it."

"Technically."

Pip rounded herself in front of Sebastian. "Tell me what's going on," she demanded.

Sebastian wasn't at all sure he wanted to, but made the mistake of looking into Pip's eyes. He saw her determination, and sighed. There would be no ducking the issue. "I, er..." He swallowed and tried again. "In my last few years at school, I used to slip out at night and do stuff."

"Stuff?"

He nodded. "I used to join in the activities of the Cave Clan."

"What on earth is the Cave Clan?"

"It's a bunch of guys who go in for urban roof climbing—the scarier, the better. And we explored the tunnels under the city."

"I didn't know there were tunnels under the city."

"Yeah, there are quite a few. Most are storm water drains for creeks that used to run across the city area. Engineers have routed them underground. You'll find the best graffiti in the city in the tunnels. The artists can work there undisturbed."

They continued walking together.

"You weren't into graffiti or vandalism were you?" she said, hesitantly.

"No. We had rules. We'd leave nothing but footprints on top of buildings—and unless you were a good artist, the only thing you did in the tunnels was to sign in."

"Sign in?"

"Yeah. There's usually a grid painted in the tunnel where you can sign your nickname and the date you explored it."

"And where's the nearest tunnel to here?"

"I could tell you, but then I'd have to kill you."

She punched his arm. "Seriously."

"Well, there are a few. One slightly collapsed tunnel leads from Wakefield Street. It ends near a Chinese restaurant."

They came to the corner at King William Street. Pip pulled him to the right and led him up the street. "Let's see the lights on the river."

The two of them headed toward the Torrens.

Sebastian was hoping that the subject of urban climbing had been exhausted, but he was disappointed.

"So you never actually did anything bad."

"Not really—although we weren't exactly angels. We were on top of a store once and saw a drunk guy staggering about in the mall. My mate started to drop ten cent coins down around him." Sebastian chuckled. "He had no idea where they came from."

"But how do you actually get up on to the roof?"

"If I remember rightly, we had to climb on top of a road sign in an alley between Rundle Mall and Grenfell Street. From there, we were able to reach a ledge." He shrugged. "It was pretty easy after that. We just had to be careful."

"Weren't you caught?"

"No, but we had some close shaves. We once made it up to the balcony of Harris Scarfe apartment store and discovered they'd left the door unlocked. When we got inside, we tripped the alarm. We had to leg it pretty quick, I can tell you." He grinned. "That was the night we discovered white men really can jump."

"You're mad."

"Probably."

They crossed North Terrace at Parliament House and walked past the Festival Centre. The splendid Victorian rotunda in Elder Park came into view, highlighted by spotlights. The river behind was reflecting the lights of North Adelaide. It was an enchanting sight.

Sebastian turned back and gazed at the soaring white planes of the roof of the Festival Centre. The complex contained a number of theaters. He'd always thought their roofs looked like folded paper boats turned upside down. "Well, well, well," he murmured.

"Well, well, what?" asked Pip.

He rubbed the back of his neck. He'd really have to be more careful with what he said around Pip.

"Er...the roof floodlights are not on at the Playford Theatre."

"And?"

"The best view in the city is from the top of its roof."

"How do you get up there?"

He pointed. "There: where the roof comes down at the side. It's actually pretty easy. The roof pitch is only about thirty-five degrees and it's an easy climb—provided it's dry."

She tugged at his arm. "Show me."

Reluctantly, he trailed after her.

They mounted some concrete stairs until they came to a small palazzo where the bottom beak of the roof swept down within five feet of the ground.

Adrenaline began to surge through him, and that old feeling of excitement, of madness, began to possess him. He ran to the wall and leaped up to a small ledge. From there, he traversed to the spine of the roof and began to climb up it. He only intended to go up a few yards to show how it was done. When he looked back, he was appalled to discover Pip beginning to climb after him.

"Get back," he hissed.

"No."

"Well, let me climb behind you in case you slip." He moved sideways and allowed her to pass him.

It was a long climb to the top, but to her credit, Pip stuck to it until they came to the relatively flat area on the top.

"Lie down about two meters from the edge. Then you won't be seen," he whispered.

He came up beside her and lay down.

Pip had her mouth open, uttering a silent 'wow.' It was not hard to see why. The view across Elder Park and the river was amazing. The plume of water from the river's fountain changed color with the lights, making a dazzling display. The lights of Adelaide's famous cricket ground could be seen behind the river, and beyond that, the floodlit spires of St Peter's cathedral soared into the night sky.

For a long time, nothing was said.

"It's beautiful," she whispered. "But I still don't know what drives you to do such stupid things."

Sebastian mulled over her comment. He'd never really thought about why before. He allowed his mind to wander back to that sixteen-year-old kid who had felt so abandoned, so abused, and so vulnerable. A wave of emotion swept over him. It surprised him. *Where the hell did that come from?* He fought against it, wrestling it to a standstill until it retreated to the wings, if not from the stage. Why did he climb? Why did he feel the need to stand on top of a building, to conquer it, and look over the city?

He cleared his throat. "I think you have to be a little bit angry."

"Angry?"

"Hmm. It's a perception thing: not real—the perception that the city has threatened you, or is trying to diminish you." He shrugged. "So you push back."

Pip was silent for a while. Eventually she said. "I've just got back from Nepal. It sort of...ruined my appetite for Western cities."

Sebastian nodded. "Conformist suburbs dominated by television."

Pip grinned. "Very poetic." She thought for a moment, then said: "That leech hope away from the eyes of the children."

"Not bad. Good pathos." He countered with: "Full of executives bent low by the misery of power."

She laughed.

It was a beautiful sound.

Pip turned to him. "You say you've been a farm hand for the last six years. How come..." she seemed to struggle to find the words, "you know things?"

Sebastian furrowed his brow, unable to understand her question.

Pip hurried on. "The things you know, surprise me. How do you know them?"

"God forbid—a farm hand who knows things."

"Seriously."

"Aah." He marshaled his thoughts. "I read, and I was quite good at school."

"Were you?"

He smiled. "Well, I wasn't always. In fact, for the first few years I just goofed around and was a right pain in the arse for the teachers."

"What happened?"

"There was a new physics teacher who believed in me. He made everything—the cosmos, the laws of physics, biology—sound so fantastic that I began paying attention and wanted to know more." He laughed. "Before I knew it, he'd bumped me up to the nerd's class, and that's when the shit hit the fan."

"The fan?"

"Well, the nerds didn't like it and made their feelings clear. Not that I blame them. I'd given most of them plenty of lip in my time." He shrugged. "I just thought: sod it, I'll show them. I worked hard; discovered I liked reading and did well."

"But you didn't follow up on it."

He smiled wryly. "The idea of university was a bridge too far. It wasn't what the guys I hung with aspired to."

"Until now."

"Maybe even now."

They were silent for a long time. There were some things he didn't feel he could share yet. He wasn't sure he could express them —even to himself.

Why did ideas come to him like visitors in the dark to tease him with possibilities? He'd learned they were delicate things that flourished only in the right mental environment—one of relaxed alertness—when his mind felt free to play. And why did the words of Pip's father strike a chord with thoughts that he'd been having recently? They'd played like wraiths, suggesting greatness, calling to him, promising unimaginable creativity. But he was mired in self-doubt—unable to break through to the brilliant turquoise that beckoned him. He was fairly sure it was not the glory of ego that was calling to him, but his real self. He was a beggar beginning to awake to disturbing memories that he was, in fact, a king—but one trapped in the gutter.

He kept his thoughts to himself.

Pip interrupted his thinking. "Does it trouble you that your father's story seems so…" she sighed, "you know…unbelievable?"

Her question surprised him. "Not really. I know he did go to prison, and was presumed dead. It all makes sense in its own bizarre way."

"But did he really hide in an opal mine for years and years?"

Sebastian drew a deep breath. "Pip, I'm going to show you something."

"What's that?"

"It's called The Fire Stone."

Chapter 19

Val refilled David's mug with tea.

David folded down the top of his newspaper and nodded his thanks. "What are you doing today?"

"Delivering a letter."

"I take it, that it's to..." David's voice trailed off.

"Yeah: to the Saracens. Sebastian and I will probably do it this evening. We might be late for tea."

The cleric looked at him speculatively. "Will it be dangerous?"

"I won't let it get to that."

David nodded slowly. "We'll delay tea and wait 'til you get back. It'll give me time to pray for you."

Val blinked. He wasn't sure anyone had ever volunteered to do that for him in his life. It was a shock. He certainly didn't expect it from someone who knew he was a killer—and was unrepentant about it.

David resumed reading.

Sebastian had already finished breakfast and was back up in the loft. Pip had yet to emerge.

Val cleared his throat. "Will you be okay if I spend most of the day with Sebastian?"

"I'll be fine. Thursdays is when I write my sermon, so I'll be in most of the day."

"Okay, then." He stood up. "I'll be off."

Once he was back in the loft, Val pulled a camping chair across to where Sebastian was sitting and sat down. It was time to address what they were going to do with the Saracens. He drew a deep breath.

"Let's talk about the place you suggest I use for my meeting with Vossik. Why on a roof in the city?"

Sebastian looked up from his Kindle. After a moment's hesitation, he said, "You'd be separated by a metal grill and have completely different routes of access. By confining him to a stairwell, you'll also limit his options."

Val nodded. He was impressed. Sebastian had thought it through well. He was also intrigued. "How do you know about these places?"

"I used to climb them during my last few years at school. It was my protest at life."

A pang of guilt struck at Val's heart. He didn't really know how to express it so instead he said, "Did you ever get caught?"

Sebastian put down his Kindle. "Only by my foster carers. They caught me climbing back in through my window a few times. The Old Man was pretty cool about it, but it was enough for him to suggest I work for his brother in the Mallee when I finished school."

"Do we have an escape route from this place you suggest?"

"A few. But they all take a bit of nerve. You'll need to jump from building to building."

"Can you get down from the buildings easily?"

"Each one has different options for getting down—stairwells and fire-escapes. You can even climb down via some ledges, although you'd be very visible during the day. I'm pretty confident of being able to get you down most buildings without being noticed."

Val nodded. "Let's fire up your computer so we can check it on Google Maps and Streetscape."

Sebastian nodded his thanks to Pip. She'd come up to the loft carrying two morning cups of coffee. She glanced at him briefly with an interrogating eye.

He lifted a hand in a half-wave.

She smiled and left without a word.

Sebastian shook his head, trying to get the memories and disturbing emotions from the previous night out of his head. He had to focus. Lives were at stake. He turned to Val. "Okay, so we know where we might have the meeting, but how do we deliver the invitation? You're not exactly on their Christmas card list."

Val took an experimental sip of his coffee. "I staked out the Saracen's headquarters yesterday and followed Vossik's car back to his house. I know where he lives."

"I'm guessing you won't be using the postman."

"No, I'll be using you."

"Whoa!" Sebastian sat up in his chair. "Back up the truck, mate. Why?"

"Because I want a method of delivery only you can provide."

"Huh?"

"I want to unsettle him."

Sebastian leaned back. "You'd better tell me what's on your mind."

Val nodded. "Before I do, can you tell me whether or not you still have your, er…finger?"

Sebastian couldn't repress a shudder. The wretched thing was macabre; he hated it. He wanted to be rid of it, but he couldn't bring himself to even touch it in order to throw it away.

"Where is it?" asked Val.

"I chucked it into the miniature tool kit I keep in the glove compartment. It's in the new car now."

"If I wrapped a message around the tube, could your drone deliver it?"

Sebastian's mouth dropped open. "Geese, mate: you are full of surprises."

"Could it be done?"

I suppose so. Particularly if I was flying line of sight."

"No, I won't allow that. I can't afford for you to be seen."

Sebastian massaged his temples. It was bizarre to have this man —his father, technically—show care.

He forced himself to return to the issue at hand. "Then I'll need to use low frequency, and that's harder."

"How accurately can you fly using low frequency?"

"If accuracy is important: I'll have to fly slow. It takes longer for the image to form in the goggle display at low frequency."

"But flying slow makes detection more likely."

"Yeah."

"If you flew slow, how accurately could you fly the drone?"

"I'm pretty good. I could put your parcel on his front door mat easily enough, if that's what you want."

"That's good enough for me." Val leaned back. "Now here's the important question: Can you take photos as well?"

"Yes."

Val nodded.

No one spoke for a while.

Eventually, Val cleared his throat. "Where would you need to operate the drone from? Assume for this purpose, you'll be operating from the road behind the block where Vossik's house is. In other words, you'll be two houses away."

"I'd need to get as high as possible to optimize control and visuals."

Val pointed to the computer. "Let's have another look at Streetscape and see what our options are."

The cypress pine was easy to climb. It had lots of branches, but they were dense and scratchy. Sebastian reflected wryly that this was not the open, accessible tree the Swiss family Robinson would have chosen for their tree house. On the plus side, the tree's many branches would hide him and his low frequency aerial.

Once he had nested himself as high as he could, he scanned the area around him. He'd need to be careful of the power lines running along his side of the road, but other than that, everything looked straightforward. Even though dusk was beginning to fall, he could clearly see the roof and carport of Vossik's place over the top of the nearest house.

Val was below him in the back garden of a ramshackle house that looked as if it had been earmarked for demolition. No lights were on, and the grass in the back garden was over three-feet tall. It looked deserted, which was why they'd chosen it.

Sebastian pulled the knapsack off his back, readied the controller, and extended the aerial. After donning the goggles, he pulled the phone from his pocket and rang Val. From his vantage point, he could see him standing beside what looked to be an old chicken shed.

Val's voice came through. It was full of concern. "Are you well concealed?"

"Yes, but I have a clear view of the back of Vossik's house. He's home, by the way. His car is in the carport. Are you good to go?"

"Yeah. The parcel's still attached."

"Put the drone on the roof of the chicken shed and step back."

Sebastian watched the scene from the drone's camera in his goggles. The reception was good. The scene in front of him wobbled and then settled.

"Any overhead wires near you?" he asked.

"No."

"Then it's showtime."

———

Val sighed with relief as Sebastian pulled away from the curb and drove demurely down the suburban street. His son looked flushed from exertion but otherwise seemed calm. That was a good sign. "Did the job?" he asked.

"Yeah. I got some interesting pictures of Vossik's woman. She was in the kitchen—dancing while she cooked tea. I think she was listening to music."

Val grunted. "That was fortunate. It would have helped mask the sound of the drone."

"I didn't see any sign of Vossik. I think he was in the bathroom. The light was on."

Val nodded. "Where did you deliver the, er…parcel?"

"Somewhere where he'd notice it."

Val paused. "You know Vossik needs to find it tonight?"

"Yes."

Val frowned. "So I don't need to contact him tonight to tell him where to find it."

"No."

Val was bewildered. "Why?"

"Because I've put it on the pillow of his bed."

"You did what?"

"The bedroom window was open."

"You flew it through an open window!"

"Yeah. The visibility was good, and I'd got caged props. They weren't going to catch on anything."

Val shook his head.

Sebastian smiled. "Told you I was good."

Chapter 20

V al watched Sebastian stand on a wheelie-bin and reach up to the fire escape above him. Moments later he swung himself up to its bottom landing. The boy made it look easy. With considerably more exertion, Val joined him on the fire escape. Dawn had not yet broken and would not do so for another hour.

Without a word, they began to climb.

Val was still torturing himself about the wisdom of involving Sebastian. Vossik would have only had a few hours during the night to digest his invitation to a meeting—hopefully not long enough for him to plan too much mischief. But there was no knowing how he would respond. Whilst he and Sebastian had prepared for the most likely contingencies, a lot was unknown. He shook his head. This was not what he had in mind when he'd vowed to keep his son safe.

The fire escape ran all the way to the roof. It was a long way up. As soon as they climbed over the parapet onto the roof, Val crossed over to the adjacent edge to inspect the building next door. The ambient light of the city enabled him to just make out its details.

Sebastian came up beside him and pointed. "The metal grill blocking the air duct at the top of the stair well is on the far side of the building."

Val nodded. From where he stood, he could see the balconies of the building on the other side of the one he needed to get to. If Vossik was going to station a man to watch out for him, he'd be behind one of those balcony windows. He turned to his son. "Sebastian, this is where you stay. You're not to come any closer. If everything goes pear-shaped, just get out of here. Is that clear?"

Sebastian nodded. "I'll watch for trouble and text you if I see it."

Val pointed to the building on the far side. "If trouble is going to come, it will come from one of those balconies, so keep the scope on them. If anyone looks threatening, switch on the laser and play it on their heart. It'll give them something to think about." Val glanced down to the roof of the building he needed to get to. It was five meters below him. "How do I get down there?"

Sebastian pointed to the raised relief of the coining at the corner of the building. "We climb down there."

"You're kidding me!"

"It's easier than it looks. Just trust your feet and hands, and don't look down."

Val, of course, did look down. He could see cars on the street below highlighted by the streetlights. It was a very long way down.

"If you're going to fall," said Sebastian, grinning, "fall to the left —then you'll land on the roof. Look, I'll show you." He climbed up onto the parapet.

Val started to protest.

"Relax, I'll climb straight back here once I've shown you."

Before he could argue, Sebastian was clambering down to the roof of the neighboring building. It took him just a few seconds to reach it.

Taking a deep breath, Val followed.

Minutes later, Val lay on his stomach against the low parapet, invisible to anyone standing on any of the balconies of the building next door. Sebastian had returned to his lookout on top of the building on the other side.

All he had to do now was be patient. Val glanced at his watch. It was 6am. Dawn was beginning to break, and he had four hours to wait.

He checked the phone was on vibrate, and made himself comfortable.

Val instantly became fully conscious when his phone began to buzz. He looked at the screen. It was a message from Pip. He glanced at the time: 9am. Pip would have been in the café opposite the entrance of the building since 8. He read the message.

"Two men in leathers entering building. One remains in car. Good luck."

Already!

Five minutes later, Val could hear steps echoing through the grill. There were some murmurings, a scuffling sound, then silence.

Val waited.

Thirty minutes later, the phone vibrated again. He glanced at the screen, tapped a brief reply, and continued to wait.

On the dot of 10am, he turned toward the metal grill and spoke. "Vossik, take your phone out and tell the clown on the opposite building, the one with the red laser sight wobbling over his heart, to leave his gun where it is and piss off."

Val heard a brief expletive and then silence.

A moment later, he could hear murmuring inside.

Val's phone again vibrated. He glanced at the text.

"Man gone."

"You've come to see me, Vossik. What's on your mind?"

Vossik's voice came through the grill. What he said was nasty— designed to shock, terrify, and intimidate. The language was vile, extreme, and savage.

Val listened to the voice, analyzing it to try and build a picture of the man he was dealing with.

Eventually, Vossik ran out of words.

"Is that the best you've got, Vossik? That may have grannies shaking in their shoes but do you really think that I'd be impressed?"

Vossik scoffed. "You're an idiot. A fool. Do you know what you're dealing with?"

"I understand what you are—vermin, who bully ordinary people. But I'm not ordinary, Vossik. When your father raped and murdered my wife, he could not have guessed what hell would drop on the Saracens as a result. I've killed eight of you." He paused and then asked, "Who was the guy I killed in Swan Hill?"

"My sergeant at arms, you bastard. We'll kill your family and everyone associated with you."

"And who was the guy who is now missing a finger?"

The silence that followed was rather too long for it not to be significant. Realization dawned.

Vossik launched into more threats and profanities.

Val interrupted him. "It was you, wasn't it? You're missing a finger." He laughed. "What's it feel like, Vossik? Do you regret attacking my son now?"

"We'll kill him next time." It was a scream.

The situation was now dangerous. It was time to cool things down. Val listened for a while to the hum of the city. After judging what he hoped was an appropriate time, he said, "Do you seriously want to be at war with me? Have you any concept of what that means?"

"You're a dead man walking, McKenzie. It doesn't matter where you go. We'll find you. If you get on a plane, I will know. You'll be followed. You can't escape."

"Shut-up, Vossik. I'm going to show you some pictures." Val slid two photographs under the grill.

The first showed a photo of the bed in Carlo's bedroom. The second was a picture of a tattoo over the left breast of a woman. It was just above her heart. The woman was Vossik's partner—the woman photographed the previous night.

Val gave him a moment to digest the significance of the pictures, and then spoke with the venom generated by years of hate.

"Hear me clearly, Vossik. Every day your woman wakes up alive, it is because I've allowed it. Every day you get out of your car and reach the gate of your home, it is because I allow it."

Suddenly, a shot rang out. The bullet ricocheted off the metal grill and thumped into something solid.

The noise was shocking, and it left Val's ears ringing.

Val continued to speak—affecting a normalcy he did not feel. "You have a brother in the Saracens. Another nasty little thug—a disease, like you. So let me give you a word of advice. Don't let him ride near the front of your next funeral procession. Every time he rides and survives, it will be because I allow it. Every moment you are awake, Vossik, be grateful I have let you live another day. You will never know when I'll be there to bring the fires of hell down on you and yours. There's going to be grief. By God, I can promise you that. You will grieve."

"McKenzie, when I shoot you—that's when, not if—I will not miss. I will put a bullet in your heart…and I'm a very good shot."

Val laughed. "I've killed eight of you vermin. Just think of that for a moment, Vossik: eight. I can go on killing—and I'd really enjoy that, or we can end the war."

Silence.

Val continued. "And what's all this lunacy with shooting up David Albright? He's just the sap that was used to get me out of prison. I don't even know him. So leave him alone. He'll just be an unnecessary complication for you."

"His mistake was being associated with you." Vossik laughed unpleasantly. "We don't do fair. And we don't do reasonable. We do what we like."

"You don't have a monopoly on terror, Vossik. Ask the grieving relatives of the thugs I put away. Leave Albright alone. You'll gain nothing from killing him except trouble."

There was silence.

"The last six years have been quiet. I can let it be quiet again. So, what's it going to be: peace or war?"

"We don't do peace. You've written yourself into our history.

There can be no peace. The brothers wouldn't allow it. You're top of the list."

"You should never have raped and killed my woman."

More silence.

Val pressed on. "The loss of your family—do you really want to endure that?"

"You ask a lot, McKenzie."

"Give me an answer. Does your family live or die?"

"It's not my choice. I'll have to ask the council." There was silence for a few seconds. "We could meet back here in a few days."

"No, I don't think so. The next time we're as close to each other as this, one of us will die." Val paused. "Fly a white flag from your TV aerial if there is peace. Fly a red one if there is war. How many days will you need?"

"Two days."

"Fine."

"I could fly a white flag, then kill you, you know."

"I don't think so. You don't know what I look like or where I'll be. I'll know you are hunting me before you find me, and the moment I find out, you'll be screaming in grief and drowning in blood. Is that clear?"

"You were the bastard with that guy on the Murray River, weren't you?"

"I'm the bastard that's looking into your windows. I'm the bastard putting the cross-hairs over your brother's heart. I'm the bastard you will never see until it is too late."

There was a pause.

"Red flag, or white flag—your choice."

"I'll see."

Vossik continued to speak, but Val had crawled away on his stomach, keeping below the height of the parapet, staying invisible to anyone with a rifle.

The Eastern sun was now shining into the balconies of the building on the far side of Val. Sebastian was grateful for it. He swung the telescopic sight backward and forward over the two balconies that presented the most danger—particularly the right-hand one where he'd seen the man with a rifle. Seeing the gun had been a shock. It was physical proof of the dangerous game he was now engaged in. For a few moments, he'd stared at a man intent on murder—*murder!* It was surreal.

He'd sent a text to Val, who replied with the instruction to 'Laser him at 10 precisely.' It was a scenario they'd prepared for, but it was nonetheless disturbing to have to put it into practice. The enormity of the responsibility hit him. In a very real sense, Val's life now depended on his actions.

Sebastian had positioned himself under the rim of a satellite dish, trusting it to make him invisible to anyone looking in his direction. He'd rested the front of the telescopic sight on the parapet ledge and continued to watch his quarry. The sun was behind him, so there was little chance of a reflection from the scope giving away his position.

At 10am, he'd switched on the laser sight strapped to the telescopic sight and played it over the would-be-assassin's heart. Now he was no longer an observer, but a participant—a participant in a dangerous game. The man was cradling the rifle in one arm as he spoke into a phone. Suddenly, the man had seen the red dot dancing over his chest and dived to the floor behind the wall of the balcony. In any other circumstance, his action would have been comical.

Val was hidden from his sight behind the rooftop building where the old fan duct was. He'd been there over four hours. Sebastian didn't know how Val could do it. He knew himself to be battling with mental exhaustion. His eyes were red with fatigue. It was only his anxiety that kept him applied to the task. *Watch, watch, watch.*

Suddenly, Val appeared from behind the rooftop building. He was crawling on his elbows and knees, keeping below the level of the parapet. Sebastian swept the scope over the balconies—and saw a movement. It came from within the room behind the balcony where the armed man had first been seen. The man was now taking station with his rifle behind the breakfast bar.

Val had nearly reached the back corner of the building. He would soon need to turn and head toward Sebastian. With a sickening sense of realization, Sebastian knew that Val would be horribly exposed—and even more so when he climbed the five meters of coining up to the parapet to join him.

Sebastian switched the laser light back on and sighted on the gunman. He played the laser across his face, flickering back and forth.

"Run," he yelled.

He had a momentary impression of Val heaving himself to feet and sprinting to the wall underneath him.

The gunman moved.

Sebastian desperately wanted to see where Val was, but he kept watching through the scope. The telescopic sight was quite long, but it was not as long as a rifle. This meant that when he moved the scope slightly, the laser swept across a hugely erratic arch. *Concentrate, concentrate.*

He was gratified to see the armed man suddenly duck for cover again.

A moment later, Val appeared on top of the parapet. He slithered onto the roof and lay on his back gasping for breath.

They were now invisible to the gunman. Sebastian felt a surge of relief. He was also impressed. For a bulky man, Val had moved quickly. He was taking to urban climbing all too well.

Sebastian crabbed his way over to him.

"You okay?"

Val nodded.

"The gunman is in the kitchen behind one of the balconies. He'll have seen you."

Val rolled over onto his hands and knees. "Then we need to go." He glanced round. "We can't risk the fire escape. It's in a box alley."

Sebastian nodded and tucked the telescopic sight down the front of his jacket. "Then it's plan B. Follow me."

As they sprinted across the rooftop, Sebastian shouted, "Watch, then do the same." He bounced up onto the ledge with one foot and pushed off, leaping across a two-meter gap to the building next door.

He hit the wall with his feet at the same time as his hands gripped the top of the parapet. There was a thump just to his left. To his amazement, he discovered Val beside him, hanging onto the same wall like a swimmer about to start a backstroke race. He looked quite at ease.

Sebastian pulled himself up over the parapet. As his feet touched the roof, he heard a feminine squeal. He took in the scene in an instant. A man and a woman were engaged in coitus on a mat in the late morning sun.

Val landed on the roof behind him, looking downright menacing.

Sebastian decided to take the initiative. He wagged a finger at the woman. "Shame on you. He's twice your age. What's he got; money or power?"

The woman jerked herself from under the man and pulled down her skirt. "Sod off," she said sulkily.

Sebastian glanced up at a small building on the rooftop. It had a door in the side that appeared to have a Yale-type lock. He forced a cheerful smile. "If you'll let us into the stairwell, we'll finish our climbing, and you can finish what you are doing."

With ill grace, the man pulled up his pants. For a moment, Sebastian thought he might make a scene, but after glancing at Val he lowered his head, padded over to the door, and unlocked it.

Sebastian smiled his thanks and said, "Don't worry: your secret is safe with us."

The man swore.

At the bottom of the stairwell was a lift door. Val pushed the down button. It seemed surreal having to wait for a lift after the drama they'd been through. Sebastian leaned on the wall, resting his head on a forearm, and tried to recover his composure.

Val gave voice to the fears that were clamoring to be heard.

"We have to expect the Saracens to be in the back alleys and by the main entrances of the buildings along the street."

The lift turned up, and they stepped inside. They were the only occupants. Sebastian was relieved. "What are we going to do?"

"I think we'll stand a better chance if we split up, and I think it's going to be easier to melt into the crowd if we leave by the front entrance." Val pushed the lift button for the third floor, and the lift slid to a halt with a jolt. "I'll get out here and join you later. You stay in the building. When you want to leave, get into the lift and stay there until a group of people want to go down to the ground floor. Leave the building with them. I'll phone you about where to meet up."

Val stepped out onto the landing but kept the doors open with a foot. "Take your time—an hour or two if necessary. Don't rush. Perhaps phone Pip and ask her to join you. Leave the building together and go for a coffee. Keep your left hand in your pocket and act natural. If you do, there's no way they'll be able to recognize you."

Sebastian began to protest. "What about you?"

But the lift doors had shut.

Chapter 21

Normally, Pip would have enjoyed spinning out a coffee in Sebastian's company but her anxiety was too high. Following Sebastian's phone instructions, she'd gone into the building and taken the lift to the third floor. She'd found him sitting in a sofa on the landing reading a magazine, looking ostensibly, very calm. The only betrayal of his feelings came from the spontaneous hug he gave her. It was perfunctory, and he let her go quickly—as if shocked by his actions.

After half an hour, they'd left the building together, crossed the road, and settled themselves in a café where they could watch for anyone loitering in front of the building where Val was.

It hadn't taken them long to spot a man in a blue donkey jacket resting against the bonnet of a car. He was in a fifteen-minute parking zone. When he was still there thirty minutes later, Sebastian had phoned his father.

"There's a bloke by a car, thirty meters to the west."

Sebastian had listened to some instructions and then rung off. "Val will stay for another hour and then come out. He'll ring to warn us."

Pip looked at her watch. That had been over an hour ago. She sighed and looked at Sebastian. He was twirling the smartphone round and round on the table with a finger.

She wanted to scream at him to stop. She wanted everything to stop—the nightmare—the threat of violence—the likelihood of death. Her shoulder bag was leaning against her leg, weighted now by the telescopic sight inside it. She put her head in her hands. This was no dream.

Suddenly, Sebastian's phone began to hum. He snatched it up to his ear. All Pip could hear of the conversation was: "Okay, we'll tail from a distance and keep you informed. Good luck." He put the phone down and turned to Pip. "Val's coming out in the next gaggle of office-workers."

In the event, they nearly missed him. Val was in the middle of a knot of people. He was carrying a sheaf of papers and had his head bowed, giving every impression he was listening to the chatter from those around him. He'd divested himself of his jacket, and the only thing that looked a little odd was his shoes. They were not those normally worn by business people.

Pip held her breath as Val peeled away from the group and made his way east. *Yes, yes, yes.* He was going to get away without being noticed.

Oh no!

She was horrified to see the man by the car stand up and frown in Val's direction as if he was uncertain. Pip groaned as she saw him begin to make his way along the pavement, some fifty yards behind Val.

Sebastian was already on his feet and had the phone to his ear. She grabbed her shoulder bag and followed him out of the café. She could only hear snatches of what he was saying.

"Go to the Botanic gardens. Use the time he can't see you when you enter the gates to get well ahead. Get to the eastern end. You'll find a path at the back of the National Wine Centre near Hackney Road. There's a footbridge that crosses the creek." Pip lost the rest of the conversation, as she ducked and weaved past pedestrians.

She had to work hard to keep up with Sebastian. Whilst they stopped at the pedestrian lights crossing North Terrace, he took her arm and whispered. "Pip, it's time for you to leave. Catch a bus home. Things could get tricky from here on."

She lifted her chin defiantly. "No way. I'm seeing this through with you."

He grabbed her by the arm—hard. "I'm serious," he hissed. "It's going to get dangerous."

She shook herself free. "I'm coming."

Sebastian closed his eyes briefly. After a moment, he glanced down at her boots. She was wearing her Doc Martens. "Can you afford to get your boots and your clothing soaked?"

She didn't hesitate. "Of course."

The lights changed and they walked across North Terrace and headed into the Botanic Gardens through its magnificent wrought iron gates.

Sebastian immediately slowed his pace to a gentle amble. He surprised her by taking her arm.

She didn't object.

He said quietly, "We need to look like lovers—taking our time."

"Oh." Suddenly, she didn't feel quite so good.

They made their way past a white, latticed pergola, then skirted round the edge of the dry desert section of the gardens. From there, they cut across the lawns and followed a line of trees. As they rounded the last tree, Pip was appalled to see the man who had been following Val standing on the path just ahead of them, looking around in apparent confusion. An instant later, he turned and scowled at them.

Pip took matters into her own hands. She forced a smile and said to Sebastian under her breath, "Don't stare, darling. Look at me and giggle."

Sebastian looked startled, but quickly got the idea. However, his actions were less than convincing. She put her hands on either side of his cheeks, steered him to her lips, and kissed him.

His lips were hard, compressed and unyielding.

She moved a hand to the back of his neck and held him to her.

His lips began to soften and part slightly. They were warm and moist. The dance began: giving and taking, shyly, exploring the novelty. It was totally convincing.

"Oi, Lovers. You haven't seen a guy with a short beard and black tee-shirt have you?"

Pip broke away from Sebastian. She looked at the man with apparent surprise and lack of comprehension.

The man glared at her. "A bloke with a short beard in a black tee-shirt," he repeated.

"Oh," she said. "Can't say I noticed. Although I think someone was on the path over there." She pointed toward the curving arch of the tropicarium.

The man turned and hurried down the path.

Just ahead of them a footbridge crossed a small creek. Sebastian led her to the water's edge, and then alarmed her by wading into the water. He turned to her and beckoned. "Come on then."

She followed. The water was chilly and came just over her boots. She sighed. It would take a lot of careful drying and dubbin to restore them. They splashed through the water toward the tunnel that took the creek under Hackney Road. She paused just inside its entrance to give her eyes a chance to adjust to the gloom. Sebastian tugged her forward, forcing her into the darkness.

She stumbled after him. "It's not coming out on the other side," she complained. "Where does it go?"

He switched on his smartphone torch. "This tunnel is about one-and-a-half kilometers long. So we'll be in it for quite a while."

She was flabbergasted.

A dark shape detached itself from the wall ahead of them. Pip grabbed at Sebastian's arm.

It was a huge relief to hear Val's distinctive raspy voice. "Are you two okay?"

Sebastian answered. "Yeah. All good. I'm pretty sure no one's following, but we need to keep moving—just to make sure."

Val positioned himself behind Pip, and the three of them set off.

Occasionally, Val reached forward to give her a steadying hand as she sloshed and slithered behind Sebastian.

She could see that the tunnel was an archway made of red brick. Occasionally, smaller water channels branched off it.

Sebastian provided some commentary. She was grateful. His voice had a calming effect on her nerves.

"This tunnel is probably one of the most commonly explored ones. It's known as 'Adelaide Darky' around the traps."

"Is it safe?" she asked.

"Yeah. The only time it's not safe is after a big rain."

The tunnel suddenly changed shape and became narrower and rectangular.

Pip shuddered. "Does it get any smaller?"

"It does. This brick section turns into concrete further on and gets lower and lower. You'll be crouching before you get out."

"Oh, joy."

"On the plus side, you'll see some great graffiti."

A hundred yards further on, they could see a shaft of sunshine lancing into the tunnel. Sebastian shone his torch up to the roof where the light was coming in through a grating. She was amazed to see that someone had painted a street address on the wall beside it. "What's that for?" she asked.

Sebastian snorted a laugh. "We sometimes ordered a pizza and directed the deliveryman here. When he arrived, we'd yell instructions up to him and he'd post the pizza through the grating. It was hilarious."

Pip steadied herself against the wall and tried not to think of what she was walking on. "Your sense of humor is warped. Do you know that?"

"You insisted on coming along."

"Let's keep moving," growled Val.

It was forty minutes before they emerged from the narrow end of the tunnel. Their exit was bizarre. The tunnel ended in a small suburban park. They emerged into sunshine to the squeals of children playing. Pip recognized the park instantly. Charles Street ran alongside it. They were only a few blocks from home. It was just as well. She was cold, wet, and devoid of all humor.

When they finally arrived home, she told Sebastian that he was cooking tea, and she was going to be in the bath for an hour.

Chapter 22

The water in the sink burped, gurgled, and drained away leaving a residue of soap scum and whiskers. Sebastian looked at himself in the mirror. So much had changed—and not just his appearance.

It was Saturday, and nothing particular was scheduled to happen during the day. What on earth should he do?

There was precious little he could do. It was now a waiting game. Would there be peace? Would he be able to get on with his life? Would Pip and David be safe? Waiting wasn't easy. He imagined prisoners feeling much the same as him as they waited for a jury to come to its verdict. It was a nasty feeling. Everything was outside of his control. The reality of this left him feeling both vulnerable and angry. It was unfair that evil men should have the power to determine whether or not he would live in dread, or not.

Val took charge of the wet shoes. He'd removed the laces, stuffed the shoes with newspaper, and they were now drying in front of the slow combustion heater. It was a humble service that left Sebastian feeling curiously warmed.

Val was currently beside his camping bed doing press-ups—pushing himself up so fast he was able to clap his hands before

146

falling down on them again. Sebastian shook his head. The man was a machine. "Bathroom's free," he said.

As he waited for breakfast, Sebastian reflected on the events of the previous morning. As dramatic as they were, it was the kiss that haunted him the most. How real was it? He shook his head. How could it not be real? The kiss was unlike anything he'd ever experienced before. It wasn't the open-mouthed, saliva-rich, cannibalistic mouthings of lust, but something altogether different. He searched for the right words to describe it. It was golden honey; it was a warming hearth; it was the headiness of intimacy—with all its vulnerability and delight. Above all, it was indescribably Pip.

He tried to read but was too restless to persist with it. Sebastian wished he was back at the farm where he could collect the dogs and check on the sheep—and let the wind blow away the bewilderment of life.

His other fallback position was to make something, but there was nothing to work with. The small bronze clasp he had made in the engineering laboratory two days ago was finished. He took it out of his leather pouch, then reached for the Fire Stone. After unwrapping it, he fitted the gem between two small metal caps on his clasp. Tiny arms connected each cap to a central spine, which came in two parts, enabling it to be screwed together. This allowed the gem to either be worn as a pendant, or to be removed. Val had told him that, for some reason, the best opals lost value when they were mounted as jewelry. Sebastian could understand why. There was something special about holding the jewel, unadorned, in your hands. Gems like The Fire Stone needed to be felt, examined, rotated, and wondered at.

When he'd first hung the gem in its clasp around his neck, it had rolled over, presenting the bronze spine at the front. That would never do. Nothing must be allowed to interfere with the view of the opal. He'd solved the problem by braising a small bar across the stem to stop it rotating when resting against his chest.

What would it look like against Pip's chest: between…?

He slapped his cheek. That was not a place he would allow his mind to go.

Pip had made herself a cup of tea and retreated back to bed. She needed its comfort as she wrestled with her sense of dread at the reality of the dangerous game she was now caught up in. Pip wanted to scream; she wanted things to be as they were eight days ago. She wanted to be complaining about the excesses of Western cities and the fact that her father never remembered to eat again. She wanted it all back.

Although there were a few things she wouldn't change. That extraordinary night on the roof of The Dunstan Playhouse, and, of course, the kiss.

She'd forced the kiss, she knew. And Sebastian's first reaction had been resistance. That was telling. She knew that it would be a huge mistake to read any significance into the kiss. Nonetheless, she savored the memory. The kiss had ended so beautifully, so completely. It was giddyingly satisfying. She sniffed and resolved not to dwell on it any more.

One of the Saracens had interrupted the kiss. That action was, in many respects, a parable of her life. The Saracens were ruining everything. Yesterday, she had seen them for the first time. It was chilling to think she was seeing the people responsible for trying to kill her father.

She'd once thought Val's story had been so unbelievable, fantastic, and shocking that it beggared belief. But Sebastian had spoken of seeing a man with a gun on the roof—a gun! And she herself had seen a man intent on finding Val for reasons that could only be sinister. The nightmare of yesterday was real enough, and Val's story was now all too believable.

It was extraordinary to think of him hiding for so many years in a remote opal field. She hadn't believed it at first, but seeing the Fire Stone on the roof of the Playhouse had persuaded her that he had. Its electric flashes of red, green, and turquoise had been breathtaking.

For some reason, they reminded her of the kiss.

Sebastian filed into a pew behind Val and Pip toward the back of the church. It was an odd feeling. He'd never been to a Sunday service in his life. What he had experienced so far surprised him. The people seemed friendly; kids were chattering, and a band had set up their gear at the front ready for the service. He hadn't expected that.

He sat with his arms folded in front of him, unsure of what was to come. Pip sat next to him. Val was on her far side. Sebastian noticed that Val also had his arms folded. He realized that the pair of them must look comical, so he uncrossed his arms and began fiddling with the pew sheet.

The band led the singing; the kids went out to Sunday school and prayers followed. Sebastian didn't sing. He stood and sat—following the cue given by the rest of the congregation. Eventually David got up to speak. Sebastian resigned himself to hearing a moralistic lecture—almost certainly boring.

David began.

"The nineteenth century German philosopher, Ludwig Feurbach, said that God is simply a projection of our own needs onto reality. God does not create us, we create God."

Thumbs up for Feurbach.

Boring!

"It morphed into Communism which caused nine million deaths in the Russian Civil War. Later, Stalin's purges resulted in twenty-five million deaths; and Mao Zedong's Cultural Revolution in China killed fifty million. The deaths caused by Communism were more than the combined deaths of World War I and World War II."

Wow! Really?

"This highlights the fact that no one is doing very well without Jesus. Certainly, if there is no God, there is a moral vacuum. If there is no God, no one exists to guarantee what is ultimately good and right. Without God, this brief, meaningless life is all there is, so get comfortable and entertain yourself as much as you can before you are dead. The miracle of existence is meaningless. You and your achievements will simply turn to dust before the universe runs out of fuel and fades away as low level radiation."

Sebastian had never really thought about why everything existed. He kept his face impassive.

"Today's militant atheists trumpet their slogan 'There's probably no God. So stop worrying and enjoy your life.'" David slapped the top of the pulpit. "An awful lot of Indian beggars are extremely grateful that Mother Teresa was not an atheist bent on self-focused enjoyment."

Sebastian shifted uncomfortably in his seat.

"In the midst of our confusion and the multitude of our religions—God turns up in history as Jesus, and says: 'I am the way, the truth and the life. No one comes to the Father except through me.'"

That's a pretty arrogant thing to say.

"...which would be an arrogant thing to say, except for one tiny proviso, and that is: unless it is true." David paused. "I don't want anyone to come to church merely because of tradition. Only the truth is worthy of you. I invite you to find that truth."

Sebastian didn't take in much more of what was said. It was too disturbing.

After the service, people milled around in the foyer of the hall next door drinking coffee and chatting. It was noisy. Pip steered Sebastian to the counter to get a drink. Val had said he didn't want one. "It's instant coffee," she warned. "Sorry about that."

The lady behind the kitchen counter smiled at Pip and said, "And who is this young man, Pip?"

Pip momentarily seemed lost for words. Eventually she blurted out. "Oh, he's just someone who needed a place to stay for a while."

The lady smiled. "You and your father have always been wonderfully charitable."

Something cold gripped Sebastian's heart.

Pip spoke again, slightly more loudly than was necessary. "Actually, we invited Sebastian and his father to stay in response to a kindness they showed us."

"Oh, that's nice, dear," the woman said.

Pip bustled Sebastian away from the counter. "I apologize for that, she whispered. "It's just...well...I wasn't prepared to answer questions about us."

"About us?"

Pip blushed.

David always felt weary on Sunday nights. Conducting two morning services took its toll. When he was younger, he used to fret about whether his sermons were effective. He was beyond that now and knew that he was called to be faithful, not successful. And God's faithfulness toward him had never failed. He was always given something to say. Sometimes ideas came from his reading. On other occasions, it came from a conversation—an innocent comment from someone he met. Sometimes a message would come in a rush. On other occasions he felt he had to chisel it out of rock. No two sermons were born the same way. But the fact that inspiration never failed to come week by week was the miracle that assured him that God's hand was still on him.

He sat in an armchair in the family room. Pip and Sebastian were seated at the kitchen bench poring over an article on how to make a cello out of plywood. Sebastian had expressed his intrigue at the possibility. Pip was disdainful. She was sitting on a stool arguing whilst turning her new copper bangle round and round on her wrist.

It was their way of dealing with the tension of waiting.

Val had gone out for a drive. The fact that he had done so without a license told David that what he was doing was important and probably dangerous. There could only be one reason he would do so.

He settled into that still place within himself, and waited for Val to return.

When Val finally arrived back, David could see that his face was pale and stricken.

"What flag was it?" Sebastian blurted out.

Val held up a hand to signal quiet and looked at David—almost beseechingly.

David nodded toward the study.

Val lifted his chin in acknowledgment, and the two of them made their way down the hallway.

As soon as they were in the study, Val hung his head and leaned on the desk with both hands. He looked emotionally spent.

"Why don't you sit down?" David gestured toward the new armchair.

Val didn't move. He drew in a deep breath. "It was a red flag; and I don't know what to do."

"Sit down," ordered David.

Val did so and began massaging his forehead. "I honestly don't know what's best."

"You feel you have to carry the burden for your son's safety, and our safety, solely on your shoulders." David poured Val a glass of sherry and handed it to him. "Perhaps it's time to let the rest of us share the load."

"It means that I'll have to continue to kill." Val's chest heaved. It might have been a sob. "And I don't want that. I really don't." He looked up at David. "The fact is: they've called my bluff—and I'm not sure I can deliver on my threats. You, Pip, and Sebastian will have to go into hiding: and I will stay."

"And kill."

"If I have to. Perhaps I can hold some of them to ransom and force a peace of sorts. Whatever happens, it will involve violence. And to be honest, I'm over it."

David nodded. "Do the Saracens know we've seen the red flag?"

"I left the aerial bent at a thirty degree angle. I'm pretty sure they know I've got the message."

"How on earth…?"

"I fired from the top of a chicken shed; a subsonic round at a hundred-and-twenty meters. It wasn't difficult."

David slapped his hand down on the desk. "Why?"

"I want them to keep their heads down until we can get to a place that's safe."

David glanced at the crucifix hanging above his desk. Christ, in agony on the cross, said nothing. There was just a peace. That usually meant that the answer was already somewhere within him, or within reach. David searched for it, but nothing came to mind. He resolved to give it time.

"And where, do you suppose, that safe place might be?"

Val passed a hand over his face. "I have no idea."

The idea, when it came, hit him with a force that was almost physical. David turned on his office chair. "Val, I've been fairly passive in this affair to date, wouldn't you agree?"

Val shrugged.

David continued. "Well, I'm now asserting my authority—at least as it pertains to my family."

"What's on your mind?"

"You may not be able to keep your son and my family safe in Adelaide, but I know a place where I can definitely keep them safe."

"And where's that?"

"In Vanuatu."

"Vanuatu!"

"Yes. I was a missionary there for ten years. Once we get there, we can go seriously off grid where no one will find us, and be among friends."

"But how would you get there?"

"Fly to Port Vila."

"Vossik said he'd know if we got onto a plane." Val rubbed his temples. "It's probably a bluff, but I wouldn't want to put it to the test."

"It's a risk I'm prepared to take."

Silence hung between them for some minutes.

Eventually, Val sat himself up in his chair. "What if I could get you to Vanuatu another way, a way that could not possibly be traced —where we'd be away from everyone."

"How?"

"We could sail there."

"Sail!"

"I'm part owner of a thirty-eight foot cutter. It's moored at Coffs Harbour." Val shrugged. "It would be about a twelve day passage. No one could find us."

Silence.

David nodded slowly. "It's been a while since I've done any sailing."

Val expressed surprise. "You've done some. That's good. Where?"

"Port Vila: with friends when on holiday. But I'll be very rusty now."

"I think you'd pick it up again quick enough. Don't forget, I'll have to spend a few days teaching Sebastian and Pip the basics before we sail."

"Can we live on board in the meantime?"

"It's frowned on by the marina, but we can probably get away with it."

David turned round to the computer.

"What are you doing?" asked Val.

"I'm sending two emails. One to my curate and another to my bishop."

Val started to urge caution, but David interrupted. "I won't tell them where I'm going. I'll just plead the need for stress leave in view of the recent violence."

"Will they be all right with it?"

"I doubt it."

"So what will you do?"

David smiled. "Exactly what we need to do. They'll get over it."

He typed two brief emails as Val paced the floor. When he'd finished, David looked up at the crucifix, nodded his thanks and turned to Val. "I think it's time to call in the kids."

Chapter 23

Sometimes Pip was able to forget that people were trying to kill them—and today was one such occasion. She watched as the whale again erupted from the ocean depths, arched itself, and crashed back into the sea. Seawater lifted into the sky in slow motion.

Pip tried not to think of the damage a forty ton cetacean might cause if it fell across their boat. The whale was only a hundred yards away. She'd been able to clearly see the white encrustations around the whale's face marking it as a southern right whale.

Val was standing beside her at the mast, he'd been instructing her on how to set the storm trysail.

She wrinkled her nose. "Are you sure it's wise to sail across the South Pacific in a concrete boat, where grumpy whales are liable to lob on board?"

"Concentrate, and clip on your safety harness," said Val. "Picture yourself doing this in a full gale at night with the boat trying to buck you off it."

Pip clipped on her harness and heaved on the halyard. The tiny sail straightened itself against the mast. "Why is this sail different from the rest? It's thick and feels like plastic."

"It's made of Kevlar. We only use the storm trysail in extreme conditions, so it's got to be tough."

She didn't think Val noticed her shudder. She was wrong.

"Worried?"

"Yes."

Val worked his lips as if seeking to conjure the right words. He was dressed in a canvas smock-top. Its sleeves had been rolled up, allowing his muscled arms to be clearly seen. Pip reflected again on how different his body shape was from Sebastian's. And yet she could see a likeness in their features. She glanced back to the cockpit. Sebastian was on the wheel—chatting with her father. It was a good sight.

Val interrupted her musings.

"*Whisperer* was built by Ferro Cement Marine Services at Burnham on Crouch in the UK. They were one of the best in the business in the 80s. She's thirty-eight feet long—and that's bigger than some boats that have sailed around the world. And being a cutter rig, she's easy to handle." He patted the mast. "We'll be fine."

Pip flexed her hands. They were chaffed and raw from three days of pulling on ropes, sheets and halyards. "It doesn't feel as if she's easily handled to me."

Val sniffed. "You'll get used to her." He pointed to the cleat. "Make the halyard fast."

"I still don't think it'd offer much protection from an overenthusiastic whale."

"Relax. Whilst the East Coast is a highway for all sorts of whales during the winter, we'll be lucky to see any once we're out in the ocean."

Pip didn't admit it, but she was saddened that their days would not continue to be punctuated with sightings of the magnificent creatures. They had seen them every day they'd been out learning how to sail *Whisperer*. It was something she hadn't expected.

Val called back to the men in the cockpit. "Right, let's reset the main, staysail, and jib, then head back to the marina. David: it's your turn on the helm."

Pip groaned. Another sail change. And Val would doubtless

spring the challenge of reefing the mainsail again whilst they were on the way back. The man was relentless.

Pip hadn't really thought about what would happen after their two-day road trip to Coffs Harbour. She'd vaguely formed the idea that they would buy a few things, climb aboard *Whisperer* and head across the Pacific to Vanuatu—a relaxing cruise—well out of reach of thugs with guns. Two things had brought her back to earth with a bump. The first was the size of the yacht. *Whisperer* had looked tiny when she first laid eyes on her. She was appalled that anyone would venture out of sight of land in her. The second surprise had come when Val told them that they wouldn't be leaving until Sunday morning. That would give them four days in which to learn the basics of sailing, buy the necessary stores, and repair everything that needed fixing before they sailed.

For the last four days, they had risen early and been well offshore by eight o'clock. Six hours of sail training followed, after which they returned to the marina for more instruction on how to handle the boat under power. She'd learned how to move the boat around the marina's pontoons using bowlines, stern-lines, and springs. Pip shook her head. Quite why anyone came to call a rope running diagonally from boat to shore a 'spring,' heaven knew.

Val yelled again. "David, let go of the wheel. Imagine you've been knocked unconscious by the boom and that I'm attending you." He pointed to Sebastian and Pip. "What are you going to do?"

Pip's mind froze.

Whisperer rocked and bucked in the water, waiting for someone to take charge.

She scrambled to get her thoughts in order. "Er…I'd start the engine, head the boat into wind, and put the sails up."

"Imagine that there are lines in the water that risk fouling the prop." Val pointed at Sebastian. "What would you do?"

Pip secretly thought that she'd head for the nearest port and vow never to go to sea again. She wondered what Sebastian would say? He'd taken to sailing with enthusiasm—and had rolled with the schooling dealt out by his father without rancor. She thought, somewhat sadly, that he was probably relating to Val more as a stranger than a father. *It must be weird...*

Sebastian interrupted her thoughts.

"I'd set the staysail. It's small and easily handled on a moving deck. It will stabilize the boat while we get the other sails up."

Damn the man; he sounded confident. He also sounded right.

Val turned to Pip. "And at what point of sailing would you sail with the staysail?"

If he can do it, so can I. She racked her brains, piecing together what she'd learned over the past few days.

"As close to the wind as possible so it's easy to put the other sails up."

Val nodded. "Good. Get on with it. The boat's in your hands."

Sebastian had a feathery sensation across the back of his neck. He glanced up but could see no one watching. The nearest people were a gang of men working on a section of pontoons that had been damaged—presumably in the last cyclone. Some parts of it were cocked askew and semi submerged.

Val was also about—somewhere. He was under the water with his scuba gear scraping weeds off the bottom of *Whisperer's* hull. The man had spent at least an hour in the late afternoon of each day on the task. Evidence of his presence came with the occasional scraping sound heard through the hull and bubbles of expelled air breaking the surface of the water. Sebastian could sometimes see him when he looked over the side—a black figure surrounded by clouds of small fish eager to feed off the dislodged marine growth.

Sebastian reapplied himself to the task of sanding the forehatch. Val had, over the last few days, smeared two layers of epoxy over it to fill up the cracks and make it watertight. The second layer now needed to be sanded before it was painted over to protect it from the sun.

Then he saw her.

Pip was watching him covertly from behind the canopy over the cockpit.

He affected not to notice and kept working—but his heart gave a lurch. Living in such close proximity with her over the last six days had been…he searched for the right words: 'disturbing,' 'beguiling,' 'frustrating.' She trailed fascination and mystery behind her like a perfume.

One moment he'd be completely at ease in her company, laughing and talking naturally with her—and on other occasions he was a tongue-tied buffoon. As if by mutual consent, the two of them had settled on relating to each other at the level of rivalry. It was mild stuff, but they competed at everything: saying clever words, and pretty much everything to do with sailing a boat. Val was partly to blame for it as he was always pitting one of them against the other in different sailing tasks.

The only area where Sebastian felt he had ascendancy over her was navigation. But even with that, Pip had a good understanding of the basics. In truth, *Whisperer's* satellite navigation unit made everything pretty easy. The real trick was plotting a sailing track that took account of the forecast weather conditions. Val had spent the evenings with both Sebastian and David teaching them what they needed to know. Pip had rebelled, declaring that the evenings were her own. She usually walked across the car park of the marina complex to the public toilets for a long shower.

Sebastian glanced up again and caught her looking at him. She waved, climbed out of the cockpit—lithe, like a cat, and made her way up the side deck to where he was working.

Her shadow fell across him.

"Were you checking me out?" he asked.

Pip stood there with her hands on hips. She'd knotted a shirt under her breasts and was showing a bare midriff—finely textured satin. He lowered his gaze and continued to rub the sanding block over the forehatch.

"You'd better make a good job of that. I'm sleeping underneath it."

Sebastian nodded and didn't trust himself to say anything.

When he couldn't stand the tension of the silence any more, he risked glancing up.

He shouldn't have.

He saw two long legs—already beginning to tan—emerging from frayed denim shorts cut at the very limit of modesty. They were twelve inches from his nose.

He returned his attention to the forehatch.

But she'd seen him looking at her. He knew it, and she'd just stood there, saying nothing. She might have even dropped one hip. Was that a hint of provocation? Had she? Really? Or did he imagine it?

He rubbed at the epoxy.

His sexual turmoil was brought to a sudden end when she clipped him around the head with her hand.

Sebastian rocked back on his heels. "What was that for?" he protested.

"I could list a number of things, but it was mostly to get your attention."

He swallowed. "Why?"

"Because buddy, we need to talk."

"Sure. Now?"

"No. I've got to go with Dad and do the last bit of the shopping. We need to do it before the shops shut." She screwed up her nose. "It's a pity we're setting off tomorrow morning. I'd have loved one more day so we could get some fresh stuff from the Jetty Markets. But they're only open on Sundays."

"Have we got any more space to put it?" Secretly, he doubted it. On Val's advice, they'd brought shopping on board every day—progressively so as not to give the impression they were setting off for a long voyage. *Whisperer's* hull had been gradually stuffed with goods and provisions. They'd stored it in lockers, under seats, and even under the floorboards.

Pip ignored his question. "Let's go for a walk after dinner, perhaps to the Muttonbird Island Nature Reserve at the end of the breakwater. We shouldn't be disturbed there."

Sebastian nodded.

That evening, they dined more sumptuously than usual at one of the restaurants in the Marina Village. The complex provided a number of places to eat. It also boasted a hairdresser, some specialty stores including a chandlery, and, as Pip had discovered, an ice creamery.

Dinner was a muted affair. The seriousness of what they were embarking on seemed to infect them all. Sebastian chased the last of his peas around the plate with a fork and said very little.

David was the one who seemed most at peace. He sat back in his seat and said. "That was lovely. Thanks, Val, for your generosity."

Sebastian couldn't help but think, uncharitably, whether he'd just eaten the last meal of a condemned man. Even the prospect of spending time with Pip failed to dissipate his apprehension. What they were doing was dangerous—plain and simple, and the future was far from certain.

David folded his napkin. "Val, what happens about customs? Don't we have to report in before we go? It's just that I'm a bit concerned that doing so might make our movements visible to anyone who wanted to find us."

Val grunted. "Yeah, they've got international customs clearance here in the marina, but we won't be using them. If anyone asks, we're just learning how to sail—and planning to finish off the schooling with a trip up the coast."

"Is it really as simple as that?"

"And we'll be taking down our radar reflector."

Nothing was said for a while.

Sebastian gave Pip's ankle a tap with his foot under the table and cleared his throat. "Um, Pip and I are going for a quick walk along to Muttonbird Island."

Val nodded and growled. "Don't be late. We sail early tomorrow morning and you'll be standing four-hourly watches from 8 o'clock on. You'll need all the sleep you can get."

It wasn't the most comforting of benedictions.

Sebastian and Pip walked along the curving sea wall toward

Muttonbird Island. He wondered whether he should take her by the arm. It felt like the natural thing to do.

But he didn't.

The lights of the town were behind them as they headed toward the brooding silhouette of the island. Sebastian could already smell the guano on the sea air coming from the colony of wedge-tailed shearwaters that nested there.

He was acutely aware of Pip walking beside him—and wished that he could offer her more safety than a sailing trip in a small boat across the Pacific.

He drew a deep breath. "Are you doing okay?"

She didn't answer immediately. Eventually, she said, "Don't you think all this—is kind of crazy?"

He nodded. "Yeah."

"But better than being a city slicker with their..." she pointed to Sebastian, challenging him to finish the sentence.

Sebastian rubbed the side of his temples. He had hoped for a conversation free of competition, but played along. "Aah, with their vegan world of political correctness, wispy beards, and bodies shaped in expensive gyms."

She nodded appreciatively. After a moment's thought, she responded: "With vistas restricted by what they can see bent over their mobile phones."

He fired back: "With trendy ideologies learned from media personalities—giddy with power but untested by responsibility."

She laughed. "There's no way I'm going to better that."

They began walking again, content now with the silence.

The moon was up—on the wane, he noticed. Its light silvered the wave tops, highlighting their restlessness.

He decided to risk taking things to a deeper level. "It's going to be an adventure—in all sorts of ways."

"And it's by no means clear how it's going to end," she finished.

"I just hope there's not going to be..." he paused, and started again. "I just hope you'll be okay."

Pip kept her gaze straight ahead. "You and I are going to be cooped up in a boat together for a long time."

Sebastian swallowed. "Do you mind?"

"It could get...interesting."

He stopped walking. "Interesting! Is that all you've got to say?"

She laughed, then the two of them lapsed into silence.

They moved off the sea wall onto the island and headed along the path to the eastern lookout.

Sebastian cleared his throat. "I actually asked whether you would mind...you know...with you and me being in a boat together."

She threw her head back and looked at him. "No, I wouldn't mind." She paused. "Would you?"

"I think you know...that I wouldn't."

"But I do have reservations," she added.

"What?" he demanded.

She took his arm and pulled it back, bringing him to standstill. Pip looked him in the eyes. "There is a lot that you and I don't have in common, and a lot I still don't know about you Sebastian McKenzie."

He began to protest but she shut him down by thumping his chest with a fist. "Hear me out."

He closed his mouth.

She took his hands in her own and looked up at him. "Sebastian, you still don't know who you are, or why you exist." She paused. "And that's the foundation for everything."

Sebastian frowned, not understanding.

She shook his hands in irritation. "Oh...talk to my dad."

"What? David?"

"Yes. You and he will be sharing watch together over the next week or two. You'll have plenty of time."

"Why?"

She ignored him. "And another thing: You, Sebastian, are changing so quickly that I'm not sure I know the guy of today. And I'm not confident that I'll know the guy of tomorrow. Things are happening so quickly to you that I'm a bit scared." She paused. "I'm not sure that a shipboard romance is a wise thing right now."

Silence hung between them. The only sound came from the

haunting, rising cooing of shearwaters getting comfortable for the night.

Sebastian disengaged one of his hands. "Ignoring you romantically would be a whole lot more helpful if you weren't so dammed attractive." He reached out to hook back a strand of hair from her face. "But if you weren't so attractive, you wouldn't be you, would you?"

She looked at him without expression, then lent forward and kissed him on the cheek. "That was a lovely thing to say. But let's leave it at that, and see what the voyage does to us."

Sebastian said nothing.

Pip paused, and laid a hand on his chest. "Just…don't push your luck, because I mightn't…"

The shearwaters cooed.

He whispered hoarsely, "And what sort of luck do you think I might push?"

She took her hand from his chest and stepped back.

He held on to her other hand. "We could…*carpe diem*…you know, 'seize the day.'" He couldn't but fail to note the desperation in his own voice.

But she pulled free and gave him an old-fashioned look.

Silence hung between them, screaming its possibilities.

"The problem with that, Sebastian McKenzie, is that you might very well seize the day, but lose a lifetime possibility."

"A lifetime?" Sebastian's mind began to spin.

"And I wouldn't like that," she finished.

Chapter 24

Whisperer seemed impatient to leave. She had been fueled, pumped out, and her water tanks were full. Now she was doing what she was made to do. Her bow was dipping and rising in the sea, shouldering the waves into spray.

Pip had wedged herself into the pulpit at the bow to be alone with her thoughts—and wished she felt as eager.

The thudding and spluttering of the engine had been stilled and there was now only the sound of whooshing water. They'd managed to set all the sails by the time they headed through the gap between the Southern Breakwall and Muttonbird Island, and a brisk southerly wind was now driving them along.

No one had said much that morning. Everyone seemed content to nurse their own thoughts as they'd gone about their tasks.

What lay ahead?

Pip looked up at the eastern horizon. It was on fire with the morning sun, its light gilding the wave-tops with pink.

Perhaps there was hope.

Val interrupted her reverie as he called from the cockpit. "Pip, can you join us?"

She made her way aft.

Sebastian handed her a mug of coffee as she stepped down into the cockpit.

She nodded her thanks.

David was at the wheel. The early morning start had left his face looking a little pinched, but he seemed content enough.

Val turned to David. "Head north for a bit. Steer zero-two-zero. That'll give the illusion we're heading up the coast—but we don't want to go so far that we get tangled among the islands of Solitary Marine Park. We'll change our course and head to the north-east in about two hours time." He glanced at his watch. "That will be around 8am when our watch system begins for real."

David nodded.

Val scratched at his beard. "Just a couple of other things it's important to say right now. The first is: If you are in doubt about anything: call me. I'd rather be called twenty times unnecessarily than not be called on the one occasion I'm really needed. Is that clear?"

Pip nodded.

"Secondly: sailing a boat on a four-hour watch system will put everyone under pressure. We'll all get tired—and tiredness exaggerates the flaws in people's character." He looked around at them. "So keep a grip on yourself and make allowances."

The brutal no-nonsense demeanor of the man made it easy for Pip to imagine him instructing a squad of soldiers in the army. She wondered how she would cope being on watch with him—just the two of them together—over the next two weeks.

Val continued to growl. "Thirdly: Our watch system will allow us to eat our meals together. Other than that, get as much sleep as you can when you're not on watch." His gray eyes fastened on Pip. "Pip; David: if the boat's motion is too violent for you to sleep in the forepeak cabin, let me know. It can get pretty lively. We might be able to move people around." He looked up at them. "Any questions?"

Pip experienced a wave of anxiety. She crossed her arms and jammed her fists under her armpits.

"Problem, Pip?"

Damn the man.

"Um, no. It's...I was just wondering whether...I'm up to it."
And I'm putting my life in the hands of a serial killer!

"Everyone's schooling will continue on the voyage. We'll be doing a 'man overboard' drill after lunch. It'll be our watch by then Pip and you'll be on the helm."

No assurances. No comforting words. Pip sighed.

"Any more questions?"

There were none.

Pip collected the empty mugs and climbed down the companionway steps into the main cabin.

Val had laid claim to the bunk behind the kitchen table, presumably because it offered quick access to the deck; and Sebastian had a little pipe cot beside the companionway. After depositing the cups in the sink, she made her way past the toilet to the forepeak cabin that she shared with her father. *Whisperer* pitched and rolled—alive in her element. Pip had to brace herself and hang on to anything within reach. She tried to think what it would be like to live at a permanent angle whilst bouncing up and down for days on end.

It was impossible to imagine.

She lay down on her bunk in a storm of emotion.

But as she lay still, she began to allow the sounds of the boat to reach her. She listened to the thrum of the wind in the shrouds vibrating through the hull, and the sound of the water.

She'd been told that the hull was essentially made from bent pipes, chicken wire, and concrete—*absurd*. Yet this didn't stop her being able to hear the musical sound of water trickling, splashing and whooshing along the side. It was a surprise to her, and strangely comforting. The roll of the boat and the sound of the sea seemed to hold her, as if in a womb. Perhaps she might survive after all.

"Hey Pip, come and have a look at this." Sebastian's voice shouted through the hatchway.

She heaved herself up and made her way on deck. Sebastian was on the bow beckoning to her.

Immediately, she saw why.

Bottle-nosed dolphins were jostling for position in front of the bow wave—impossibly close to the pitching stem of the bow but never bumping it. They weaved among themselves in a fabulous display of dexterity. One of them, in particular, was a show off. It was surfing the bow wave upside down, exposing its pale belly and looking at her as if waiting for her applause. Then, in an instant, they all spiraled down deep into the sea and disappeared leaving *Whisperer* alone on the ocean.

"How's the seasickness?"

Sebastian was jolted out of his ruminations by David's inquiry. The two of them were the only ones on deck.

"Um, not bad. A bit queasy yesterday. Good today."

He'd actually suffered a good deal from seasickness on the first three days of their sail training at Coffs Harbour. It irked him that he was the only one who'd been affected by the malaise. Pip was fine.

Val, of course, showed no sign of it. Sebastian thought, uncharitably, that seasickness wouldn't dare afflict him.

It was late afternoon on the second day of their voyage, and they were well out of sight of land. Their only company through the day had been a group of gannets diving for fish. They'd tucked in their wings and speared into the water, giving a fantastic display.

But now they were alone, and Sebastian was brooding like a sulky school kid. He knew it, and wasn't at all proud of himself.

Why couldn't he stand watch with Pip? He'd love to speak with her—to have her to himself during the long watches of the night. And why didn't he have a physique like Val? He'd enjoy her seeing it.

He thrust his hands in his pockets. Val was paired with Pip, and that was that. Their watch system was perfectly sensible and only to be expected—*dammit*.

He glanced at the sail and the compass bearing. The wind direction was more easterly. Sebastian reached for a chrome handle, inserted it into the mainsheet winch and gave it a turn. *Whisperer* signaled her thanks by leaning harder to the wind. She butted the sea so that the spray shone like a rainbow before dying in the sea.

Sebastian staggered across the cockpit and returned the handle to its storage pocket.

David grinned at him. "Don't drop it."

"Why?" He was being petulant.

"I've had a look at the chart. The sea is four kilometers deep at this point."

Sebastian blinked. *Jeeesh.* "Sorry David, I'm being an asshole."

David waved a dismissive hand.

Sebastian decided to repair things with better conversation. "Do you think we're crazy doing this?"

"What?"

"Sailing to Vanuatu. It's not exactly sensible."

David smiled. "Well that's it, you see: we never really grow up. We only learn how to act in public."

Sebastian laughed.

It was enough to reset the mood.

His thoughts went back to Pip's comment on Muttonbird Island. Unsure of where it would lead, he asked, "Why would Pip suggest I ask you about my identity? What would she be on about?"

David pushed his spectacles up his nose. "I expect she's signaling her willingness to hang around with you."

"But?"

"But she's reluctant to team up with someone who is a feckless, beer binging, self-sabotaging wastrel with no apparent reason for living."

It took a moment for Sebastian to digest David's merciless reply. It was all the more shocking coming from someone so mild mannered and affable.

"Wow! That's telling it…"

"…like it is?"

"Yes." Sebastian tried to marshal his thoughts. "Presumably, you wouldn't be too keen either if I dated your daughter."

David kept his eyes on the sails. "I would be reluctant to trust my daughter to a man who has no foundation for knowing what good is, and no foundation that would allow him to love her sacrificially in good times and bad."

"If you're talking about God, I've never seen much evidence of his existence."

"So you've done some serious research?"

Sebastian thought for a while and decided to be honest. "Nah, not really—although I've heard a few quotes from some high profile atheists."

"Paddling around in the shallow end of Google is a culpably lazy response to the miracle of existence."

Sebastian couldn't think of a reply.

"I invite you to go deeper, Sebastian." David gestured around him. "The universe is shot through with signs of mind. To believe otherwise is to believe that everything came from nothing, and that fractures the law of 'cause and effect' that underpins all science."

Sebastian had never had a conversation like this in his life. He rubbed the back of his neck, unsure of what to say. Eventually, he said, "The religion thing: you know—it's not really my thing."

David banged the top of the wheel. "Willful atheism should never masquerade as a carefully researched intellectual objection to God. If you want to not believe, that is your prerogative, but you may not claim an academic mandate for doing so."

Sebastian reeled before David's brutal exposé of his spiritual vacuity.

"You're, er…pretty passionate about this." Sebastian had hoped his comment would be seen as a mild reproach.

David gave no indication of hearing it as such. "If you expect me to be indifferent to someone my daughter is interested in, you're mistaken. Love cares, and truth matters."

The albatross was sweeping backward and forward, working its way upwind toward the smells coming from the yacht. The great bird wouldn't be visible for very long. Night was closing in. Not that it would bother the albatross. It could sleep on the wing.

Val turned his attention to the girl sitting on the coach roof. Pip was hugging her legs and looking pensive. She was about to experience only her second night under sail, so it was understandable. On the previous night, he'd set the self-steering gear so that she hadn't needed to be on the helm at all. Tonight it would be different.

She looked vulnerable and innocent, so much so, it disturbed him. Something deep and visceral within him stirred as the memory of another woman swam into his memory—a woman he'd been unable to protect.

Val looked again at the girl. The wind was blowing her hair across her face. He shook his head to forestall the memories she evoked, memories that haunted and accused him.

Activity: he needed to do something to redirect his thinking. He reached into the ditty bag for a sail-maker's palm, a needle and some Terylene thread. A corner of the cockpit canopy had become unstitched and needed mending. He folded the canopy down and set to work.

"What are you doing?" Pip asked.

"Redoing some stitching." He pushed the needle into the canvas. "Cruising is the art of traveling to exotic locations in order to do maintenance."

Pip smiled, unwound herself, and climbed into the cockpit. "Show me."

Val showed her the technique of holding the needle into the sail-maker's palm and doing a stitch.

"That's not too different from normal sewing—just heavier. Can I have a go?"

Val surrendered the palm, and she set to work.

"Where's the nearest land from here?" she asked.

"Middleton Reef. It's about a hundred nautical miles to the south."

"A hundred...but that's over a one-hundred and...what? Eighty miles?"

"Yeah. Roughly."

"But we're doing okay?"

Val nodded.

Darkness was now falling rapidly. The albatross was no longer visible. Pip was putting on a brave face, but Val could hear the anxiety in her voice. He wished he could assure her that he would allow nothing on God's earth to harm her.

But he didn't, and he couldn't. Instead, he said: "It's my responsibility to get you to Vanuatu. I fully intend to honor that responsibility."

She looked up at him and searched his face. Then said, "I believe you will."

She trusted him.

The knowledge of it amazed him.

Pip did not know it, but she had just given him a precious gift. He looked away. Perhaps there was a chance he could redeem himself. He put his hand into his pocket, felt for the tiny handkerchief, and caressed it between his fingers.

Pip reapplied herself to the stitching.

Val kept his attention directed elsewhere.

"How's this?" she asked, eventually.

He glanced over. "Not bad, particularly considering the lack of light." Val decided to put the bit of confidence she'd just generated to good use. "Can you get on the wheel and steer for a while. I'm going to disengage the self-steering. I want you to get confident at steering the boat at night."

Pip's eyes opened wide. "I'm…I don't think I'm as good a sailor as you think I am."

He moved out of the way so she could take the wheel. "Let me be the judge of that."

Pip took hold of the wheel.

Once Val was confident that Pip had the boat under control, he said, "All you need to do is to learn the right technique. Get the boat settled on the compass bearing; then line up the bow or forestay on a prominent star. You'll find it easier to steer toward a star than to chase a compass heading. But it's important to recalibrate every ten minutes. Stars move."

The evening wore on, and after an hour, Val re-engaged the self-steering.

"You did well, Pip."

She flopped down on the cockpit bench. "Aren't you afraid of anything, Val?"

The question surprised him. In no way was he ready to voice things he didn't even understand himself. He searched for something to say that had at least some semblance of truth. "I...have no fear of the living, but I'm disturbed by the dead."

It was a massive understatement. He desperately sought the forgiveness of the dead, but they only offered their curses.

It was now completely dark. Pip hung her head over the stern and watched the phosphorescence burble and curl away in *Whisperer's* wake.

Val was grateful for the silence.

Inevitably, it was broken. "Being in prison must have been pretty horrible. How did you survive?"

Val frowned.

She looked up at him. "I'm sorry. I don't mean to pry. I just wondered what stopped you going mad."

He grunted. "There's plenty of time for thinking. But that's not always a good thing."

"Why's that?"

Val avoided the real reason and said instead, "Bored people can get creative."

"Yeah? How so?"

"Some prisoners discovered that if you light a Panadol tablet, it catches fire."[1]

"Really?"

"Yeah. You can flick it onto someone's back where it will burn into their skin like Napalm."

"Woah!" She paused. "Didn't any of their creativity extend to trying to escape?"

"Of course. One bloke kept ordering a lot of dental floss and toothpaste. It turned out that he'd used it to cut through all but one bar of his prison cell. Took him three years. Dental floss and toothpaste are abrasive—particularly when used together."

Pip shook her head.

"Another guy ordered a lot of Kenacomb cream, the stuff that's normally used to treat skin rashes. It turns out he was using it to simulate the gray grout between bricks which he'd removed in a bid to make his escape."

"Wasn't any of this creativity ever put to good use?"

"It depends what you call 'good.' Someone discovered that Metamucil speeds up gin production by twenty-four hours—which cut detection time down by a third."

Pip laughed. "How can you possibly make gin in a prison?"

"From fruit, but it's important not to add the skin of the fruit or you'll make too much methanol. They used Vegemite as a source of yeast."[2]

Pip laughed again.

Chapter 25

As the days passed, Pip became more at home on the sea. Life was simple and regulated, and part of her was now in no hurry to reach Vanuatu. All sorts of complications and demands would doubtless be waiting for them when they arrived.

She marveled at the changing moods of the ocean. One moment the sea was covered in low swells with velvety surfaces; the next, it whipped itself up into waves with foaming tips.

Whisperer took it all in her stride.

Occasionally, they were entertained by the acrobatic antics of sea birds. A Cape petrel fluttered its stiff wings between glides as it inspected the yacht on their fourth day out. How such a small bird could be so far from land amazed her. The nearest land was Norfolk Island, three hundred nautical miles to the south-east.

They had been at sea for five days when Pip put a mug of coffee beside Val. He was seated at the chart table. She and Val were off watch and she'd just finished washing up after the evening meal.

Val was listening through some headphones whilst staring at a weather map on the computer. His grim expression caused her to pause and ask if all was well.

Val took off his headphones and pointed to the weather chart.

"This storm cell is coming a lot further north than anyone predicted." He chewed his lip. "I'm sorry to say it Pip, but I'm afraid we're in for an uncomfortable time."

Pip gulped. "What do you mean by 'uncomfortable?'"

"Eight hours of storm conditions by the look of it—with things pretty rough either side of that."

"Will we be okay?"

"Yes, if we prepare well."

"What do we have to do—to prepare well?"

"Strap everything down. Use gaffer tape to seal the top of any jar or container that might spill if turned upside down."

"Upside down!" she squeaked.

"We have to expect to at least be knocked flat a few times." He shrugged. "It's going to be a pretty wild ride. One of the safest places to be will be in your bunk. You can't fall far there. But you will need to double-lash the lee cloth on your bunk if you expect it to hold you in."

"Anything else?"

"If you can, empty your bowels and your bladder before the worst of it." He shrugged. "Sorry about that, but it's a reality." Val glanced again at his watch. We'll have a hot meal before the storm breaks, and prepare another meal that can be eaten during the storm. Stews are best. We'll put some in the wide-mouthed vacuum flasks. You can eat from them. We'll also need to drink, so put water into all the travel mugs. They've got lids that can be shut."

"How long have we got before the storm hits for real?"

"About six hours, I reckon."

"Right."

It wasn't right at all. Her head was spinning.

A remote part of her said, "What do you want me to do?"

"Can you get a stew warmed up?"

She nodded.

"And perhaps get Sebastian to help you secure all containers in the cupboards."

"Will the cupboard doors actually remain shut—if we get knocked flat?"

"Yeah. Those locking catches are designed for these conditions."

Pip remained seated trying to overcome the shock of what she was hearing.

Val put a hand on her shoulder. "Are you okay?"

No!

She nodded.

Val stood up and headed for the companionway.

But she wasn't sure she was ready to be alone yet. "What are you going to do?"

"I'll get the sails off her—rig her down to storm staysail and trysail. The wind will start rising in an hour or so."

"We will be okay, won't we?" she asked again.

"Yeah. The trick to riding out a storm is to prepare for it early."

When he'd gone, she looked out of the cabin window. The sea looked benign enough. Oily four-meter swells glided past. She shivered. She'd heard the term 'the calm before the storm,' and she very much suspected she was in one now.

Val could think of nothing else that needed to be done. He wiped the spray off his face, content that they'd readied the boat for the storm as best they could. There was nothing more to do now but wait.

As if by common consent, everyone was on deck in the cockpit. No one wanted to be alone.

Val looked at the glowering sky. It was dark, swirling, and menacing. *Would they be able to handle it?* He glanced at his crew.

Pip was wide eyed.

Sebastian was working hard at looking nonchalant.

David had his eyes closed.

He felt for them. In a few hours, they'd be hearing noises they'd never heard before, and be shaken with a violence that was nothing short of maniacal.

Rain added to the mix of spray that dashed in their faces and whitecaps dotted the sea.

Val shouted above the wind. "If it gets too hairy in the cockpit, get down below and shut up the hatchway. The boat is quite capable of looking after itself—even if we lie ahull with all the sails down."

Sebastian broke in. "What about our watch system? Will that stay the same?"

"We'll stand normal watches until things get too extreme. At that point, David and I will stand watch together." He turned to David. "Is that okay?"

David nodded.

The wind moaning in the rigging rose to a shriek.

Val yelled again. "Keep your safety harness fastened at all times. Clip on to the jack-line that runs the length of the boat if you have to leave the cockpit. That'll be particularly crucial in the next twelve hours. If you go overboard, we won't be able to see you, and we certainly won't be able to sail back to pick you up. This is one occasion when the wind is boss and we've got to bow to its demands."

Two hours later, it was pitch black. The storm had turned the night's darkness into a blackness that could be felt. *Whisperer* was now bucking and rolling like a battered and tormented being.

Val was on the wheel, trusting the boat to no one but himself. He'd ordered Pip and Sebastian down below, and now only David was with him.

It was wearying work fighting the wheel, and he was already tiring.

A vicious squall suddenly howled out of the darkness and knocked *Whisperer* onto her ear. All Val could do was hang on to the wheel as the cockpit floor tipped sideways and filled with water.

He turned instantly to check on David.

David was hugging the mainsail winch like a drowning man to stop himself from being thrown out.

Relief flowed over him.

Bang!

It was the sound of something breaking, clearly audible even above the storm. Instantly he heard the flogging of an untethered sail.

As *Whisperer* rolled upright, he could see that the clew of the storm staysail had been ripped out, and the sail was thrashing itself to bits.

Even more alarming, David was clipping his safety harness onto the jackline and starting to make his way to the staysail halyard at the base of the mainmast. He yelled in alarm. "Leave it, David. Get back."

But the wind whipped away his words before they could be heard.

Whisperer fell off a cliff of water and plunged into the deep. A massive wall of water rushed across her decks. It picked David up and threw him over the side.

For a moment, his safety harness held.

But then the jackline parted.

David's arms flailed in the sea trying to reach the gunwale. But *Whisperer* lurched away from him, putting it out of reach.

Val instantly unclipped his harness and threw himself forward along the side deck reaching out for David from under the guardrail.

Miraculously, he found David's hand. He locked on to it and tried to haul him up the side.

But the storm would have none of it.

It snatched and pulled on David. One moment he hung like a dead weight; the next, he was being jerked away. With each jerk, Val was being tugged further and further over the side.

He was faced with an impossible dilemma—to let go of David and save himself, or hang on and hope.

He hung on.

It was excruciating.

The muscles in his forearm screamed in protest as the boat reared and plunged.

Another jerk tried to tug him into the maelstrom below.

He must have screamed, but he couldn't remember.

Suddenly, he could feel arms grabbing at his legs—two sets of arms.

"Hang on," he yelled as *Whisperer* dipped her gunwale into the water. Val seized his chance and hauled David in under the guardrail.

"Pull," he yelled.

Pip and Sebastian pulled at his legs.

He slithered along the side deck and felt himself being manhandled into the cockpit. Val discovered he was still holding on to David only when the man fell on top of him.

Whisperer was not under command. She was rearing and rolling from side to side like a person in torment.

Val found that his muscles had frozen, and he was unable to let go of David's arm.

He shouted "Get on the wheel. Bring her off the wind."

Sebastian lurched for the binnacle and grabbed the spinning spokes of the wheel.

Once everyone was untangled, Val began to flex his hands, coaxing his abused muscles back to obedience. Eventually, he had them back under control.

"Everyone: get down below," he yelled.

Then he took the wheel—and stayed there for the next six hours.

Sebastian was hunkered down in the cockpit trying to keep out of the wind. David was now on the wheel. Val had told them that it was necessary to hand-steer the boat to avoid putting excessive strain on the self-steering gear.

Val was in his bunk. Pip had told them that he'd fallen asleep almost immediately after she and David had finished seeing to his cuts and abrasions.

The sea was still rough but was now without malice. *Whisperer's* mainsail was reefed down to the third reefing point, and her normal staysail had been reset. However, there was still too much wind for the jib to be unfurled. Rain squalls occasionally caused *Whisperer* to lean and shudder, but she was pushing through the heaving seas with the ease of a veteran.

Sebastian, however, was not at ease. He was shivering as he replayed the drama of the previous night over and over again, reflecting on the appalling tragedy that had so nearly engulfed them.

David interrupted his reverie.

"How do you feel about finding your father, Sebastian?"

Sebastian blinked. He was surprised by the question and not at all sure he could answer it—particular amid the storm of emotions he was currently experiencing.

After a moment's reflection, he decided that talking, however uncomfortable, was preferable to brooding.

"I, er...don't think of him as my father. I can't. He's kind of... dark: you know—scary."

"Think kindly of him, Sebastian. He's having to survive the crushing weight of his own history."

Sebastian said nothing

David continued. "And he's trying to care for you—for all of us, in his own way."

"Yeah, I suppose so. But he's still..."

"Disturbing?"

Sebastian nodded. "He's so driven, so uptight—even at night. He barely sleeps; just thrashes about."

David nodded. "He's desperate to find redemption by protecting those he cares for. And his love has driven him to unleash terrible violence." He paused. "That can't help but conflict a man and make him slightly mad."

"He's mad all right—ballsy for sure."

David raised an eyebrow. "And this from a young man who climbs buildings at night."

Sebastian grunted. "Yeah, well..."

"He's been enduring a living death, Sebastian, and that can make a man a little careless of his life."

Whisperer reared up on the flank of a large wave, shouldering a sheet of green water across her deck.

Sebastian instinctively ducked.

The water sluiced off the decks, and *Whisperer* powered on.

David cleared his throat. "And what has made you careless of life?"

"Me?" he said surprised. "Careless?"

David nodded. "The drinking, and all the rest?"

Sebastian leaned back on the cockpit seat. "Oh, I dunno. Boredom, probably."

"Boredom comes from having no purpose; and having no purpose comes from meaninglessness; and meaninglessness comes from not knowing who you are." David paused. "Haven't you ever experienced anything that suggests there might be something bigger than yourself to believe in?"

"Not until the other day—when you spoke to me. You were pretty rough with me, you might remember."

"But did I make sense?"

Sebastian avoided giving a direct answer. "Not according to the philosophers I've been reading. Their thinking suggests getting drunk isn't such a bad option."

David raised an eyebrow.

Sebastian sighed. "Jean-Paul Sartre said the road to atheism is a cruel affair. Nietzsche said that the true atheist must be willing to risk madness; and Camus said that atheists need to embrace the absurd."

"And what do you think?" asked David.

"I reckon that's about enough to drive anyone to drink."

David was not put off by his attempt at humor. "Or there's something in your spirit that grates against their nihilism."

Sebastian rubbed the back of his neck. "Hmm. Recently, I've experienced something pretty special." He shrugged. "I'm getting an idea that it's all a bit too special for it to be meaningless."

"So maybe God does exist?"

"But not necessarily the Christian God."

"Ah, then you've become a deist. Welcome to the boring majority. Most Australians are deists or atheists."

"Deists?"

"Deism is simply a belief that God exists, but remains mysterious—hidden behind the masks of a thousand different religions.

Most Australians unconsciously flip-flop between deism and atheism depending on their emotional state."

"And what's wrong with that?"

"Atheism promises freedom, but only delivers hopelessness. It traps people within the smallness of themselves, from where they can't see either their meaning or identity."

"That's bad, I suppose?"

"A drawer full of holiday tee-shirts from Bali is no substitute for meaning."

Whisperer shuddered as she heeled to a gust of wind. David wrestled with the wheel and brought the boat back on course.

Sebastian glanced at him. He seemed to be quite at ease—appearing to be even enjoying himself. Damn the man! It was ridiculous. He had no right to be. What drove him?

He decided to probe.

"You don't have much time for atheism, do you?"

"Atheists, like anyone else, should be honored. But atheism... well, let's just say that I am suspicious of a belief system that blinds people to the bigness of the universe and discourages them from asking why they exist."

"But what about all the other religions? Are they okay?"

"Trendy self-focused spiritualities look a little shabby in the face of a God who came in history to die for our sins to rescue us back to himself. This is something that is either a lie or it is true. If it is a lie, discard it. If it's true, it is worthy of your life's commitment. But the one thing you cannot do is patronize Christianity by relegating it to being just one of a number of equally valid religions."

They were silent for a while.

Sebastian wiped some spray from his face. "Why are you telling me all this stuff?"

"Because I want you to find hope."

"Hope?"

"A hope you can pass on to your children."

"Why?"

"Because atheists can only expect to see the ruin of meaninglessness in the eyes of their children."

Sebastian hunched himself over, keeping his face from the wind. David's words heaped up in his mind in a jumble, waiting to be understood.

But one word stood out: 'Hope.'

It was a disturbing word.

Chapter 26

It was very evident to Pip that Val had been more damaged by the storm than he'd first led them to believe. He had some nasty grazes—probably caused by the winch barrels, guardrails, and sheet blocks during his desperate rescue of David. But his main damage was internal. Whilst there were no broken bones, Val had torn muscles both in his torso and arms. David was also concerned that Val might be dehydrated. He'd seemed only dimly aware of what was going on around him when he and Pip put him in his bunk—no easy task with the boat rolling and pitching so much.

On David's orders, Pip had fed Val with warm soup and dosed him up with painkillers.

Next morning, the big man couldn't move. He made a valiant attempt, but his body simply refused to work. Even little movements caused him pain.

He was not much better today.

Pip looked at him now as he lay in his bunk. She could only guess at what it must have cost him to stand watch alone during the storm. As she'd helped her father re-bandage Val's cuts and abrasions that morning, she couldn't fail to appreciate again the immense strength of the man. Very few people would have been strong enough to hang on to David in the storm and haul him to safety as he had done. Tears came to her eyes. Val was paying a heavy price for it now.

"What's the matter?"

He was awake. She blinked the tears away.

"Nothing. How are you feeling?"

Val tried to sit up, winced, and lay back down. "Not great, I'm afraid. Sorry to be…a nuisance."

She put a beaker of water to his lips. "Drink. Dad's orders."

He shook his head. "I need to pee."

She handed him an empty plastic milk container.

He could barely hold it.

"Do you need help? I can get Dad."

"Nah."

She looked away.

Above her, she could hear the rattle and clunk of a foresail block banging against the deck. *Whisperer's* movement was still lively, and Pip could feel the boat shudder in the wind gusts.

He handed her the filled container.

She called up the companion steps to Sebastian and passed it on to him.

Pip returned to Val with the beaker of water. "No heroics. Let me hold it for you."

He drank.

"That's good," she encouraged.

He nodded when he'd had enough.

"I'll make you some soup now."

Val grunted. "Better keep the milk container within reach, then."

It was a poor attempt at humor, but it was good to hear his gravelly voice. As she turned to go, he said: "Pip…" He paused then started again. "You and Sebastian…you broke every rule the other night. You didn't clip yourselves in; and you saved my life." He closed his eyes. "I'm grateful."

Pip looked at him for a moment, bent over and kissed him on the cheek.

David glanced at the compass in the binnacle behind the wheel. "Our course is zero-four-eight…and the self-steering is on."

Pip nodded as she wedged herself up on the cockpit bench against the doghouse, trying to keep out of the wind.

David watched her raise a hand in salute to Sebastian's welcoming smile.

Hmm, things were progressing on that front…'deepening' was probably a better word.

David reflected on the night Val and Sebastian had first met Pip at his home in Adelaide. He'd experienced a curious peace at the time, a peace he'd learned to recognize over the years. It was a peace that had nothing to do with the conversation that had gone on, which—goodness knows—was disturbing enough.

"How's the patient?" he asked.

Pip wrinkled her nose. "Hard to say. Eyes closed but awake. Still not moving much."

"Hmm, I'll have a look at him before I get to my bunk." He glanced up at the sails. *Whisperer* was on a fine reach, sailing close to the wind—as she had for most of the voyage. It had made things uncomfortable because it was a point of sailing that caused the boat to heel a lot. If they sailed back from Vanuatu, they could expect an easier time, as they'd be riding an easterly wind on a broad reach for most of the way.

'If they sailed back.' David wondered what the next few months would bring. He was returning to a place that had been his home for ten years, to a people who had been his family and who had taught him so much.

He made his way down the companionway and crossed over to Val's bunk.

Val's gray eyes opened. "Where are we?" he asked.

David glanced across to the sat nav.

"Approaching the southern end of New Caledonia."

Val nodded. "Keep clear of the barrier reef surrounding the island—well clear. It extends thirty-five nautical miles to the south."

"Relax. Sebastian's got the navigation in hand. We've already planned a track around it. We'll head north once we've cleared the Isle of Pines."

"Is that the little island at the southern end of the reef?"

"Yes. And there really are pines there. We looked it up. Evidently it's a good place for a holiday—good beaches and great snorkeling."

"Just make sure you don't hit it."

David folded Val's bedclothes back and checked Val over.

Some spectacular bruising was now evident. Val would be sore for a good few days yet. He covered him up again. "Your job is to get fit again."

Val grunted.

The two men said nothing for a while.

David broke the silence. "You know you should have let me go. You're indispensable to the kids right now."

"Probably."

"Why didn't you?"

"Instinct. You don't have time to think."

"Hmm."

"And I couldn't have faced Pip."

David raised an eyebrow. "Pip?"

"Yeah."

They were silent again.

David cleared his throat. "You know, of course that great love means being prepared to die for another, don't you?"

Val looked away. "Yeah? Who says?"

"Someone rather famous." David handed him a traveling mug of water. "Keep drinking, then see if you can get some more sleep. I'm going to get my head down."

———

Pip watched as Sebastian glanced at the sat nav on the tablet set up in front of him. The screen repeated the image that was on the computer below.

He caught her looking at him and grinned.

"Here goes," he said. "Our first major course change since leaving Australia."

He turned the wheel.

Whisperer nosed round to the left.

Once Sebastian had settled the boat on her new track, Pip attended to the winches. She eased out the sheets until the leading edge of the sails threatened to back-wind—then made them fast.

Whisperer signaled her thanks by increasing her speed to six knots. The wind was now on her beam—her best point of sailing.

Pip resumed her position on the cockpit bench, hard up against the doghouse, and cast a covert eye on Sebastian.

He looked older than when they'd begun their voyage, she decided. She was pretty sure it wasn't just the tiredness that she was seeing in his face. He'd matured. Perhaps they all had. Being responsible for the lives of others whilst on watch for days at a time could not help but change a person.

Sebastian seemed to read her thoughts. "Together at last," he said.

He'd aimed at humor but he'd hit rather more truth than she wanted to admit.

The watch system was now being shared among three people. They'd decided that one person should be on watch during the day and two people at night. This meant that Sebastian and Pip were occasionally together.

They hadn't talked much on their previous watches. Both of them seemed content to simply savor each other's company. However, Pip now felt the need to talk. The dramas of the storm had highlighted the fact that life was an uncertain thing—and that if there were things she wanted, she had to pursue them.

Sebastian reset the self-steering and flopped down on the bench beside her. Their thighs were touching. Her skin began to warm.

Dammit, I hope he doesn't notice.

It wasn't the first time it had happened. Heat seemed to emanate from him. She'd even coined a name for it—his 'gamma rays,' she'd called it.

Stupid.

He surprised her by speaking first. "Here, I've got something to show you. I'd like your opinion on it." Sebastian fished inside the leather pouch on his belt and removed a small parcel wrapped in a handkerchief. She guessed straight away what it was—The Fire Stone.

She was partly right. However, the stone was now clasped between two tiny metal cups mounted on a cross-shaped frame.

He showed her how the clasp could unscrew to separate the cups and release The Fire Stone. "Val told me that the stone has more value if it is not permanently mounted on anything." He lifted up the clasp. "I thought this might be a good compromise. It means it can be worn as a necklace."

Sebastian screwed the gem back into place and handed it to Pip.

"The question is: Is the clasp too clunky and ugly? What do you think?"

Pip had never seen the gem in the sunlight before. The stone glinted aqua and blue; and from its depths a fiery red erupted. It was hypnotizing. She turned her attention to the clasp. It was ingeniously made, intricate, yet strong. She held it against his chest. The crossbar at the back stopped it hanging backward. He'd thought of everything.

She was impressed and wished for the umpteenth time that Sebastian could really appreciate the potential that was in him. He had extraordinary gifts.

"Sebastian, it looks great. Not too clunky at all. How did you get the idea for it?"

He shrugged. "I just…sort of worked it out."

"But how do you actually get all your ideas?"

"You'd have had plenty of ideas too, I bet."

"Not like you. How do your ideas actually…arrive?"

Sebastian blew out his cheeks and thought for a while. "Um, er…ideas are like unexpected visitors. And they're sort of…delicate."

"Delicate?"

"Yeah. They only come with the right mental mood."

"And what's that?"

"I've never really put it into words before." He scratched his stubble. "I reckon it's one of relaxed readiness. You're relaxed enough for the mind to play, but ready enough to catch the results." He grinned. "That's the best I can do, I'm afraid."

She nodded. "If you don't use all that creativity you've got, Sebastian McKenzie, I'm going to haunt you for the rest of your life."

He faced her. "You already haunt me Pip, and I suspect you always will."

It was not the reply she'd expected.

But she enjoyed hearing it.

The gamma rays intensified.

Blast them!

Val felt himself to be slightly better after the second day and even managed to make it up the companionway to the cockpit a few times—not that he was required to do anything. The boat was sailing well, and he knew it was in good hands. He scratched at his beard. It was an odd feeling to be redundant.

Whisperer had threaded her way between the Loyalty Islands and was surging northward. The first of the two-hundred islands making up the Vanuatu archipelago were somewhere just over the horizon to the east. This was a part of the world David was familiar with. Val saw the excitement of anticipation in the man's eyes. David was on watch, having taken over from Pip.

Pip was now in her bunk. She'd gone below with some reluctance as she'd seen her first flying fish. Val reflected on her kiss. It was the kiss of affection, of innocence, and it had warmed him to the core. He couldn't remember when he'd last had such a kiss.

David pointed to one of the larger Islands now beginning to be visible on the sat nav. "That's Tanna—home to one of the most active volcanoes on Earth. It's a very strange place."

Val raised an eyebrow.

"They have some very odd beliefs there. The rest of Vanuatu is highly Christianized. It's resulted in sociologists calling the Vanuatu people the happiest people on earth." He tapped the sat-nav screen. "But the people of Tanna resisted Christianity. They kept to their own beliefs, morphed it with their experiences of western civilization and developed a cargo cult." He grinned. "On the south of the island, they have a particular reverence for Prince Philip.

"What? As in the Duke of Edinburgh?"

"Yeah. They see him as a god."

Val shook his head.

The two men remained silent for a good while.

Whisperer pitched and surged her way through the crests kicked up by a steady force four wind.

David broke the silence.

"Val, in a couple of days, we're going to be making our home among the Nivan people in a fairly remote corner of Malekula Island."

Val waited for him to say more. David looked as if he was searching for the right words.

"The, er…social structures are complex and delicate. They can easily be damaged by Western cultural values and behavior."

"Why are you telling me this? What's on your mind?"

"I don't want these people hurt. So, when we get to Malekula, we play by my rules."

Val remained silent.

"Seriously, Val."

He weighed up David's words, trying to consider their implications. After a moment he nodded. "Okay, we play by your rules— except in situations of extreme danger." He looked up at David. "Then I reserve the right to do what I think is best."

"Fair enough."

David's words had disturbed him more than he would have liked to admit. He felt the guilt of bringing danger to his son; bringing danger to David and to Pip; and now he'd been cautioned against being a danger to a community in Malekula.

Voices started to scream at him in his head. He held his temples with his fingers.

"What's the matter?" David had noticed.

"Nah, nothing."

"What's the matter?" he repeated.

Val grunted in irritation. "Um, I just feel…responsible."

"Responsible?"

"Yeah; sorry that I got you all into this mess."

David waved a hand dismissively. "You didn't choose the actions of the Saracens. Don't lay claim to guilt which is not yours to bear."

Val grunted. "At least I can try and make amends."

"You're already doing that." David leaned forward to check the heading on the compass. "Both you and I survived the storm, and that's a fair indication that we've both got more work to do."

Val grunted. "I think I've lived too long; been given too long to repent of my sins."

The two men fell silent again. *Whisperer* burst through the crest of a wave sending a shower of spray across her foredeck.

David cleared his throat. "Val is short for Valentine. That was the name of a goodly number of Roman emperors. If memory serves me, the name actually means 'valiant.'"

Val laughed bitterly. "Not in my case. Remember? The prison governor gave me the nickname 'Val' from the Valkyrie of Norse mythology. The Valkyries drift around a battlefield choosing who will die. Stoddard would say, 'You are my Valkyrie.'" He rubbed his forehead. "And I was. I've killed a lot of people." Val gave a derisive laugh. "No God will forgive that."

"Rubbish. He already has. It cost the death of his son—so your forgiveness hasn't come cheap. Don't spurn it."

David's words lanced into his soul—into that dark part where he tried not to look—the part that held his grief, self-hate, and guilt. Nothing usually reached it. But David had.

Val couldn't decide whether his words were wounding or healing. Whatever they were, they were disturbing. He shook his head. "Why would he…" he paused, "do that…?"

David glanced up at the sails. "Because that's what love does."

Chapter 27

D avid was experiencing a storm of emotions as *Whisperer* edged closer and closer to the Island of Malekula. He was coming home to a community that had owned his soul for ten years. Being a medical doctor had given him a door into the community. And being a minister and a friend had given him a door into their hearts. They had taught him the richness and frustrations of being part of a society in which everyone knew everyone else's business. And they had taught him to find joy in the small things, and how to live with almost nothing. Now he was coming back—but this time without his wife. Her sickness had forced him to leave. The community had been heartbroken.

Whisperer ghosted past the Maskelyne Islands southwest of Malekula in a light breeze. Sebastian, who was at the helm, was keeping her well clear of the fringing reef.

David could see the island of Ambrum twenty kilometers off to the northeast. The smoke from the twin vents of its volcano was clearly visible through the tropical haze.

Sebastian pointed to it. "Looks pretty dramatic."

"It is. They're the twin volcanic vents of Mt. Benbow and Mt.

Manum. You can see the red glow from the volcanoes easily at night from Lamap."

Sounds like an interesting place to visit.

David grunted. "It has a reputation for witchcraft, so the locals at Lamap are ambivalent, to say the least, about going there."

All four of them were now in the cockpit watching the coast as they crept toward it. This was the morning of their thirteenth day at sea, and the prospect of being on land again was making them all excited. David glanced at Pip. She had both hands on top of the coaming and was staring at her old home. God alone knew what she was thinking.

He inspected the reef that extended beyond Lamap headland. Somewhere out there lay the remains of a crashed American fighter plane from World War II that he'd once explored at low tide.

His thoughts turned to Sebastian and Val. How could he prepare them for what they would experience? He should probably try and forewarn them. But what should he say? He pondered for a few seconds then cleared his throat.

"I, er…should probably tell you a few things that will help you fit into the community here."

Val glanced at him.

"First the language. You can expect to hear three languages. There's their local language that they call, rather prosaically, 'language', and there's French. This Island was once under French rule. But the main language is Bislama. It's a form of pidgin English."

"What—Pidgin English like they speak in Papua?" asked Sebastian.

"It's a bit like it, yes. When westerners came here to capture and cajole men to work the Australian sugarcane fields, they were frustrated by the inability to communicate because of the many of languages they spoke. The westerners therefore came up with a form of phonetic English, with Spanish, French and colloquialisms added for good measure. It's now the official language of Vanuatu. The good news is that you can sometimes follow the gist of what's being said because of the English words. You've just got to use your imagination."

David racked his brains for what else he should say.

"You'll also need to watch out for coral cuts. They turn into ulcers very easily. Wear wetsuit boots when you're swimming over the reefs."

He turned to Sebastian. "You should probably be aware that Westerners are seen as being both exotic and rich. Expect to attract the attention of the girls. They'll want to sit beside you, fan you with their fans and feed you. Just be careful. They are a very tactile people who will invade your personal space. Be ready for it and be polite."

Sebastian nodded. "Would it make things simpler if we, um…let it be known that Pip is my girlfriend?"

David smiled. "It might simplify things for you both. But be warned, you'll get lots of very personal questions."

Pip rolled her eyes. "You bet I will."

David tried to find the words to explain the dense social network Val and Sebastian were about to experience.

"Social etiquette requires that you try not to greet anyone bare chested, so put on a tee-shirt. And don't walk between people who are speaking to each other." He paused. "Other than that, it's just a case of using your common sense."

The wind finally died away altogether, seemingly content that it had done its job in getting them to their destination.

They took down the sails and started the engine.

Val took over the wheel and asked David to hoist Sebastian up to the top of the mast in a boson's chair. "Winch him up on the main halyard," said Val. He turned to Sebastian. "Your job is spot the coral bommies. Those are pillars of coral that balloon up from the seabed. They'll rip a hole in us if we hit one."

Sebastian looked alarmed.

"Relax. You'll see them pretty easily from up there. With the morning light behind us, there'll be almost no reflection." Val pointed to the cockpit locker. "The boson's chair is in there. It's the thing that looks like a plank of wood on a child's swing."

Whisperer began to nose her way into the harbor.

David watched as the harbor opened up before them. Port

Sandwich harbor cut its way into the island for seven kilometers, and the village of Lamap was strung along its southern coast. In truth, the village was little more than a scattering of huts that extended from the harbor mouth to Port Sandwich three kilometers into the bay.

Up ahead, a fisherman was standing up in a dugout canoe. When they drew closer, David could see that the man was wearing a Manchester United T-shirt. He didn't recognize him but nonetheless gave a cheerful greeting. *"Olsem wanem?"*

The man grinned and waved. *"I gud. Yu kam wea?"*

"Mi blong Australia."

Val interrupted. "What's he saying?"

He's saying 'hi' and asking where we've come from. I've said we've come from Australia. David turned back to the man in the canoe. *"Old Fella Seule gud?"*

The fisherman nodded. *"Si. Gud."*

That was good news. The village chief, Seule, was still alive.

The fisherman called out. *"Wanem nem blong yu?"*

David drew a deep breath, knowing that things could get interesting from this point on. *"Nem blong me Doctor David."*

The fisherman frowned, then his mouth dropped open, and he stood up and started to dance about. David was sure he'd fall overboard.

Whisperer was now too far past him for David to continue the conversation. When he looked back he was not surprised to see the fisherman paddling for the shore.

Val interrupted his thoughts. "David, the chart shows two places we can anchor; one off the village a mile or so ahead, the other off Port Sandwich further on. Do you have any local knowledge that might point to which is best?"

David replied without hesitation. "Anchor off the village. *Big Sista* comes into Port Sandwich during the night, and it would be best if we keep out of her way."

"Big Sista?"

"Yes. It's the ferry that goes between Santo and Port Vila."

He smiled to himself. *Big Sista*, or Big Sister—it was a beautiful name for something so many relied on to link them with the outside world. Its imagery helped him think fondly of the café where Pip worked: *Little Sister*. Both names spoke of community—and he liked that.

Whisperer edged toward the shore as Sebastian shouted directions from the masthead.

David made his way forward and began preparing the anchor so that it was ready to drop. As he did, he couldn't help but wonder what might lie ahead.

Chapter 28

Sebastian and David picked up the inflatable dinghy, and carried it through the shallows over the coral outcrops and up the beach. After setting the dinghy down under the trees, Sebastian glanced back at *Whisperer*. She was looking very much at peace. He smiled. She deserved to be. *Whisperer* had delivered them safely across two-thousand kilometers of ocean.

As this was Sebastian's first time ashore he was keen to explore. David and Pip had gone ashore earlier that morning to greet people, show respect to the local chiefs, and to endure the enthusiastic welcome of old friends. Evidently, it had been an emotional experience for everyone involved.

Shortly after they arrived, Val insisted that *Whisperer* be reprovisioned with water and food so that they were ready to move at a moment's notice. Accordingly, he and David had set about ferrying jerry cans of water back and forth to the boat. The water came from a communal tap stand. Evidently, they were fortunate it was working.

Finding food was less straightforward. David volunteered himself for the task but asked Sebastian to help him. "It will mean a visit to the trading store which is a two mile walk up the track that goes back to the headland."

Sebastian had readily agreed.

Once the dinghy was tethered to a tree, he and David shrugged the empty rucksacks onto their backs and set off down the track.

Soon, Sebastian was exchanging '*bon jours*' with cheerful locals along the road.

He tried to take in all that he was seeing. The local huts seemed to be made of woven bamboo strakes, and had roofs constructed from coconut fronds. Pigs, dogs, chickens, and cattle roamed freely among the huts.

He was intrigued to see that most fence posts were sprouting green leaves—a fair indication of the richness of the volcanic soil on the island. Rather more disturbing was the sound of falling coconuts. One could be heard falling every few minutes. He commented on it.

David smiled. "Yes. The locals have learned not to spend unnecessary time under a coconut tree."

Occasionally, young men would pass them, usually carrying strange looking vegetables.

"They're coming from their gardens," explained David.

Sebastian could see no sign of any gardens. "What gardens?" he asked.

"Most families own a semi-cultivated area of land from which they harvest sweet potato, taro, yam, bananas, and papaya. They're further up in the hills."

Many of the men he saw sported Rastafarian, Bob Marley hairstyles. One of them carried a boom box on his shoulder blasting out reggae music.

After fifteen minutes of walking, a pick-up came bouncing along the rutted truck behind them.

David hailed it. "*Yu save sakem mi long Lamap?*"

The driver smiled. "*Si*," and cocked his thumb at the back.

Sebastian and David joined three smiling Nivans in the back of the pick-up, and they were soon bouncing and lurching on their way. The three Nivans immediately began peppering them with questions. *Wanem nem blong yu?* and *Yu kam wea?* Sebastian was slightly alarmed at their lack of inhibitions. David answered them good-naturedly. During a lull in the conversation, he leaned across to Sebastian. "They're fueling the 'coconut wireless.' Relax, it's quite normal."

After a few minutes, they were dropped off at the administrative center of Lamap. From what Sebastian could see, it didn't consist of much—just a trading store, a school, and the ruins of some buildings presumably left by the French. The locals had not bothered to try and rebuild them, preferring their own buildings made of plaited bamboo and palm fronds. Sebastian was not surprised. The native huts would be infinitely cooler in summer.

The trading store was a brutally utilitarian thing. It had bare wooden serving benches and shelves stacked with sacks and tins containing the basic foodstuffs of life. There were no luxuries.

The store manager nodded to them and asked, "*Yu save toktok Bislama?*"

David nodded. "*Si.*" He started pointing to various sacks and cans, and asking, "*Hamas long hemia?*"

The storekeeper named the prices.

They bought all the goods they could fit into their rucksacks and then organized for their mobile phones to be in credit through Digicel. Once everything was completed, they began their walk back.

At one point along the track, Sebastian took out his phone to take a photograph of some decorated wooden frames on a derelict building. The posts standing over its entrance were carved like totem poles.

He was surprised when David pushed his arm down.

"Please don't photograph that, Sebastian."

Sebastian looked at him in puzzlement.

"Sorry to startle you." David paused. "You heard me tell you that the big island offshore, Ambrum, is reputed to be a center for black magic. What I didn't tell you was that the people of Lamap also have a reputation for this." He nodded to the ruined building. "That's the remains of the chief's meetinghouse which was used for witchcraft. It's not a good place, and the locals don't like anyone photographing it. It can awaken things."

Awaken things! Sebastian put his phone away. "I thought you said this was a Christian place."

"It is, mostly." David rubbed his head as if struggling to explain. "Christianity has been good for Vanuatu. It's encouraged the best of the Nivan's own culture—their friendliness and sense of community, and it has kept a lid on the worst of it—fear, black magic and violence." He smiled. "Sociologists call the people of Vanuatu 'the happiest people on Earth.' But evil is never very far from the surface."

There were only two sets of snorkels and flippers on board *Whisperer*. Pip and Sebastian commandeered both late in the afternoon and were floating over the reef about sixty yards away from the boat.

It was soon evident to Pip that Sebastian was not particularly at home in the water. He didn't have that easy fluidity and confidence of a seasoned swimmer. She, however, had pretty much lived in the water during her ten years in Vanuatu and was relishing being back in it.

There was not a lot that could remain hidden when a girl was in the water, and she knew that Sebastian was trying not to make it too obvious that he was watching her. She couldn't repress a sense of glee. Neither could she resist a bit of mischief.

"Just keep an eye out," she said. "The locals say they've seen a tiger shark around here recently."

Sebastian gulped and twirled around in the water, looking this way and that. But before long he was distracted by the schools of tropical fish beneath him. She was not surprised. There were exquisitely colored butterfly fish, triggerfish, rainbow-colored parrot-fish, and a few blue starfish. The coral itself was also beautiful. Most of it was lilac and pale green in color. Some of it was yellow.

However, it was the stag-horn coral, with its beautiful blue tips, that she particularly loved.

Sadly, not all of the coral was healthy. Some of it was covered in silt and other bits were bleached—quite dead. Pip wondered whether the silt had come from the last cyclone, and hoped the bleaching was not a symptom of global warming. It was a stark reminder to her of the fragility of life in Vanuatu.

The thought caused her to look across at Sebastian. He was floating on the surface, absorbed by what he was seeing.

What he didn't see was a canoe full of children sneaking up behind him.

They bumped the canoe into his feet.

Sebastian reacted with shock and spun around in the water.

The children shrieked with delight.

When Sebastian realized it was a prank, he swam to the canoe's outrigger and began to lift it up.

The children squealed in alarm at their imminent capsize.

With honor apparently restored, he lowered the outrigger back down.

The children were soon in the water with them, laughing and splashing. One of them kept calling out to Sebastian, "*glas, glas.*"

"He wants to borrow your mask," Pip explained.

Sebastian passed it to him—and was rewarded a few minutes later when he returned with a cowry shell.

Pip duck-dived and swam among the coral, causing schools of colored fish to dart back among the horny filigree to seek safety. The child with the mask swam down with her. He tapped her on the arm and pointed at a round-shaped fish.

When they came to the surface, she asked, "*Wannem ia?*"

The boy spluttered, "*Fis i gat naef long tel blong hem.*"

She nodded and reflected on the sensible names they had for fish. Its name was literally, 'fish he got knife on tail belong him.' It was a fish to be handled with care.

Eventually, she and Sebastian returned to *Whisperer* and climbed up the ladder into the cockpit. As they toweled themselves dry, Sebastian said, "There's coral everywhere. It's beautiful, but frightening. It can only be a matter of time before we put a hole in our inflatable dinghy."

Pip couldn't disagree.

Sebastian flopped down on the bench. The sinewy strength of his arms and legs was plainly evident. Pip swallowed. He looked good. She leaned forward so he wouldn't see her reaction.

Fortunately, the man's mind was on other things.

"Do you suppose we could get the use of one of their old canoes? I've seen a few without their outriggers pulled up under the trees at the top of the beach." He pointed. "See; there's one over there."

Pip glanced up. It was not uncommon to see discarded canoe hulls along the coast.

"If it's not too badly holed, and the rot isn't too bad, there might be a chance I could mend it."

Pip raised her eyebrows. "Seriously? Their owners would have already tried to patch them up."

"Yeah, but we've got epoxy. There's not much you can't fix with that."

She nodded. "Okay. Let's ask Dad to make inquiries."

Val and David returned to the boat in the inflatable just as Pip and Sebastian were preparing the evening meal. David dropped a hand of bananas down on the cooking bench. "Seule, Aunty Lorie, Monique, and Tatiana are putting on a banquet for us tomorrow night to welcome us." He smiled. "I'm afraid there's not going to be anything very anonymous about us being here."

Pip nodded. She never expected anything else.

"Dad, can we get the use of one of the old canoes? Sebastian reckons he could mend it." She shrugged. "It would save us holing the inflatable on the coral."

"Really? I suppose that's a good idea. I'll ask Seule about it. It's Friday, so there's a worship service in the village tonight. I'm going to it and will ask him then. Val's coming, too. He insisted on escorting me."

Later that evening, Pip and Sebastian were alone again in *Whisperer's* cockpit. She could smell wood-smoke in the air from cooking fires and the copra ovens dotted among the coconut plantations. The orange lichen on the trunks of the coconut trees caused them to glow with warmth in the setting sun.

Night came quickly as it always did in the tropics, and soon it was dark. In the distance she could hear the sound of singing. "*Me blong him. Him blong me.*"

She knew the song well.

Next day, Sebastian was introduced to an old man called Jean who was the owner of the derelict canoe on the beach. The old man poked a finger in one of the holes in the hull and shook his head. "*Samting ia hemi bugarap.*"

Sebastian grinned. He didn't know Bislama but he was pretty sure that *bugarap* meant 'buggered up.'

He smiled. "Mi fixim." Sebastian wasn't sure that what he spoke was correct, but it sounded sort of right.

Jean seemed to understand for he nodded.

Sebastian didn't trust himself to say anything more so he turned to Pip. "Pip, can you ask Jean to show me around one of the good canoes so I can see how it's put together."

"Sure." She spoke to the old man.

Jean beckoned them over to an intact canoe that had been pulled above the shoreline and began chatting away.

Pip translated, occasionally stopping to ask for clarification.

During a pause in the conversation, Jean reached inside the canoe, picked up the tin that was being used as a bailer and went down to the water's edge. He came back with it full of water and tipped it into the bottom of the canoe. Sebastian had no idea why, and continued to examine the dugout.

The top edge of the hull had been built up with two planks of wood to increase its freeboard. Notches in the top plank took the staves that reached out to the outrigger. There was nothing sophisticated about the outrigger: it was simply a log with a boat-shaped bow. It was secured to the staves by a series of angled wooden braces.

Sebastian pointed to the outrigger. "What sort of wood is that?"

Pip jabbered away, and the old man answered.

"It's whitewood," she answered.

"And the staves?"

More jabbering.

"Mangrove wood."

Sebastian pointed to the hull of the canoe.

Jean knocked on the canoe's hull. *"Blu wota."*

"What?"

The man beckoned and pointed to the water lying in the bottom of the hull. Sebastian was amazed to see that it had turned a milky blue.

"Blu wota," the man repeated.

Blu wota…'Blue water.' Of course.

Pip broke in. *"Blu wota* is actually rosewood—very valuable I understand. Sap from the wood of a new canoe turns the water slopping around the bottom blue; hence its name, *blu wota*. Pretty cool, eh?"

Sebastian nodded.

He was now confident he could repair the old dugout. All the pieces of the canoe were still there although not in place. The children had removed the outrigger log to play with in the water. Sadly, the children were not around this morning as they were at school. He'd heard them singing as they made their way along the track.

Everyone seemed to sing.

The trestle tables on the veranda of Seule and Aunty Lorie's home were covered in dishes. The children were milling about, and the gaunt village dogs hung back in the shadows coming as close as they dared to explore the smells.

Pip walked with David, Val and Sebastian up from the beach to Seule's home where many of the community had gathered. She had already met some of her old friends but was eager to catch up with the rest of the community.

When they arrived, David introduced Sebastian and Val to the chiefs, uncles, and aunts. After the formalities, she and David were mobbed. David was hugged by the men, and Pip was hugged by the women. They caressed her hair and stroked her, exclaiming, *Mi no lukum you longtaem* (me no look at you longtime) and *mi glad tumas* (me glad too much).

She could see Sebastian edging away to the back of the throng. Pip stepped forward and took him by the arm. Taking a deep breath, she said, "*Sebastian blong mi.*"

Her comment drew a chorus of oos and aahs from the aunties and ensured that Sebastian would have to spend the rest of the evening trying to answer their questions.

Seule called for quiet and made a speech of welcome before saying grace.

As guests of honor, they were shepherded forward and enthusiastic aunties filled their plates with food. She was pretty sure Sebastian wouldn't recognize much of what he was eating, but noticed that he was tucking in pretty well.

Once everyone had eaten, both she and David were required to make a speech. It was not hard. She spoke from the heart, thanking them for their love and speaking of her sadness that her mother could not be with them.

As the evening wore on, people began chatting in groups and things started to quieten down.

Pip looked around and couldn't see Val. She extricated herself from the children who had surrounded her and went to find him.

He was some yards away in the darkness, patting one of the dogs.

She stood beside him for a while, saying nothing—just listening to the strident chirruping of the cicadas. Eventually, she spoke. "I can't imagine not being part of a caring community. It must have been horrible for you not to have one."

He grunted and continued stroking the dog's ears.

"How do you go; you know—living a life that's anonymous, not being able to own a driving license, or anything?"

"It's inconvenient, but not impossible."

"But what do you do for money? How do you buy things?"

"I've got an account with a bank in an offshore tax-haven. They're a little less discriminating about in-depth identity checks. Any income from mining got paid into it, and they gave me a credit card." He shrugged. "For the rest, I operate in cash."

"It's as easy as that?"

"It's not easy, but its doable."

They were silent for a while.

Pip drew a breath. "Are we going to succeed in being anonymous?"

"I can't answer that."

Val straightened up from patting the dog and gestured to the throng of people on the veranda. "They seem to be good people."

She nodded. "They are the best."

"Nothing much seems to happen here other than subsistence farming and harvesting copra, but they seem pretty happy." He glanced at her. "That is all they do, isn't it?"

"Almost. Every tribe has something it is particularly good at. Some are good wood carvers. The Lamap people are known for their dancing."

"Dancing?"

"Yes."

At this point they were interrupted by a young man. He approached Pip and spoke to her enthusiastically. She recognized him as the son of one of the chiefs. He was also the local policeman.

Pip forced a smile and waved her thanks as he went back to rejoin the party.

Blood drained from her face. She unconsciously reached out and took hold of Val's arm.

"What's the matter?"

"That was Jayz, the local policeman. He lives down the track in the house next to the big banyan tree; the one with the fiberglass boat beside it."

Val nodded.

"He just said that someone rang him today to ask, quote: 'if the Albrights had arrived.'"

Val frowned.

"Jayz told them we had. He came to tell me just now how pleased he was that the good news was spreading to everyone." She bit her lip. "And before you ask: No, he has no idea who was on the phone."

Chapter 29

V al put his head on his hands. Someone knew they were at Lamap. It was inconceivable that it was possible, but the shocking reality was that someone did. Try as he might, he could think of only one group of people who would be looking for them. It was deeply disturbing, and it meant that he had to give thought to their immediate safety.

He was seated at the table in *Whisperer's* cabin. David, Sebastian, and Pip sat on the bench seats either side of him.

"How safe will we be in the village, do you think, David?" he asked.

David didn't hesitate. "Pretty safe: probably safer than if we stay on board *Whisperer*. I'll let Seule know that there may be some men coming after us seeking revenge for something Pip and I are innocent of." He pushed his glasses up his nose. "They understand the notion of revenge pretty well here, I'm sad to say. The village will look out for strangers and close ranks to protect us as best they can."

Val nodded.

Pip had wedged herself between himself and Sebastian as if seeking safety. The thought of her did nothing to ease the crushing sense of responsibility he felt. He alone was the cause of the danger everyone was facing.

Pip spoke up. "Aunty Lorie has asked me to help teach English in the local school while we are here. And she's asked me to stay with them in the village."

Val glanced at David. "What do you think?"

"It's difficult to imagine a safer place for Pip to stay."

Pip interrupted. "I'd also be at the center of village gossip. If anyone new arrived at Lamap's airstrip or by boat, I'd know about it very quickly—particularly if I recruited the eyes and ears of the children. They see everything."

Val raised his eyebrows. "There's an airstrip?"

David nodded. "Of sorts. It's just a grass strip down by the Maskelyne Islands. A twin Otter lands there once a week from Port Vila."

What about boat arrivals?

"*Big Sista* comes in twice a week. She arrives in the early hours of the morning. Nothing else. Just the copra boat."

Val remembered the copra boat. He'd got up early that morning when he'd heard the sound of its engine. The rusted, dumpy little boat made a noise that quite belied its size. It looked like something out of a cartoon. A derrick sat over its hold, and a tarpaulin had been rigged over the foredeck—presumably to allow its crew to sit in the shade. He'd taken careful note of it. The boat represented another way of leaving the island without the authorities knowing.

David broke in on his thoughts. "I've been asked to run a medical clinic from Seule and Aunty Lorie's house some mornings of the week." He shrugged. "That would probably also mean staying overnight." David turned to Val. "Is that okay with you?"

Val nodded and looked at Sebastian. "That leaves you and me. I think we need to stay with *Whisperer*, but she's way too visible where she is moored offshore from the village." He turned to David. "Is there a place we can hide her, a place that's not too close to the shore, yet which is still fairly hidden?"

David chewed his lip. "The only thing I can think of is to go deeper into the harbor, beyond Port Sandwich wharf." He shook his head. "But it will be very dangerous. There's no navigation channel, and the area is a maze of corral bommies. You'd need to be very careful."

Sebastian interrupted. "On the plus side, no one will be able to sneak up to us by boat."

Val nodded. "Then that's what we'll do." He turned back to Sebastian. "We'll need your outrigger to get to and from the boat. The inflatable would be shredded by the coral. Is your canoe waterproof enough to remain tethered to *Whisperer* without sinking?"

Pip wrinkled her nose. "No local leaves their canoe floating when not in use. They don't want them broken by the waves and filling with water."

Val looked at his son. "How good are your repairs?"

Sebastian rubbed the back of his neck. "I've cut out all the rot, plugged the holes with new wood and epoxied it into position. It reckon it should be fairly good. Old Jean is amazed it hasn't sunk already, so he's pretty excited." He shrugged. "Time will tell, I suppose."

Val grunted. The boy had shown ingenuity and resolve. He liked that…but then the crushing weight of guilt descended on him again and spoiled his enjoyment.

"What's next?" asked Pip.

Val turned to David. "I'm assuming you're taking *Whisperer's* first aid box."

David nodded. "Yes. I know what's in it because I provisioned it. The thing is, if I take it, it will leave you with nothing."

"Doesn't matter. Take it." He leaned back. "Are you and Pip packed up and ready to leave?"

They both nodded.

"Then Sebastian will paddle you to shore."

"What do I do after that?" asked Sebastian.

"You come back here. I need to hoist you back up the mast so that you become my eyes when we make our way up the harbor."

Pip glanced up at him. "Do please be careful—both of you."

It took Sebastian forty minutes to paddle the dugout back to the village from their new mooring. He and Pip had organized to catch up in the middle of the afternoon when her work was done. Sebastian didn't allow himself much time to look at the rugged ranges that ringed the harbor. Keeping the canoe moving took all his energy. He'd cut down one of the dinghy's oars to use as a paddle and although it worked well, it was still hard going. It was four o'clock in the afternoon before he arrived.

Sebastian pulled the canoe up the beach and trudged up the path, being careful to avoid the holes dug by the mud crabs. Their holes pitted the ground for twenty yards inland of the beach, and it was easy to twist an ankle in them.

A green backed pigeon with an orange beak and white shoulder patches watched him from the safety of a palm tree. He wondered idly what it was.

When he arrived at Seule's house, he found Aunty Lorie pounding some sort of vegetable on a bench in the outside kitchen. She told him that Pip had not yet come home from the school.

Sebastian nodded and said he'd wait for her on the beach.

He trudged back down to the water's edge and climbed up into the crook of a tree bough that overhung the sand. Gradually, the distant sounds of village life and the peace of his surroundings began to have a narcotic affect on him. Peace, of a sort, settled on him.

He was disturbed only twice. The first was when a copper-colored lizard with a blue tail ran over his hand, and the second was when one of the local men made his way along the beach and stopped before his tree. The man pointed to the beach in front and asked, "Walk here?"

What sort of community is so mindful of other people's sensibilities that they ask permission to walk in front of them? "Yeah, sure," he said.

The man nodded his thanks and kept walking.

He drifted off again in a semi doze.

Only one thought nagged at him and prevented deep sleep. It was the memory of Val assembling a brutal looking rifle on *Whisperer's* cabin table.

Hopefully, it would never be used. Hopefully, they could stay here for a long time until those who pursued them grew tired of their quest and gave up. Hopefully—but the more he thought about it, the more agitated he became, and the peace he'd been enjoying began to evaporate.

He craved a beer.

With some amazement, it occurred to him that he'd not actually had a beer since he'd left the Mallee. Extraordinary! He rubbed his forehead. So much had changed. He was in no doubt that Pip was largely to blame. She'd awakened a hunger in him. David too had much to be responsible for. Through the long watches of the night, he'd dismantled every philosophical preconception he'd surrounded himself with, and introduced him to the loving designs of a relentless God. His words had got under his skin…and warmed him with something that might have been hope.

He forced himself to engage with the reality around him and turned his attention to the mud crabs sidling in and out of their burrows. Pip had told him that the crabs needed to be quick otherwise children would catch them, tie them up with strips of palm leaf, and take them home for supper.

His thoughts darkened. He wondered if they too would be caught. To be caught after having done so much to avoid it was a scenario to terrible to contemplate. His hands balled into fists. Nothing must be allowed to ever threaten Pip again.

He stared out across the harbor. As the minutes passed, the turmoil within him subsided…and he was rewarded with the sight of two dolphins. One leaped out of the water in a somersault.

Perhaps it was a sign of hope.

"Hi there, stranger."

Sebastian spun his head round. Pip was back. She was looking fantastic in a white blouse and patterned sarong. Affecting a nonchalance that was far from the truth, he waved and climbed down to the beach.

"You're late," he said. It was a banal comment. What he really wanted to do was kiss her.

"I had to print out a page of English phrases for the kids to learn."

"And this took most of the day?" Another stupid comment. He still wanted to kiss her.

She sighed. "Sebastian, you have a lot to learn. Nothing in Vanuatu happens easily."

He raised an eyebrow.

Pip put her hands on her hips. "Let me explain, young man, the process of printing out a piece of paper in Lamap. First, you have to push-start the pick-up because it has a dead battery. Next, you get driven to the Catholic school because that's where the only computer in the village is located. Then you have to set up the portable generator—not easy because it is heavy. But it is out of fuel. So you push-start the pick-up again and buy some petrol for the generator. You return to the school, but discover that the ancient MS Dos commands of the computer are written in French. Once you decipher that, you need to fix the paper jam in the printer. The last person couldn't fix it and simply left it. Then, and only then, are you able to print your piece of paper."

Sebastian started to laugh.

Pip continued. "But no, it's not over. Then you have to push-start the pick-up yet again and drive off to pick up an 'aunty' with a bad hip in order to drop her off at someone's home. And finally, you get taken home—with your wretched piece of paper." She turned and stabbed a finger into Sebastian's chest. "So cut me some slack, buddy."

As if by mutual consent, they stood on the beach together and said nothing, seemingly content with each other's company. On the other side of the harbor, a steamy mist hung between the steep-sided ranges. For one magic moment, a shaft of sunlight pierced the clouds and highlighted their flanks.

Pip pointed to the northeast. "Can you see that faint outline of an island north of Ambrum?"

"Only just."

"That's Pentecost Island. The young men on the island dive

with vines tied to their ankles from huge towers built of wooden poles. It's terrifying."

The thought was disturbing enough for Sebastian to lose his sense of tranquility, so he turned and shepherded Pip back up the path to Aunty Lorie's house.

When they arrived, Pip crossed over to a large stone that protruded from the crabgrass, squatted down, and stroked it.

Sebastian looked at her quizzically.

"This stone is pretty special," she said.

"Why?"

"Did you know that Seule is David's adoptive father?"

"What! The local chief?"

Pip nodded. "Being adopted is quite an honor. Most local chiefs are elected to office for two years, but Seule has his position as a result of his royal blood-line. That gives him particular authority. To be adopted by Seule is pretty special." She shivered, "Even though the adoption ceremony was pretty gruesome."

"Why? What happened?"

"Ah," she waved a hand dismissively.

"Seriously," he insisted.

"I still have nightmares about some of it—although some of it was beautiful."

"Really?"

"Yeah. It begins nicely enough. Everyone gathers, and the master of ceremonies blows a conch. Then there's a prayer and welcoming speeches from the local chiefs." She furrowed her brow, trying to recall the sequence. "Um, I remember Seule giving a speech; and then Dad..." She shivered. "And then the pig was killed."

Sebastian raised an eyebrow.

"Yeah: not pretty. Dad was given a rock and instructed to kill a trussed up pig. I remember the pig well. He was big tusker—and a tough blighter. He'd evaded capture for two days. But on the morning of the ceremony, I remember hearing the yelping and baying of the dogs. That told me they'd finally got the pig. But it wasn't easy. The pig killed two of the dogs."

"Wow! Did David actually kill the pig with the rock?"

"That was the horrible bit. He tried three times but couldn't kill it. The pig just squealed and tried to kick free. They cut its throat with a knife later. It was terrible to watch."

"Woah! Can't see much that would be lovely about that."

"Oh, the ceremony had its good bits. Mum and Dad were draped with garlands and peppered with white powder. Dad was half naked and dressed in vine leaves. And the local women had dressed mum in a native dress. You'll see them wearing them on special occasions. They're long floral things with flaps on the hip." She grinned. "They look as if a series of pockets have been turned inside out."

"All sounds pretty amazing."

Pip laughed. "Oh, the ceremony was only half completed at that stage. Gifts had to be exchanged and then all the chiefs made a speech. I remember them filing past, laying a hand on the pig, then shaking Dad's hand. That bit was rather moving."

"Wow!"

"There were probably other things that happened but I was taken home by an auntie at that point. Judging from the halooing and singing I heard through the night, the rest of them went off and drank cava."

Sebastian pointed to the stone. "And this…?"

"Dad and Seule buried this stone. It's the covenant stone that marks Dad's adoption."

"Oh, right." He lapsed into silence.

"A penny for them," she prompted.

"Hmm."

"Come on: out with it."

Sebastian cleared his throat. "Um…you know we'll be…sort of separated, with you staying in the village and teaching."

She nodded.

He undid the flap of his belt pouch and pulled out The Fire Stone. "Would you let this be…" um, our sort of…a covenant stone." Sebastian rushed on. "Will you keep this with you, for me… until we're back together again?"

Pip frowned. "But how would I keep it safe?"

"You could wear it, but keep it under your blouse. Only you would know…and me."

"But it's worth a fortune."

He nodded. "Yes, it's worth a fortune."

Chapter 30

The young boy came to him with a suppurating wound on his hand wrapped in a dirty white cloth. It was a machete wound. David had seen many such wounds during his time in Vanuatu. Children used machetes at an early age, and he was surprised there weren't more accidents. Every coconut tree he'd seen had multiple scars at its base caused by the men and children hacking at them with their blades.

David cleaned the wound, bandaged it, and injected him with an antibiotic. He then instructed the boy to keep the wound clean and to dab it every two days with oil from the local tamanu tree.

A sizable dent had already been made in his medical supplies, and David wondered how long they would last. He waved goodbye to the boy and began packing up the medical box. As he did, he reflected on Val's medical well-being. It had been over a week since the storm, and Val was now moving more freely. His wounds were almost healed, although his torn muscles would take more time.

David sighed. Val's mental state was of more concern. He was a tortured soul. It would require a seismic shift in his heart before Val found peace—and that was well beyond anything he could bring about. But David was used to being out of his depth and was no longer overly troubled by it. There came a point where you just had to trust.

Aunty Lorie emerged from the kitchen outhouse holding a plate containing a baked banana. He nodded gratefully and began to eat. It was good fuel—which was about all that could be said about it. The large local bananas were almost devoid of flavor.

David sat down at one of the two wooden benches in the bamboo patio he'd used as his clinic. It was lunchtime and the children who were lucky enough to go to school would be returning, singing as they always did. He could expect to be busy again as their mothers brought them to him. There was no such thing as official open hours in Lamap.

Two pigs were rooting around the weed patch behind Aunty Lorie's kitchen searching for the food scraps she threw there. Everything seemed normal. It was as if nothing had changed during the years he'd been away.

His thoughts turned to Sebastian. He was someone who definitely was changing. The reading Sebastian had done in philosophy had taught him the value of reason. David suspected it was this, coupled with his native curiosity that made him open to new truths. He couldn't suppress a smile. Pip would be pleased. He knew that she was in love with Sebastian—and had been almost since they'd met. If their behavior around each other wasn't proof enough, confirmation came when he had caught her composing a piece of music for Sebastian on her tablet in Coffs Harbour. He wasn't given a chance to examine the score as she'd banged the tablet shut when he'd looked over her shoulder. The only thing he'd seen was the heading, 'Sebastian,' and that it was written in the key of C major— a key noted for being both cheerful and natural.

He was watching an orange hornet explore the palm tree beside him when his mobile phone rang. It was Jayz, the local policeman. As he listened, he got to his feet and pinched the top of his nose. *No, no, this couldn't be happening.*

After a brief conversation, he cut the call off with a perfunctory thanks, and walked round the back of the house to find Pip. She was outside washing her undergarments in a bucket of water. Pip hung a bra over the bush beside her as he approached. *Baskit blong titties* was its name in Bislama. *Stupid time to remember.*

"Pip, I've had a call from Jayz. Evidently, he isn't feeling all that great about confirming our presence here to someone he didn't know and putting us in danger. So he's put the word out that he should be contacted if any strange boat is seen in the area."

Pip frowned. "And…?"

"A boat has been seen—a big modern thing, apparently. It's currently moored off the Maskelyne Islands. The people in it are poking about the islands in a speedboat that's been launched from it."

Color drained from Pip's face. "Do you think…?"

David nodded. "I think we have to assume it could be. And you and I are far too accessible here if they choose to come up the coast into the harbor. Everyone knows we're at Seule's house."

"What shall we do? Should we get back to *Whisperer?*"

"No. Even though *Whisperer* can't be reached easily by land or sea, she's still fairly conspicuous. You'd still be too vulnerable."

Pip began snatching her washing from the bush. "Then what shall we do?"

"There's only one place you'll be safe, and that's in the tiny village of Barmandrin across the harbor; you know, the place I used to have a clinic once a fortnight."

Pip nodded.

"If we move now, no one here will know where you are. We'll take Seule's canoe. Everyone here will think we're going back to *Whisperer.* But once we're round the point and can't be seen, we'll cut across the harbor to the village. It'll be a forty minute paddle." He laid a hand on her shoulder. "Are you up for it?"

"She nodded."

"Grab your essentials and meet me down at the beach as soon as you can."

She called after him. "Do Sebastian and Val know?"

"Not yet. I'll ring them once I've launched the canoe."

Ten minutes later they were paddling Seule's dugout across the clear water, gliding over the coral and the brilliant tropical fish below. As they paddled, David's mind was whirring. How many nautical miles was it from the Maskelyne's to Lamap? How long would it take a modern motor launch to cover the distance? He sighed. *Too late now.* They were committed.

Once they rounded the point by Port Sandwich, they headed across the harbor.

David felt terribly exposed in the middle of the large expanse of water. His muscles burned as he drove the canoe on.

As far as he could see, there was only one other canoe on the harbor, but it was somewhere well behind him.

Slowly, the far shore, and the densely forested range behind it began to creep closer. He could see the tiny village on the flat land just behind the beach. Deeper in the harbor, the coast became siltier. Mangroves could now be seen growing at the water's edge, and sea grass grew in the shallows. He was not surprised to see a dugong—such a weird creature—swimming where the sea grass grew. It rolled over onto his back and showed him a blunt, pale flipper.

His momentary distraction was cut cruelly short. David heard the rumble of diesel engines. He glanced round in despair.

A large black motor launch was cruising past the buoy that marked safe water for *Big Sista*.

Perhaps they hadn't seen them? He continued to paddle hard for the beach one hundred meters away.

The children of the village met them first. They splashed in the shallows and helped pull the canoe out of the water. Behind them, men with big smiles came down to welcome them.

As soon as the locals had overcome the surprise at having him back in their midst, David explained that bad people were looking for him to exact vengeance for something he didn't do. He pointed to the motor launch and said that they could be on board. Was it possible for him and Pip to hide with them until it was safe?

One man walked to the chief's hut and disappeared inside it. A moment later, an old man dressed in long shorts and a ragged tee-shirt, emerged and walked down to join them on the beach. He moved slowly and with obvious pain, but carried himself with dignity. David dearly wished he could get away from the beach to a place where no one with binoculars could see him. However, it would be rude to enter a village without permission. Hugs and greetings were exchanged, and the story was told yet again. David wanted to scream. Everything was taking an inordinate amount of time.

The old man nodded, asked a few questions, and then glanced across to the motor launch.

David noticed that it had come to a stop. However, what really alarmed him was that an inflatable with an outboard engine had been launched from the back of it. The inflatable was now creaming across the harbor toward them.

The old chief asked David what he would like them to do.

With relief, he said, "Take Pip and hide her at the old Frenchman's well. It's very thick cover there and they'll never find her." He pinched the top of his nose and tried to think. He felt dreadful about bringing trouble to the village. It was a fragile community. What could he do? *Think, think.* He racked his brain.

After a moment's thought, he told the chief that he would make himself visible on the beach, then lead those in the boat away from the village up the jungle track beside the creek up the flanks of the forested range. Perhaps he could make things so uncomfortable for his pursuers that they would give up any ideas of trying to hunt them down.

The chief nodded then walked over to a bench that had been placed under a large tree. He sat down and stared at the inflatable skimming across the water toward them. David noticed that his lips were moving, but he made no sound.

As the men spirited Pip away, David began jogging along the beach, making no attempt to hide. He passed the tiny village church with its immaculately tidy grounds and headed further up the beach to where the creek spilled its tannin-rich water into the sea.

Once he got there, he bent over to catch his breath.

Disturbingly, he saw the inflatable change direction and begin heading towards him. It was now possible to see that it had two occupants: a dark-skinned man—probably a Nivan, and a large white man.

David had seen enough. He turned and began walking up the hill along an overgrown track.

David regretted that he was not fitter. Whilst he regularly rode a bike in Adelaide, his job was essentially a sedentary one, and his level of fitness reflected it. He wiped perspiration from his face. The game he was now playing was quite probably deadly, and required him to be fit enough to carry it out. He hoped he was up to it.

The track through the dense tropical foliage beside the creek was barely discernible. He'd not walked it for many years and hoped he could remember the way. Progress was slow, as he didn't have a machete to cut his way through the vegetation. He pushed on.

Every now and then, the path ran beside the creek. It was dank and muddy. The villagers regularly rummaged in it searching for fresh water mussels. He remembered that they were horrible to eat, even when cooked.

A kingfisher flashed past, showing off its iridescent coloring.

David fought his way through the vegetation, snapping branches and leaving muddy footprints.

Before long, he came to the bog. He remembered it because he'd once lost a boot there. It was probably still under the mud somewhere. The thing he remembered about the bog was that it was impossible to cross unless you used fallen logs and low tree boughs as stepping-stones—and this was almost impossible to do without the aid of a rope that had been rigged as a handrail.

David crossed the bog with great care, and untied the rope.

The path then turned to the left away from the creek. David followed it and soon found himself in a different world; surrounded by majestic trees with massive buttresses. They soared upward to the heavens. It was a land of giants. On any other occasion, he would have found the experience magical.

Not today.

There was still plenty of undergrowth, enough to constrain anyone from deviating from the path. David began to search the bushes beside the track for one particular plant—a plant with large oval leaves and purple veins. It was called *nagalat*. He'd already seen it growing beside the track, but he wanted to find a place where *nagalat* grew in profusion.

Eventually, he found what he was looking for. But did he have time? How far behind were the men who were looking for him. Were they even following? He had no idea.

David backed his way past the stand of *nagalat*, breaking the stems of the plant so that its leaves hung across the path.

Then he heard a noise. He stopped to listen. In the distance, he could hear the sound of twigs breaking and muffled cursing. He paused to listen. But it was quiet again.

There was now no doubt that he was being pursued and that those tracking him were not far behind. David turned and made his way uphill as quickly as his lungs would allow.

After fifteen minutes, he arrived at a gently sloping hillside where the tropical vegetation gave way to open space. The entire area was covered with coconut trees. He'd arrived at a copra plantation. He could smell the wood-smoke from the copra oven half way up the hill. As he stared at it, he saw someone moving about beside it.

A wave of anguish washed over him. In no way did he want to bring danger to any of the locals in the area. This was his affair, not theirs.

He made his way up to the hill.

The man attending the oven paused mid way through pushing a branch into the furnace and waited for David to reach him.

The oven had been made from a number of forty-gallon drums tipped on their side and joined together. A large metal tray of desiccating coconut sat on top of it. The furnace was protected from the elements by a crude roof made of corrugated iron and palm leaves.

When he approached, David could see that the man was quite old and that he was smoking contentedly on a clay pipe. The stem of the pipe had obviously been broken at some stage because a wooden substitute had been lashed to the broken stub. David wondered how old the pipe must be. It would have to be a hundred years old at least.

The man puffed away and waited for David to speak.

David wasted no time. Speaking in Bislama, he told the man who he was.

The old man nodded and smiled. He remembered David from years ago.

David hurried on and explained that two dangerous men were pursuing him. He urged the man to hide in the adjacent tropical jungle until they had passed.

To his dismay, the old man shook his head and replied in Bislama, "This my place. I will stay."

David pleaded with him, but the old man was adamant.

The sound of men cursing could now be heard clearly.

David urged the old man to take care, then jogged toward the safety of the jungle. Once he got there, he hid himself in a place that still gave him a line of sight to the copra oven. He only just got himself settled when two men emerged into the clearing.

They were not in good shape. Both were rubbing their faces and arms, and were in obvious pain. David could hear them cursing.

He was not surprised. Stings from a *nagalat* leaf were vicious. They left a burning welt across the skin that took up to two weeks to heal. The worst thing to do was to rub it. The best thing to do was to dab sap from the stem onto the rash.

He watched as the men made their way up to the old man and his copra oven.

David was in despair. He'd banked on the men being so brutalized by their experience of the bog and the *nagalat* that they would have given up the chase.

But they hadn't.

David had no idea what to do next.

He remained perfectly still and watched.

A large white man led the way. He was heavily muscled and well over six feet tall. When he reached the old man, he drew a pistol from his belt and fired it into the air.

The sound of the gunshot startled a flock of red-faced parrots, causing them to fly away, squawking.

A hush descended.

David watched in horror as the man then pointed the pistol at the head of the old Nivan and yelled out, "Albright: You've heard us and know we're here. Come out or I'll put a bullet into the old man's brain."

The tropical jungle held its breath.

David was appalled. What should he do? He couldn't let the old man suffer over an issue that was entirely his. But neither could he allow himself to be captured. If he were taken prisoner, they would use him to get to Val. David was in a torment of anxiety and indecision.

The man yelled again. "Albright, I enjoy violence and don't make empty threats. Yell out that you're coming, or this man gets killed."

Before David realized it, he had called out, "I'm coming. Don't harm the man," and was stepping through the undergrowth toward the clearing.

Inside him, his soul shrieked. Everything was unraveling. Pip, Val, and Sebastian were now in real danger, and he had no idea how to protect them.

When he approached the two men, he could see that both were covered in mud and had lurid red rashes over their arms and faces. The Nivan accompanying the white man hung back as if trying to distance himself from the drama being played out.

The armed man aimed the pistol at David.

David was conscious of a curious peace coming over him. Death was not something he feared. He knew himself to be the responsibility of someone greater than himself.

David's calm did nothing to settle the armed man's temper. The man stepped forward and smashed the pistol across the side of David's face.

David fell to the ground only half aware of the profanities that followed as the big man gave vent to the level of discomfort he was feeling. When the tirade was over, the man hauled David to his feet and aimed the pistol at him again.

David had no idea what would happen next. He was too traumatized to think.

BANG!

The shocking crack of the sound whipped David's ears.

In the same instant, the head of the man holding the pistol exploded.

David had the vague sensation of being splattered with brain pulp and blood.

The big man fell to the ground. The top of his head was completely blown off.

It was all too much for the dead man's colleague. The Nivan turned and ran.

It took some time for David to register what had just occurred. When he did, he spun around looking for who had been responsible for the killing.

Nothing moved.

He waited some more.

Still nothing moved.

The old man was the first to break the spell. He returned the pipe to his mouth and gave the corpse lying in front of him a push with his foot. "He's dead," he said.

David was appalled. He was also bewildered as to what he should do. Was this a police matter? Who should he tell about what had just happened?

He must have voiced the question out loud, because the old Nivan simply shrugged. "No problem. I'll put him in the copra oven and cook him." He took another puff on his pipe. "When he's done, I take his bones, put them in a sack, and drop him in the harbor."

David was incredulous. "Is that...is that the right thing to do?"

The man shrugged. "Yes. It is good." He spat on the ground. "Bad men should have no grave." The Nivan waved David away. "You go now."

David bent down and picked up the dead man's pistol. "What about this?"

"You want?"

David shuddered. "No."

The old man grunted. "I put it in the sack with him."

Chapter 31

The coppery smell of blood permeated not only his clothes but his very soul. Was the smell just in his mind? David shivered. One thing was certain; the memory of what had happened would haunt him for a long while.

He was eating fish in the communal meeting hut with Pip, the village chief, and his family.

Eating fish—as if nothing had happened! It was bizarre.

Nothing was said about the drama of the day. There seemed to be a conspiracy of silence. All he'd been able to learn from the old chief was, "A friend come to help you."

"What friend? Where is he now?"

"He gone."

"Where has he gone?"

The old man had shrugged. "He gone," and wouldn't elaborate.

When he'd asked the chief about the other 'bad man,' the chief had waved his hand dismissively. "City Nivan man. No good. He gone too."

"Where did he go?"

"To big boat."

The chief didn't comment on the fact that two men had arrived but only one had left.

David glanced at Pip. Her attention was fully taken up by the children. One was plaiting her hair and another was resting across her lap. They were asking her questions and laughing at her replies. It was probably the best therapy she could have. He'd not told her what had happened that afternoon and had blamed the gash on the side of his face on a fall.

David glanced outside. The trees were in dark silhouette against the dusky pink twilight. Night was coming quickly. To the east, clouds were beginning to bank up and block out the stars.

One of the aunties disturbed his reverie by handing him half a cocoa pod.

He voiced his thanks, scooped out two seeds, and put them in his mouth. Once he'd sucked off their soft coating, he spat the seeds out. The sweet white flesh was delicious. David walked across to Pip, squatted down, and handed her the rest of the pod.

She began to feed the children with it.

"Pip, I've been thinking. The people in the boat know we're in the village here. It's a very small community, and I don't want to bring them any trouble. I think we should get back to Val and Sebastian on *Whisperer* and plan our next move."

Pip nodded. "But how do we get there. They'll see us if we go by canoe."

"We go tonight. In an hour."

She glanced outside. "But it'll be pitch black. How will we know where we're going?"

"I've taken a bearing with the compass app on my phone. In an hour's time, it will nearly be low tide and there won't be a current to sweep us off course."

"We still won't be able to see *Whisperer*."

"When we're getting near, I'll ring Val and ask him to shine a light to guide us in."

She nodded then reached for his arm. "Dad, there are things I'm not being told. What went on today?"

He lowered his head. "I really don't know, darling. All I know is that these people have rallied around to protect us." He conjured a smile. "I think this is one of those occasions when it's wise not to ask questions."

Pip was right. It was pitch black. There was no sign of a moon or a star. She was sitting in the bow of the canoe staring into the inky blackness willing herself to see something that might orientate her as to where they were. But she could see nothing.

David was behind her. He was paddling steadily, occasionally stopping for a rest. She noticed that the time between rests was getting shorter. The bang on the head, and the dramas of the day had taken more out of him than he was admitting. He'd sustained a nasty gash. She'd asked to share the paddling but he'd refused. As there was only one paddle, all she could do was to stare into the darkness and nurse her anxiety.

Time passed as they continued to paddle into the blackness. It was only the bobbing and swishing of the canoe that told her she was experiencing reality.

She was startled into full awareness by David. He paused from paddling and whispered, "Did you hear that?"

Her heart started to race. Pip listened. She could hear nothing. "No."

She glanced back at her father. He was only just visible from the light of the mobile phone showing their compass course. The light was reassuring.

She turned back to the darkness in front of her.

Then she heard it. *What was that?* There was a clunk of something solid dropping onto the bottom of a boat.

Her blood froze.

The sound was immediately followed by an outboard being gunned into life.

No, no no! This couldn't be happening.

The sound appeared to be fairly close by.

Pip instinctively ducked down low and held her breath.

But it was to no avail.

A boat came howling toward them.

Seconds later, it had bumped into them, none too gently.

The next instant, she was blinded by torchlight.

The engine cut to a burble, and a voice called out. "Got you, ya bastards. Don't move, or I'll blow your heads off."

Pip put a hand up to shield herself from the light. She squinted through her fingers, trying to see who was speaking.

All she could see through the glare was the sheen of light on the barrel of a pistol.

The light played briefly between Pip and David, before settling on Pip.

"Get into the boat, bitch," the voice snarled.

David called out. "Don't move, Pip."

"Get into the boat, or I'll put a bullet into your father. Now!" he shouted.

Pip didn't pause to think. She scrambled across the slippery sides of the inflatable. A hand reached out, grabbed her by the hair and hauled her onto the floor of the boat.

Pip yelped in pain.

David called out in alarm. "Don't hurt her. Take me instead."

The voice laughed. "Oh no. We need you to take a message to McKenzie. We'll be in touch."

"No!" yelled David, throwing himself forward, trying to reach them.

The outboard gunned into life, backing the rigid inflatable away.

The voice called across to David. "If you go to the police, your daughter will be killed—probably after we've had a good deal of fun with her. That's a promise."

"Don't you dare…" but David's voice was lost in the revving of the outboard as the boat reared up and began to skim across the water.

The torch switched off, leaving only darkness.

Pip had never experienced pure terror before. She was catatonic with shock and with fears too terrible to imagine.

The man pressed against her. She could smell him. A moment later, a hand came round and began to grope her.

"What a nice little bitch you are." The man snorted a laugh. "You and I are going to have a lot of fun."

She screamed, and was rewarded by a backhanded slap across her face.

The hand reached for her again.

"If you want to stay alive, you need to please me, girl." The man laughed. "I like to be pleased."

Pip could feel his fingers bumping up against The Fire Stone hanging around her neck.

The man's fingers closed around it and gave it a yank trying to break it free. However, Sebastian had put a good chain on it. Her head jerked forward, and she felt the metal cut into her skin.

"Stop!" she screamed. Pip reached back and pulled the pendant over her head and thrust it at the man.

He took it. An instant later, torchlight shone on the pendant resting in his lap.

The Fire Stone leaped into life. Writhing flames of red swam among a sea of turquoise and gold.

"Well, well, well; this must be worth a pretty sum," he said, turning it over in his hand. "See, you're already being quite generous."

Pip noticed that the man was careful to shield it from the person driving the boat.

Her mind whirled.

Before she consciously thought she had a plan, she found herself saying. "That opal is worth at least two-hundred thousand dollars."

The man whistled.

She continued. "If you lay another hand on me, I'll tell your friends that you have the stone, and then you will have to share its value, or even lose it altogether. So what's it going to be: messing with me, or losing two-hundred thousand dollars?"

"Don't threaten me, bitch."

"I didn't threaten you. I just made a promise."

The boat continued to skim across the blackness.

Chapter 32

"You did what!" Val said, glaring at him.

Sebastian looked at his father with a hint of defiance. "I had a look at the motor launch." He pointed to his computer. "Do you want to see the pictures?"

"How did you do it?"

"With the drone."

"Ah," said Val, sounding only slightly mollified. "Did anyone on the boat see it?"

"Don't think so. I flew it just above the water between the boat and the tree line: It would have been difficult to see."

"What about when it got to the boat?"

"I flew above the main deck for just a few seconds to take pictures and then I was gone."

Sebastian was sitting at the chart table in front of his computer. Val stepped behind him and looked over his shoulder.

Sebastian scrolled through the pictures.

The photos showed a black-hulled motor launch—about twenty meters long. She had once been an elegant vessel but was now showing signs of age. Sebastian stopped at a picture that showed the boat's stern. The boat's name was painted on it: *Galactic*. The charter company's name was written below, as was the boat's home base—Port Vila.

Val grunted. "She looks quite quick: probably cruises at eighteen or twenty knots." He returned to the main table in the cabin and continued to clean the rifle that was set up on top of it. The thing sat on its bipod with its innards resting in a neat row on a rag beside it.

There was only one reason Sebastian could think why Val would be cleaning it so soon after he'd last done it. It had been used.

Sebastian remembered how Val had turned up in the dugout late that afternoon. He'd placed his rucksack on the deck, climbed aboard stiffly and gone down below without a word. Whatever Val had done, it was evident that he'd significantly overtaxed the muscles that were trying to heal.

He'd not got much more out of Val since then—mostly because Val had fallen asleep. When the man had woken, he'd set about cleaning the gun.

It was only after the evening meal that Sebastian confessed to having had a look at the motor launch with the drone. He'd found it impossible to do nothing. When they'd learned from David's phone call that a motor launch had arrived, washing *Whisperer's* decks of accumulated salt seemed an inadequate response.

He was deeply troubled at the possibility that the Saracens had found them. They had sailed so far and been through so much in order to find safety—all now, apparently, to no avail.

Sebastian turned to his father. "Are you sure Pip and David will be safe in the village?"

"David thinks so. We didn't talk much. He was trying to save the battery on his phone."

"But the Saracens…it is the Saracens, isn't it."

"Yes."

"The Saracens know we're here?"

"Oh yes." Val paused. "They know."

Sebastian gained no comfort from the tone of Val's voice. He leaned back in the chair. "What will we do? We're caught. They may not be able to reach *Whisperer* easily, but equally, we can't get through the coral bommies and escape—except during the daytime. They'll see us and easily overpower us. Sebastian closed his eyes in anguish and groaned. "We're caught like a fly in a bottle."

Val looked at him dispassionately. "Not a fly; a wasp."

Sebastian frowned.

Val didn't elaborate.

Sebastian put his head in his hands. "Whatever happens, it has to end here, doesn't it?"

"Yes."

"However that plays out, we've got to ensure that Pip and David remain safe."

"Yes."

They were silent for a while.

Outside, Sebastian could hear the evening winds from the hills begin to sigh through the rigging. *Whisperer* tugged on the anchor warps testing their strength. They'd been streamed fore and aft to hold her in place.

Val broke the silence. "Did you and your drone see anyone on board?"

"In real time, yes. But I didn't manage to take a photograph."

"What did you see?"

"A dark-skinned man, probably a Nivan, on the aft deck; and two pale faces visible behind the glass in the main cabin."

Val nodded.

The silence again hung heavily between them.

Sebastian felt the bile in his gut churn. "What are you going to do?"

"I'm going to bed. You have first watch. Wake me if you hear anything suspicious—and I mean anything. Don't use any lights, and sit in the cockpit. Wake me at midnight."

Sebastian wanted to yell.

Val crawled stiffly into his bunk in the main cabin. The gun, now reassembled, sat on the table within his reach.

Sebastian did not wake Val at midnight. His father was obviously in need of rest, so he stood watch until 4 am. In truth, Sebastian needed that time to deal with his own thoughts.

When he finally did get to sleep, it was only for a few minutes, or so it seemed.

Val was now shaking him by the shoulder.

He opened his eyes. It was still dark. Adrenaline rushed through his veins. "What's the matter?"

"I've had a call from David. He's back at Seule's house."

"What?" Sebastian levered himself up onto an elbow. "I thought he and Pip were staying in the village."

"They decided to paddle back to Lamap last night. The trouble is, the Saracens caught them and have taken Pip."

"What!"

"Yeah. They've threatened to kill her if we go to the police—and we have to expect that they'll use her to get to me."

Sebastian tried to comprehend what he was hearing. It was impossible—a nightmare. He flopped back down and passed a hand over his face. "We've got to get her back."

"Yes. But I'm afraid David's taken the initiative. He rang Pip's phone and has organized to meet with the Saracens. He's hoping to persuade them to swap Pip for him." He shook his head. "If I know David, he won't care much what happens to him, as long as Pip is safe."

Sebastian's head was spinning. "When did he ring you?"

"Just now. He wants us to know, so we're in the picture."

"But it's crazy. The Saracens won't..." he trailed off.

Val nodded. "I know. He says that the Saracens have agreed to meet with him. That probably means they've decided to take him captive as well to boost their chances of forcing me to give myself up."

Sebastian groaned.

But even as he did, an idea pushed its way through the confusion. He grabbed Val's arm. "What if we ring the Saracens and say that I will take the place of Pip. I'm your son, so I'm closer to you. They might agree to that."

Val said nothing.

The storm clouds of emotion that had been building up in Sebastian began to break. He choked back a sob. "Val, I've only just discovered Pip…and I love her. I can't just…" He tried again. "I can't just do nothing." He felt himself wanting to rant and rave. Just one thing stopped him—the sight of tears in his father eyes.

Seconds ticked by.

Val cleared his throat. "They won't part with Pip. You know that."

"Then what does David think he's going to achieve?"

"He's a desperate man. He's prepared to do anything."

"What, exactly, has he agreed to?"

"He's organized to meet with them on the wharf at Port Sandwich at sunrise." Val pushed himself away from the table. "So I've got to get there. But I'm not happy leaving you on your own. You're unarmed and fairly conspicuous here. I want to ferry you ashore so you can lose yourself in the village."

Sebastian remembered how stiff Val was just eight hours earlier and realized that the man would have to push himself to the very edge of endurance to paddle to Port Sandwich in time to meet David.

Sebastian pulled himself out of his swag. "No, I'll take you. Otherwise you won't be in any sort of shape to deal with things when you get there."

Val shook his head. "I don't think that's a good idea."

"Why?"

"I'll be taking the Barrett."

"The rifle?"

Val nodded. "It could get…bloody."

Sebastian pulled on his shorts. "If they have taken Pip, I want it to get bloody."

"You…" Val paused. "You don't know what you're saying."

"Probably not. But I'm still paddling you there." He glanced at his watch. It was 5:30am. "Dawn is in half an hour. We need to go right now."

———

David had arrived at the wharf early. Dawn was still a while off and the village was not yet awake. It was frustrating. He couldn't even work out his impatience by walking up and down the wharf. Many planks were rotten and some were missing, making walking on them a treacherous exercise.

David chewed at his lips, willing the ghostly predawn to grow into sunrise. The waiting was tortuous.

He reflected for the umpteenth time on the decision he'd made. Was there anything else he could have done?

David could think of nothing. He was glad he'd rung Val to put him in the picture. He was glad too that Val wouldn't have time to interfere with the plan he'd put in motion.

Finally, the morning sun began to spill over the horizon to the east, lending a pink cheerfulness to the morning that quite belied the drama that he knew must soon play out.

Almost on queue, the rigid inflatable he'd seen briefly during the night came sweeping up the harbor. It throttled back and edged toward the wharf. David could see that a different white man was sitting in it. He wore a black tee-shirt and a denim waistcoat adorned with patches. The man looked nonchalant, almost indolent, showing a complete lack of concern.

The Nivan at the control consul brought the boat alongside the wharf with a gentle bump.

The white man leaned over and grabbed the rungs of the steel ladder that led to the top of the wharf. David noticed that one of his fingers was missing.

"Get in," the white man ordered.

David stayed where he was. "Mr. Vossik, we thought we'd see you before long."

David had thought nothing of the sort, but he hoped his comment would unsettle him.

"Get in," Vossik ordered again.

"No, I don't think so. You were meant to bring my daughter here."

Vossik reached behind him and produced a pistol from his waistband. He aimed it at David.

A momentary sense of déjà-vous flitted through his consciousness. It was soon replaced by a sense of the ridiculous. David laughed and pointed to the pistol. "You don't think I'm worried by that do you, not while you have my daughter held captive?"

There was silence.

Vossik put the gun back in his waistband, reached for the ladder and climbed up onto the wharf. Without any further ado, he grabbed David by the scruff of the shirt and propelled him to the ladder.

David, disorientated by the sheer physicality of the man, climbed down into the boat. He'd lost the initiative and had no idea what would happen next.

Vossik was climbing in after him...when he suddenly twitched.

An instant later, David heard the 'crack' of a gun.

He knew that sound. Without thinking David threw his arms around Vossik and hung onto his back like a limpet.

"What the..." Vossik tried to elbow him away.

"Stay still, you fool, I'm saving your life. Don't move. Let me cover you."

"What?"

"Let me shield you. Stay still. There's a gun."

Something in the urgency of David's voice caused Vossik to stop moving. David yelled at the driver. "Go, go."

The water boiled under the boat as it backed away from the wharf.

As the boat turned and sped back out into the bay, David moved around Vossik keeping himself between Vossik and the patch of mangroves half a mile away where he suspected Val was hidden. How on earth had the man got himself into position to shoot at Vossik? David realized that he'd seriously underestimated Val's capabilities.

The thought of another death had caused him to act instinctively to preserve Vossik's life. He hoped he wouldn't live to regret it.

Vossik remained on his feet, supporting himself by hanging onto the windshield of the boat's central consol. David clung onto him.

By the time they had reached the diving platform at the back of the motor launch, blood was flowing freely from Vossik's arm and dripping onto the bottom of the boat.

David turned Vossik round to examine the wound.

Vossik pushed him away.

David snapped at him. "I'm a doctor. Let me look at it."

Vossik stayed still.

The wound was bloody but superficial. The bullet had plowed its way across the surface of his upper bicep.

"Do you have a first aid kit on board?" he asked.

"I expect so."

"Then let's get you on board and fix you up."

Twenty minutes later, David closed the lid of the first aid box. Vossik's wound had been dressed, and the man was sitting on one of the cockpit's bench seats. He'd said very little as his wound was being dressed.

David slid the first aid box away. "I'd like to see my daughter now," he said.

Vossik shook his head. "That's not going to happen. Not until we get McKenzie."

A wave of despair washed over him. David had hoped that he'd earned enough merit to be allowed to see his daughter.

For a while, no one said anything.

"You've complicated things, Albright."

"How so?"

"We have a code: If you save the life of a Saracen, we are forever in your debt." He snorted a laugh. "It means that you come under our protection."

David said nothing.

Vossik rubbed his chin. "But we have an outstanding matter."

David suspected that he knew what he was about to say.

"McKenzie."

He was right.

Vossik nodded. "I'll allow nothing to get in the way of us nailing the bastard."

The motor launch rocked gently at its mooring.

David knew that they had come to a critical moment. "So how will this play out? Will it be the life of my daughter for your life?"

Vossik shook his head. "While we have your daughter, we reserve the right to do whatever we like with her, whenever we like. But you get returned to shore unharmed." He stood up and spoke to the man cleaning the bottom of the inflatable.

David began to protest.

Vossik held up a warning finger.

David fell silent.

"If we get McKenzie, no harm will come to you or your daughter ever again." He lifted a hand and inspected the missing finger. "But that all depends on you delivering McKenzie to us within the next twenty-four hours."

Chapter 33

"You missed."

"Hmm."

"I can't believe it!"

Val could hear the anguish in Sebastian's soul. This was the third time he'd given vent to his frustration, and Val could understand it. In truth, he felt frustrated himself. With so much at stake, he'd missed his target. Val was in no doubt about the terrible consequences of his failure.

Sebastian made the canoe fast to a cleat on *Whisperer's* stern and climbed up onto her deck.

Val handed him up the Barrett and followed after him. As he stepped down into the cockpit, he glanced up at his son.

Sebastian was pressing the palms of his hands on his forehead whilst he rocked backward and forward. "Why?" he wailed.

Val swallowed. "I told you. You'd be put off too if you had a hornet visiting your right ear."

Sebastian groaned.

Val's own soul writhed in a torment of guilt. The guilt was in no way assuaged by the knowledge that he'd again told a lie. He screwed his eyes shut and lowered his head trying to come to terms with what had happened.

There'd been no hornet. The shot was an easy one—the first shot at least. David's bizarre behavior in clinging onto Vossik's back ensured he couldn't fire again. He'd watched everything through the telescopic sight and not tried to fire again. And he knew why.

The reason had surprised him. He'd not factored it in because it hadn't occurred to him that he might need to. Val glanced again at his son. The hands he'd pressed against his forehead were now bunched into fists.

Val looked away. The real reason he'd missed was simple. It was the realization that his son would be watching him kill a man—and that was not a memory a son would ever forget. The shock of it had been enough for Val to pull to the right—to wound rather than kill.

Val's mind had been working furiously during the canoe trip back to *Whisperer* trying to come up with another plan—one that did not involve Sebastian witnessing a killing. And a plan, of sorts, was already coming to mind, but it would put Sebastian in danger. He was loath to consider it. It was only the depth of his son's despair that prompted him to pursue the idea. The boy needed hope, and he needed it soon.

He cleared his throat. "Are you up to paddling me the three kilometers to the Saracen's motor launch, and then back again?"

Sebastian's head jerked up. The look in his eyes was disturbing. Flashing amid a look of incredulity, was the fire of hope.

Val swallowed. He was far from sure that his plan deserved it, but he pressed on.

"Can you?" he repeated.

"Of course."

"It could be dangerous."

Sebastian waved his hand dismissively.

The boy had courage. Val looked away to stop the emotion he felt from being seen. When he'd got himself back under control, he turned back. "I need to turn you into a fisherman."

Sebastian's eyes widened. "A fisherman?"

The black face was startling. It stared back at him from the mirror in *Whisperer's* bathroom. Sebastian didn't recognize it as his own, so he doubted anyone else would. He'd spent the last fifteen minutes using Val's camouflage cream to blacken his face, arms, and legs. By the time he'd put on Val's baggy shorts, tee-shirt, and a battered straw hat, the transformation was complete.

He made his way through the cabin, up the companionway, and stepped into the cockpit.

Val was over the side in the canoe arranging a piece of netting over two hessian sacks. A plastic bucket and a hand fishing line had also been put into the dugout. His father glanced up. "You ready?"

Sebastian had no idea what constituted 'being ready,' but nodded anyway.

Val stripped off his tee-shirt and reached for the diving mask and fins on *Whisperer's* deck. He'd already strapped a diving knife to his ankle.

Once Val had the fins on, he lay down at the bottom of the canoe. He was bulky, and it was a tight fit. When Val was settled, he said, "Cover me up."

Sebastian laid the two hessian sacks over the top of him. The sacks still had the rancid smell of copra. They had come aboard with David when he'd used them to carry supplies of sweet potato, taro, and yam. As a flourish, Sebastian arranged the piece of netting over the top. The net had actually come from a string hammock and had nothing to do with fishing, but he hoped it would give the illusion.

Not daring to think about what they were attempting to do, Sebastian took his place in the stern of the dugout and began to paddle.

He had to be a Nivan fisherman. One or two of them were always to be seen on the harbor. Given the abundance of fish on the reef, Sebastian was surprised he didn't see more. He had also been surprised at how primitive their fishing techniques were. The local women would wade out onto the coral reefs, unwind a hand-line from their waist and begin to fish. They'd stand there for hours. Men in the canoes fished in deeper waters, but their techniques seemed no more sophisticated. Perhaps there were so many fish around that they didn't need to be efficient.

He glanced down at the plastic bucket. Val had put a lump of tinned ham at the bottom. Bait, presumably.

Sebastian was grateful he was paddling. He needed to do something physical to keep the waves of anguish at bay.

He heard Val's muffled voice. "How are you going?"

"I'm passing the point at Port Sandwich, and I can see the motor launch."

"This is where you start acting. Take your time. Stop now and then to fish for a few minutes. Don't paddle at all when you get two-hundred yards from them. Just fish with your back toward them and allow the ebb tide to carry you past."

Sebastian grunted.

It came as shock when Sebastian actually hooked a fish. He brought the silvery flipping thing aboard and dropped it in the bucket. Sebastian thought it was probably a mullet.

The motor launch came closer and closer.

He'd caught three fish by the time they were two-hundred yards away.

"We're there," he murmured.

Sebastian stood up and lifted a hessian sack holding it up like a curtain.

Val sipped over the side of the canoe into the water whilst being shielded by the hessian sack. The man was now hanging onto the outrigger strut, protected from view by the hull of canoe.

Sebastian finished the theater by pulling the hessian sack over the bucket of fish. Then he baited his hook and continued fishing.

The ebb tide carried them nearer and nearer to the boat.

Sebastian counted down the distance. "One hundred and fifty; eighty; forty; dead abeam," he murmured. "One Nivan—at the barbecue on the back deck. No one else seen."

Sebastian realized that the Nivan was probably cooking breakfast. The day was still young.

He glanced over the side.

Val was gone.

Val came up to the surface underneath the dive platform at the back of the motor launch. He glanced up through the grating and could see no movement.

Taking hold of the edge of the platform, he gradually let it take his weight. The last thing he wanted was his presence to cause any sudden changes in the rocking movement of the boat. He then slithered onto the platform. After removing his mask and fins he risked a quick look over the cockpit coaming.

A Nivan was turning sausages at a barbecue located against the cabin wall.

Four seconds later, the same Nivan was frozen with fear as Val held a knife across his throat. In six seconds, the man was unconscious and on the floor.

Val put the sauce bottle he'd used to club the man back on the table, and turned off the gas. He didn't want the smell of burning sausages to alarm anyone.

The rigid inflatable was gone. At least that would mean that there were fewer people to deal with. The downside was that he had no idea when it would return. He needed to act quickly.

Val pressed himself beside the open door into the main cabin and listened. The only noise was a faint clinking sound coming from underneath him. Someone was in the engine compartment under the aft deck—one of the permanent crew, no doubt.

With knife in hand, he stepped into the main cabin.

Almost immediately, he saw one of the Saracens. He was a big man whose tee-shirt didn't quite cover the underside of his belly. The man saw Val immediately, dropped the magazine he was reading and reached for a pistol lying on the coffee table. He moved quickly for a big man.

The pain and stiffness in Val's muscles meant he couldn't react with his usual speed. His muscles screamed in protest as he launched himself into the air to deliver a diving dropkick. Val's feet crashed into the man's chest and neck.

The pistol spun to the floor.

It had been way too close.

Neutralize your opponent. Dead is safest.

Val bounced back onto his feet, spun round and lashed out, kicking the man in the neck.

The Saracen fell sideways.

A second later, Val was behind the settee holding the man's head in a chokehold.

The big man grabbed at his arms trying to prize them loose, but when Val applied more pressure, the man held his arms out signaling surrender.

"Where's Pip?" he hissed, giving the man's head a jerk. "Where's the girl?"

The Saracen coughed a laugh. "Not here." He coughed again. "She's out with Carlo. He had a case of cabin fever and had to get out—and play with her."

The man again tried to shake free.

Val tightened the pressure on the man's neck.

The Saracen was tough. In a strangulated voice, he managed to choke out, "If you hurt me, the girl gets hurt. If you kill me; she dies."

Val eased the pressure on the man's neck as despair washed over him.

Pip was not there. It was a cruel twist. Everything seemed fated to go wrong.

The Saracen seemed to sense Val's lack of energy, and managed a hoarse laugh.

"There's nothing you can do, McKenzie." He paused. "It is McKenzie, isn't it?"

Val was keeping an eye on the set of stairs that spiraled down, presumably to the cabins below. The pistol was close to his feet, and he was confident he could take care of any danger that came from that direction.

He glanced around the saloon. The pistol wasn't the only

weapon in it. Two machine pistols sat on the bench beside the boat's control consul.

They'd come ready for war.

The man tried again to shake Val off. "Let go and piss off McKenzie. You can't win. Anything you do to me will get taken out on the girl—and you've already caused me pain."

The Saracen's comment succeeded in snapping Val out of his anguish. He tightened the chokehold. "So you'd hurt Pip would you?"

"Y…y…yes." The man coughed then continued. "I'm looking forward to it."

Val's blood ran cold.

The big man attempted another laugh—and failed to realize the terrible peril he was in.

Val continued. "Well, I can't allow that, matey."

Something of the danger he was in seemed to reach the man, for he fought again to remove Val's arms.

But it was too late. Val twisted sideways, viciously.

The man slumped on the settee, lifeless, his neck broken.

Another face would now haunt him at night.

Val collected the machine pistols and hid them under some cushions. Then he picked up the pistol. It was a Glock, and he was familiar with it.

He checked the magazine was full, cocked it, and flicked off the safety switch. He descended the stairs and began pushing open the doors to the cabins.

All were deserted.

Behind the spiral stairs was a thick, fireproof door that he reasoned must lead to the engine room. Val could hear faint noises coming from behind it. He jammed a chair from a neighboring cabin under the handle and returned to the main saloon.

A search of the dead man's pockets revealed no more weapons, but it did produce something that shocked him: The Fire Stone. He stared at it in bewilderment before putting it into the pocket of his shorts.

Whilst he was delighted at retrieving The Fire Stone, he was sick to his stomach at not finding Pip. He breathed in deeply. What could he do?

He glanced round and saw a pad of paper and a pencil on the coffee table. Val scribbled a note.

He said he would hurt Pip. If you make the same mistake, you'll be next. That's a promise. If she stays well, you live. I'll be in contact.

He placed the note on top of the dead man, collected the two machine pistols, and made his way to the aft deck.

Chapter 34

Pip was seated in front of the inflatable's driving consul. Vossik was at the controls, steering the boat toward the harbor entrance. As they got closer to the open sea, the wavelets increased in size causing the boat to pound. Wind whipped Pip's hair against her neck. In any other circumstance, it would have been exhilarating.

But this was not another circumstance, and Pip's situation was dire.

Vossik had said nothing to her. He'd simply dragged her into the boat and set off.

She didn't know what to expect and was surprised when he said, "What's there to see to the north of the harbor?"

Pip racked her brain. "Er...Banam Bay."

"What's that?"

"It's about ten kilometers away. The track from Lamap to Norsup drives along the top of the beach there. It's pretty."

He nodded and said nothing.

Across the water she could see the smoke of the cooking fires coming from the village of illegal settlers on the northern headland. They'd settled there a few decades ago from Pentecost Island. The locals were upset about it, but there appeared to be no mechanism to deal with the issue.

She decided to try and foster a degree of cordiality.

"What do I call you?"

"Carlo." He smiled. "And I promise; it's a name you won't forget."

She tried to keep things positive. "It's good to be away from… the other man?"

"Mason?"

"Is that his name?"

"Yeah." Vossik laughed. "That's one of the reasons you're with me." Vossik laughed. "He'd planned an interesting day for you."

Pip shuddered.

"So I'm protecting you."

"Why?"

"He's aah…particularly cruel, and I've got an arrangement with your father."

"My father! What's been going on between you and my father?"

"He saved my life this morning. I owe him a favor."

Pip was incredulous. "How did he do that?"

"He protected me from being shot by McKenzie."

"What? When?"

"Before you were up."

Questions tumbled and tangled in her mind, but she kept quiet.

For a while, nothing was said.

It became apparent, however that Vossik wasn't ready to let the issue go. "Why would your father do that?"

"Do what?"

"Save my life?"

"It's a Christian thing."

Vossik snorted. "Well, there won't be anything very Christian going on in this boat today." He looked her up and down.

She felt his eyes undressing her and shivered.

"I'm inclined to beat Mason to you and sample you myself." He smiled. "Lucky for you, I'll be gentler."

Pip put a hand over her mouth and another over her stomach as it started to heave.

No Fire Stone could protect her now.

Frantically, she gripped the rope running around the rubber gunwale and tried to steady herself. She was about to be raped. How agonizing and defiling would that be?

She thought of Sebastian. The thought of not seeing him again…of not owning up to him about her love; of not making love to him. It was all too much.

She turned away to hide her terror.

Eventually, she managed to say, "Is there any way…that this doesn't have to happen?"

"If McKenzie's delivered to us within twenty-four hours, you get to live." He smiled. "But in the mean time, we get to play with you. It's part of the threat I made to your father."

The full horror of her situation was now laid bare. Pip was too stunned to respond, to imagine…to do anything. It was impossible. Everything was too shocking to contemplate. She wanted to rant and cry, to plead and beg.

But she refused give Vossik the satisfaction.

She thought frantically. If she was to change anything, she had to say something.

After a brief pause, she said, "When McKenzie learns what you've done to me, he's going to be an angry man." She conjured a shiver. "You'd better be ready for it."

"I'm terrified," Vossik said dryly.

"He's taken a bit of a shine to me."

"And that's meant to frighten me."

She shrugged. "He sure frightens me."

"Yeah?"

Forgive me, Val. She nodded. "He's a psychopath. You must know that. He has no conscience at all. He enjoys inflicting pain."

Vossik shrugged.

Her words hadn't reached him.

She turned up the heat.

"You're pretty gutsy; I'll say that."

Vossik sneered. "I can deal with McKenzie."

Pip shook her head. "No, I don't think you can. You certainly haven't been able to in the past." She looked away. "You can't control McKenzie. You know that. Once he's angry, hell breaks loose. He's unstoppable."

The boat continued to speed north up the coast.

Pip gave Vossik a moment to reflect on what she'd said, and then added more pressure. "He's got this particular thing about women. He's had it ever since your lot killed his wife." She shook her head. "I can't imagine what he'll do if I'm hurt. There will be a lot of funerals, that's for sure. Your woman will be one of the first." She glanced up at him. "How many of you has he killed so far?"

"Shut up bitch." He paused, then added, "Be grateful I'm keeping you safe—at least for the time being."

Vossik swung the boat around in a wide arc and began heading back toward the harbor.

Pip was sick with relief. She willed her stomach to stop heaving. Her charade had won a reprieve—of sorts.

But it was only for twenty-four hours.

Chapter 35

David put his rucksack and medical box down on the beach and stretched. He'd been given a lift for most of the way but had to walk the last kilometer.

Whisperer was sitting eighty meters off shore. The wind had died away and the sea was dead calm. A tree on the beach had dropped some of its flowers into the water. It made the sea look as if it had been strewn for a wedding. What were the flowers called? David racked his brain. *Narwell* or *norwell*, something like that. But then he remembered that these particular flowers were used at funerals rather than weddings. He hoped it wasn't a sign.

Sebastian was moving around on *Whisperer's* deck.

David put his fingers in his mouth and gave a piercing whistle.

Sebastian looked up, recognized him, and waved. Moments later he was paddling toward him in the dugout.

By the time the two of them had returned to *Whisperer*, Sebastian had brought him up to date regarding their failed attempt to rescue Pip.

David had been trying to manage the nightmare scenarios Pip may be enduring. He groaned inwardly and reproached himself for not also concerning himself with how Val and Sebastian were feeling.

"How are you going with all this?"

Sebastian put the heels of his palms into his eyes. "It's killing me. I'm frustrated, angry, and terrified for Pip."

David nodded, pausing a while before he said, "Thanks for caring."

Sebastian lifted his head. "It's been well beyond caring for some while, David."

"I know."

The canoe had been made fast to *Whisperer's* stern, but neither of them had climbed out.

"And how's Val?"

"Very quiet. Won't talk. Physically, he's on his last legs. I tried to help him to his bunk, but he shrugged me off."

David sighed. "Did you gain anything from visiting the motor launch? Do you think we are we in a better position or worse one as a result?"

"Two machine-guns and a pistol were removed—so they've lost most of their firepower. We chucked the machine-guns in the deep-water channel. Val's kept the pistol."

"What about the chap on board?"

Sebastian shrugged. "Val just said he'd been incapacitated."

David tried not to think what that might mean. "Okay," he said. "Let's talk with Val and see what we can do. What time is it?"

"Just past eleven."

David suspected that it was going to be a long day.

"What on earth?"

Val turned round. He could understand David's question. Val had lifted up the mattresses in the forepeak cabin to gain access to the lockers underneath. The storm trysail and the scuba tank had been pulled out onto the floor. "I'm looking for the epoxy," he said. "Sebastian, do you know where it is?"

"You won't find it there. It's in the locker beside the engine bay."

The three of them made their way to the main cabin. Val and David sat at the bench seats around the table whilst Sebastian boiled the kettle. The boy needed to remove a saucepan of water to do so. Val had put it on earlier to boil some eggs but had never got round to lighting the flame.

Instead, he'd cried.

Now he was manic with desperation and despair. But the weariness in his body was starting to shut him down.

David glanced at him. "Thanks for trying to get Pip back this morning."

Val nodded and didn't trust himself to say anything.

Sebastian put mugs of tea on the table and sat down. He had washed away most of the camouflage paste, but it hadn't all come off.

Nothing was said for quite a while.

Val forced himself to push through his weariness and say something sensible.

"We have three problems to solve. The first: how to get Pip back. The second: how we can sail *Whisperer* past the Saracen's motor launch without causing a firefight. The third: how to prevent all this happening again." He rubbed his eyes. "Any ideas?"

Neither of them said anything.

Sebastian broke the silence. "Our priority has to be getting Pip back."

Val nodded. "I've been giving that some thought, and I think there's only one thing we can do."

Sebastian leaned forward. "What's that?"

"I've got to meet with Vossik and persuade him that it will cost the Saracens too many lives to keep up their vendetta against us." He sighed. "I've got to put the fear of God into him."

David looked at him quizzically.

Val avoided his eyes.

"Will it work?" asked Sebastian.

"I'll call Pip's phone and organize a meeting with Vossik tonight."

"Will that mean we can then simply sail out of here?" asked David.

Val massaged his temple. "I'd be a lot happier if we could slip past them without being noticed. Simply sailing past, as calm as you like, might be too much of a provocation."

"Can we sail past them at night without making a noise?" asked David.

Val shook his head. "We're in a maze of coral, and the prevailing easterly wind would be against us."

David frowned. "Not necessarily. Cool air flows down from Mt. Marmatchi at night into the bay. That causes a westerly wind when the trades aren't too strong." He glanced up. "The trades are hardly blowing at all at the moment. I think we could sail."

Sebastian was fiddling with his mug. "I, er…I think I might be able to get you through the coral at night, if that helps."

Val raised his eyebrows. "How?"

"Let me do a few experiments first. But, for the purposes of this discussion, assume I can."

"There's one other factor you will need to bear in mind if we sail tonight," said Val. "I won't be sailing with you."

Sebastian straightened his back. "Why's that? We can't sail without you."

"Yes you can. If I stay here, it will draw the heat away from you in Australia. The three of you are perfectly capable of sailing *Whisperer* back to Coffs Harbour. And with the prevailing easterlies, you'd be on a broad reach—that's easy sailing."

Sebastian expelled air from his cheeks. "Whoa! Back up the truck."

Val ignored him and plowed straight on. "Be ready to leave the moment Pip arrives. Leave the kedge anchor, and tie Jean's canoe to it. That will allow him to pick it up later. Sail without the navigation lights and don't use the winches. The clinking of the winch pawls carries in the night. And don't bother with the mainsail; just set the jib." Val scratched his beard and tried to remember all the things he needed to say. "You'll probably get becalmed for a while before you pick up the easterly wind, but don't use the engine unless you're at least two miles offshore."

Nobody said anything. *Whisperer* rocked benignly at her mooring.

Val continued. "The water tanks are nearly full and you've got a reasonable supply of stores. You've got sweet potato, taro, and yam—pretty starchy and horrible, but it's good fuel. You've also got pineapple, papaya, and coconut. Eat the fresh food first."

"We've got the stuff from the trading store as well." Sebastian pushed his empty mug away. "But, mate, are you sure about this?"

Val ignored him. He wasn't sure about anything. "Now this is important: you must get rid of any evidence of Vanuatu before you reach Coffs Harbour. That means no fruit, no vegetables, and no hessian sacks smelling of copra. Chuck them overboard." He paused. "And also throw my rifle over the side, but only once you're clear of any danger from the Saracens."

Everyone was silent.

David nodded his head slowly. "And what do we do once we've arrived at Coffs?"

"Put the sail covers on, clean up the boat, and lock the keys in the cabin. Then drive away as soon as decently possible. If anyone asks where I am, say you dropped me off up the coast at Evans Head." He looked around. "Are we clear?"

David and Sebastian nodded.

Val turned to David. "David, can you get the boat prepared so it's ready to leave?"

"Yes."

"Sebastian; you'd better go and do what you need to do to get us through the coral."

"Okay. And what will you do?"

"I need to fiddle about for a bit then paddle to the wharf."

"But you can't. You're exhausted. Let me take you."

Val held up a hand. "No, Sebastian. I need to do this alone."

David glanced at him, and for a moment held his eyes.

Val looked away.

David returned his attention to his mug of tea. "So, you'll ring Vossik?"

"Yes. I want to arrange to meet with him at 6pm at the wharf when it's starting to get dark."

Please, please: no more questions.

Val was relieved when David and Sebastian got up and left for their various tasks. He was uncomfortably aware that only part of what he'd told them was true.

Chapter 36

V al dawdled among the mangroves until he saw the rigid inflatable speed away. He looked through the foliage at the two figures standing on the wharf. The smaller one was being held against the larger.

He sighed. *This was it.* Haunted by demons of fear and hope, he began to paddle.

Slow; slow. And make sure your hands are always visible.

He stopped paddling ten meters from the wharf, laid the paddle down, and stood up. It was not an easy thing to do in a narrow canoe—even with an outrigger. Val lifted his shirt to his midriff and twisted left and right. He was only wearing a shirt and shorts.

"Get up here," ordered Vossik. "If you try anything stupid, I'll kill the bitch."

"Take it easy. Take it easy."

Val made the canoe fast and climbed the ladder.

He was almost at the top when he reached underneath the planking to a crossbeam. His hand closed around the butt of the Glock. An instant later the pistol was aimed at Vossik's head.

Pip squealed in terror.

Val forced his voice to be as normal as possible. "No one has to die if you do exactly what I say."

Vossik was frozen into immobility—his gun pointed at Pip's head.

Val continued to speak. "You will die, I promise, unless you lay the gun down using your thumb and forefinger."

No one moved.

An eternity passed.

Vossik sniffed, bent down, and laid his pistol on the planking.

"Now take three steps back."

The Saracen backed away.

Val stepped onto the wharf and over to the gun. He unclipped the magazine and ejected the chambered round. With a backhand flick, he threw the gun parts into the sea.

Without taking his eyes off Vossik, he spoke to Pip. "Have you been hurt or molested in any way?"

Pip's eyes were wide in disbelief.

She opened her mouth but no sound came.

"Pip?"

"No."

Vossik exhaled a breath.

Val continued to speak. "Are you able to take the canoe and paddle back to boat?"

"Y, yes. But what about you?"

"I'll be all right. Please go. Now."

Pip gave him a searching look.

Val avoided her eyes and kept his pistol trained on Vossik.

She sniffed. "I…I don't know what's happening here, but I don't like it. I don't want anyone to get hurt."

Vossik put a hand on his heart in a mocking gesture. "Even me?"

Pip turned and faced him. "Everyone is sacred—whether they know it or not." She began to step away but then turned back. "Before I go, Mr. Carlo, I need to tell you that I seriously maligned Mr. McKenzie earlier today."

Vossik raised an eyebrow.

"He's not cruel. He's a good man who has a hatred of evil." She faced Val. "I'd be proud to have him as a father."

Val felt the warmth of her words wash over him. "It's time to go, Pip," he said with more gruffness than he intended. "Take the canoe along the shoreline until you find the boat. Don't turn back."

She walked over to him, stood on the tip of her toes, kissed him, and laid a hand on his cheek. "Please stay safe." Then she climbed down the ladder.

Val listened to her paddle away into the darkening night.

When he looked up, Vossik had an ironic smile. "Well, well, well; I think I got played this morning."

"What do you mean?"

"Tell me, McKenzie, would you ever put a bullet into the head of my woman?"

Val shook his head. "No. She has nothing to fear from me. But you do."

"I thought so."

The minutes passed in silence.

It was now dark. The only light came from a solar powered globe on a post by the ladder.

Vossik passed his hands through his hair. "So, how's this going to end? You can kill me McKenzie, but others will come after you. You know it. There will be no peace for you and yours until you're dead."

Val gestured with the pistol. "Sit down against that bollard, Vossik. We've got a long wait—and things to discuss."

Vossik shrugged and settled himself against a bollard.

Val did the same five meters away.

"How did you find us?" he asked.

"It was easy."

"How?"

"We went through Albright's rubbish bin and found a list that suggested he was going abroad to a place he was familiar with. Then we rang the church and discovered he'd lived here for ten years. He shrugged. "We asked people to make some phone calls and found you." Vossik paused. "I warned you we would."

"But was it worth it? Two of your people have died."

"What happened to Abe?"

"The first guy?"

Vossik nodded.

"He'll be buried at sea—might already be."

"Hmm, and so will Mason. He'll have company."

Silence hung between them again.

Pip should be on board *Whisperer* by now. There was at least another hour to wait.

Val broke the silence. "You didn't bring your brother."

"No."

"Wise."

"How did you find me in Queensland?"

"We had a tip off."

"And Albright?"

"We learned he was in on the game, too."

Val shook his head. "I think we've got some more talking to do."

Sebastian turned the wick of the riding light down to the faintest flicker and hung it from *Whisperer's* bow.

It cast a glow across the water. The high level haze that had obscured the sky for much of the day continued to hide the stars.

Lighting the lamp had destroyed Sebastian's night vision. He took his place beside David on the doghouse roof and stared into the darkness waiting for it to return.

The two of them were silent for some time.

Sebastian cleared his throat. "I love your daughter."

David nodded slowly and said: "I wouldn't mind."

"You wouldn't mind—what?"

"I wouldn't mind if you asked her to marry you."

Sebastian couldn't believe what he heard. Nor could he prevent a grin from breaking out.

David continued. "You've proved your worth, and I don't believe you will treat either Pip's or your own life carelessly."

Sebastian could think of nothing to say. He simply offered his hand.

David shook it. It was an oddly formal ritual that Sebastian knew he would always remember.

But first he needed Pip's safe return.

He fought to keep his anguish in check as he waited.

David interrupted his brooding. "Did you say anything to your father before he left?"

Sebastian remembered all too well what he'd said. He'd taken Val by the arm and said, "Thanks for getting Pip, Dad."

Val had looked up at him. "Dad?"

He'd nodded.

Val had smiled, and paddled away.

Sebastian sniffed. "I think we said enough."

Whisperer was ready to sail. The anchor had been hauled short, the sail covers removed, and the halliards were attached. All they had to do was drop the stern kedge and haul in the main anchor—if Pip turned up.

They stared into the darkness.

Then they heard it—the dip and splosh of a canoe being paddled.

Both of them stood up.

Who was it? Would it be Pip or Val, or both?

Pip came into the loom of the riding light.

Sebastian couldn't restrain himself. He yelled out, "Pip!" and reached for her frantically. The grief and anguish he'd been holding in for so long tumbled out of him.

She was crying.

David, rather more helpfully, took the painter, led the canoe to *Whisperer's* stern, and made it fast.

Sebastian enfolded Pip in his arms even before she was fully aboard. He dragged her to himself, his arms hugging, patting, and touching, making sure she was real.

Pip laughed and cried.

He felt a primal hunger rise up within him. His lips found hers and they kissed wildly and extravagantly, satiating the yearning he'd nursed for so long.

David finally interrupted.

"I hate to break this up, but it's time we made a move. Pip, could you untie the kedge warp and make it fast to the canoe? I'll unfurl the jib."

Pip protested. "But we can't sail. Not yet. What about Val?"

David paused, then replied. "Val can't join us at the moment. He's told us to set sail. I'll explain later. But right now, we need to get going." He turned round. "Are you ready Sebastian? Have you got the wheel?"

"Yep."

Sebastian could hear the jib flapping lazily in the breeze.

He heard Pip exclaim. "Sebastian: what are you doing? You can't see a thing!"

Sebastian had pulled the display unit for the drone over his eyes.

"I can't see you, but I can see the coral bommies clear enough. I took a film of them when I flew the drone up the harbor this afternoon. The drone's current position is marked on the picture I created. All I need to do is stop the cursor from bumping into the bommies."

"Are you seriously going to steer us through the coral wearing that?"

"Yes."

Sebastian readjusted his headset and called out. "Right David, I'm ready. You can haul in the anchor. He smiled. "Gee, it's good to have you back."

Somewhere out in the darkness, *Whisperer* would be ghosting past with only her jib set—silent and with no lights. Val listened intently for any sound that might betray her presence, but could hear none.

After another twenty minutes, he got to his feet.

"So, there'll be no peace until I'm killed?"

Vossik nodded.

"And if that happens?"

"Then it's over."

"The Albrights? My son?"

"There'd be no issues. Not any more."

Val nodded.

Vossik clambered to his feet. "Are you through playing with me, McKenzie? Because if you're going to kill me, just get on with it."

There was only a slight waver in his voice.

Val lifted his head up to the night sky, seeing none of it.

Greater love has no one...

He cleared his throat. "This is how it's going to end, Vossik. I'm going to place this gun half way between us and walk back here. Then I'll see if you really are a good shot."

Vossik furrowed his brow. "What?"

"You heard. Just take it easy and do what you have to do."

Val walked three paces forward, laid the Glock on the planking and backed away so that he was standing on the end of the wharf. Then he felt in his pocket and took out the white handkerchief.

Peace. Peace at last. Please let it come.

Vossik walked forward, picked up the pistol, and aimed it at Val. "You're a gutsy bastard, McKenzie. I'll say that for you."

"Tell me Vossik, would you do it for your family?"

Vossik fired.

There was a stab of pain, a sensation of falling, and then blackness.

Chapter 37

Pip was alone on a black, heaving sea. High clouds were shrouding the stars and visibility was minimal.

Amédée lighthouse, situated twenty-one nautical miles off the coast of Noumea, was now well behind her. According to the marine notes she'd consulted, it was a marvel of French nineteenth century engineering. The loom of its light, flashing twice every fifteen seconds, had kept her company for nearly an hour, but it had been a while since she'd been able to see it.

Whisperer was pushing her way into the loneliness of the South Pacific Ocean, as if eager to escape the recent traumas. All her sails were set, and she was bowling along in a following wind at six knots.

Pip shivered. The velvet darkness closed around her, and she felt very alone—accompanied only by her grief.

The dreadful certainty of Val's death hung over her, suffocating her joy. Val, the one who had once so shocked and disturbed her; the one on whom she had come to rely, was dead. David had explained the certainty of it to both her and Sebastian.

She was alone on watch because David had ducked down into the cabin to heat up two mugs of water laced with the juice of a pomelo. Their supply of tea and coffee had long since run out.

The watch-keeping regime was a poignant reminder of Val's loss. They continued the pattern adopted on the last few days of their voyage across. Just one person was on watch during the day, allowing the other two to prepare meals and sleep. At night, two people stood watch, and one slept. It was a demanding and fatiguing regime; one made worse by the memories of all that had happened—and what might have happened.

She had come very close to being raped. Pip shivered. She was under no illusions. The dreadful act would have been motivated by a savage need for dominance, every bit as much as lust—and it would have been brutal. But Val's protective shadow had fallen across her even at that point. It was only the fear of his retribution that had stopped Vossick.

The corybantic fires of terror that had plagued her for the last three days attacked her with fresh vigor.

"I've put some sugar with it," said David as he held a mug out to her through the hatchway. His comment succeeded in putting a temporary halt to her nightmarish reflections. The red night-light in the cabin snapped off and David clambered up the companionway to join her in the cockpit—his face now only barely discernible.

Whisperer dipped and rolled through the waves.

Pip watched David blow across the surface of his drink to cool it. She was grateful for his presence. The demons of anguish always lost something of their stridency when he was with her.

They sat in silence for a long while.

Eventually, David said, "How are you going?"

She knew the question would come, but was still not sure how she would answer it.

Pip rubbed her temples, willing herself to make sense of her stormy emotions.

She began hesitantly. "It's as if I've both been given life…and robbed of life."

"Hmm."

Silence again descended between them.

"Given life?" prompted David.

"Sebastian."

David nodded. "And how do you think he's going with it all?"

"He's conflicted—like me."

David pressed her further. "And robbed of life?"

She swallowed. "It's not easy to live with the knowledge that someone chose to die so that I could live free of fear."

Her father raised an eyebrow.

She lifted her hands in acquiescence. "I know. I know. I should be used to the concept—particularly given your calling, but nonetheless…" she trailed off.

Whisperer shuddered as she shouldered through a big wave. Pip could hear the hiss of spray in the darkness.

Minutes passed, but she knew that silence meant nothing to David. He had the patience of Job. Her conversation with him was still very much alive. He could be irritating.

"Was it worth it?" She slapped her leg, angrily. "Was '*I*' worth it?"

David reached out an arm and drew her close. "He certainly thought so."

The false dawn was quickly giving way to the real thing. Pip was on watch again after having only two hours sleep. However, her weariness was tempered by the optimism of the dawn, and her anticipation of Sebastian joining her in the cockpit. She had resolved to sit with him for half an hour as she ate breakfast. Pip could hear him moving about below getting it ready—fried sweet potato and pineapple by the smell of it.

When Sebastian came up the companionway, she recoiled in shock. He was not carrying her breakfast but holding Val's rifle, the Barrett, as she'd heard it called. The cold blue light of the early morning accentuated its chilling brutality.

She said nothing as Sebastian laid it down on the leeward bench of the cockpit.

He bent over, gave her a kiss—brief but delicious—and sat beside her.

For a long while, the only sound was the swish of water as *Whisperer* continued to surge toward the west.

Eventually, Pip could bear it no more. "What's on your mind, darling?"

Sebastian passed a hand over his face.

She took his arm. "You don't have to tell me if you don't want to."

He attempted a smile. "No, I want to tell you…"

"What?"

He screwed up his nose. "It's hard to express."

"Try."

"Well, in the last few months, I discovered that my father was alive—the man I'd always been ashamed of, and never felt I'd known. Then I met him…and the more I got to know him, the less I hated him." He paused.

Pip waited for more.

Sebastian shook his head. "And then I grew to respect him." He laughed unconvincingly. "I was even jealous of him." He tried to speak again, but couldn't. He cleared his throat. "Then, um, something else began to grow…to warm."

"And?"

"I think it might, er, have been…"

"Love?" she ventured.

Sebastian looked away. This was clearly not the sort of conversation he was used to. "Maybe." He dropped his head in embarrassment, unable to say anything more.

He cut a forlorn figure.

Pip watched him for a while, then leaned forward and put a hand on his knee. "Will you…" she faltered, and tried again. "Will you let my love compete with your grief?"

Sebastian glanced up with a look of incomprehension. He shook his head as if to rid himself of the implications of what she was saying. "Pip," he stammered, "you are the best thing to have ever happened to me. You are…amazing, and I still struggle to believe…" he paused.

"My love?" she prompted.

He nodded.

Pip sat in silence for a while, and then stood up in front of him. Very slowly, she undid the top two buttons of her blouse. Whilst two buttons ensured that her modesty remained intact—it was a close run thing. She was not wearing a bra.

Sebastian's mouth dropped open, and he swallowed.

Then she reached down and took his hands in her own. She caressed them, feeling their strength and calluses.

Sebastian leaned forward on his seat, wrapped his arms around her thighs and pressed himself against her.

Experiencing his love and desire was sheer bliss.

An eternity passed.

Thinking that she'd suffered all the sexual tension she could decently manage, she put her hands on his shoulders and eased herself away.

Sebastian let her go reluctantly. "Wow," he said.

Pip began doing up her buttons. "That, my dear Sebastian, is a down payment—a promise—of what is to come. So please don't lose hope."

Decorum was restored only just in time. David came up the companionway. The cleric glanced at the Barrett on the bench, and then said, "I've had my breakfast. So let me take over for a bit so you can have yours."

Sebastian was seated again but needed to have his arms crossed over on his lap. Nonetheless he managed to say, "You're meant to be in your bunk getting some sleep."

David ignored him and pointed to the Barrett. "What are you planning to do with that?"

"Um, I think I'm finally able to part with it," said Sebastian.

David nodded. "I take it, you've not found that an easy thing to contemplate doing."

"No."

"Do you know why?"

"It's very much…him, brutal though it is." Sebastian dropped his head. "It's sort of…the final goodbye."

David put a hand on his shoulder and kept quiet.

Pip reached across and placed a hand on his knee. She'd wanted to throw the wretched thing overboard for the last three days. It had lain fully assembled on Val's bunk, just as he'd left it—compelling her to re-live the violence it represented each time she saw it. The wretched thing had been impossible to ignore.

But it was not her business. The privilege of dispatching it belonged to Sebastian, and he needed to come to terms with doing so in his own time.

Sebastian turned to her. "Pip, I'm really sorry for all the trauma that Dad and this gun have caused you." He turned to David. "The same goes for you. I'm more sorry than I can say."

David nodded.

Nothing much was said for a while.

Eventually, David said, "I can assure you, Sebastian, Val found peace in his final act of giving."

Sebastian sighed. "Yeah, I reckon he would have." He stood up and reached for the Barrett. After weighing it in both hands for a moment, he turned and dropped it overboard.

Pip moved to his side. "Is it really all over? Have we really…won?"

David answered from behind her. "Three Saracens came to Vanuatu, and only one is leaving. I think that is retribution enough."

Pip turned and snorted. "But I hate the idea of Vossik escaping scot-free. He's a brutal murderer."

"Hmm," said David, noncommittally.

Pip furrowed her brow. "What do you mean, 'Hmm'?"

Her father shrugged. "Er, I think it unlikely that Vossik will leave Vanuatu without mishap."

"Why?"

"Seule confided in me that a couple of the Nivans were planning to unshackle the navigation buoy just offshore from Lamap and move it to a slightly different location." He grinned. "Vossik and his motor launch will be very lucky to get out of the harbor without hitting a coral bommy."

"But he'll still be alive," objected Pip.

David nodded. "Yes, and it is important he remains so. We need him to spread the word that we are under the Saracens' protection."

"But what does that really mean?" she persisted.

David put an arm around her shoulder. "It means that we will never see him again."

Pip reflected sourly on the irony of being under the protection of the Saracens. She shook her head in irritation, and sought to change the subject.

"I can't believe that we'll get away with sailing *Whisperer* straight into Coffs Harbour. Surely someone will ask us where we've been. They've got customs there."

Sebastian arched his back and stretched. "Yeah, but I've been giving that some thought. Let's make landfall to the north, which was the direction we set off on from Coff's—perhaps somewhere near Woolgoolga. Then we can linger around until we find a yacht heading south. There are always yachts sailing up and down the East coast. We can fall into company with one of them, and then break away from it when we get to Coffs Harbour. That'll make us look as if we are returning from a coastal sail." He shrugged. "Our radar reflector has already been taken down, so it'll be unlikely that we will be spotted until we are close inshore. We'll only hoist it once we're off Woolgoolga."

Pip looked up at him. "There is a deviousness about you, Sebastian McKenzie that I'm only just beginning to appreciate. I can see that I will have to be careful."

Sebastian shook his head. "Nah. I'm just a simple country fellah."

His comment did much to assure her that Sebastian had sloughed off much of the earlier conflict that had tormented him. However, it would take a great deal longer for his grief to dissipate. She was sure it would, with time. Then grief could be be replaced with gratitude…and even pride. She glanced at David. And having pride in a father was a precious thing.

The morning sun was now well up from the horizon. Pip allowed herself to feel joy in the warmth of the sun on her back.

Whisperer dipped her nose into a wave, then rose, shrugging off the water with contemptuous ease. A piece of spindrift tumbled down the side-deck and brushed against her fingers. It might have been a kiss.

Something had ended. A chapter had closed…and it had done so at a good place.

The Australian coast, just seven days away, now represented a future that had hope.

Epilogue

The sun made a half-hearted attempt to peer between the clouds but soon gave up allowing itself to be overtaken by the gloom. It wasn't, he reflected, the most prepossessing return to the land of sun and surf.

Val sat on the foredeck of the catamaran as it nosed its way into the Burnett River. The sails had been furled, and they were now using the engine.

The north bank of the river was bordered by the silty wastes of Barubbra Island. Breakwaters ran either side of the estuary as if trying to ward off the silt and protect the deepwater channel.

Val looked ahead trying to spot what he was looking for—the gap in the southern breakwater. He knew that a small sandy beach was adjacent to the gap. Val had discovered it some years ago when he'd visited the cruising yacht club next door during one of his sailing trips.

He looked down at the bag strapped around his waist. The bag contained all his worldly possessions. It did not, however, include the white handkerchief. He'd never found it.

Val glanced over his shoulder to check that he couldn't be seen.

He couldn't. The dinghy lashed down in front of the doghouse hid him from view.

Good. No one would see him slip into the water.

His muscles were still stiff but were not now quite as sore. His chest, however, continued to ache even though he'd strapped it tight. He suspected that the bullet had broken a rib.

It had so nearly killed him.

Ten layers of Kevlar cut from the storm trysail—stuck together with epoxy had saved him; that, and the scuba tank he'd left under the wharf at the bottom of the pier.

It had been a tedious and painful journey back to Australia. He'd arrived in Port Vila on the copra boat. Then hitched a ride as a deckhand on a catamaran owned by an Australian couple.

The sailing voyage itself had been without incident. His main concern had been avoiding the amorous advances of the woman, and not choking on the marijuana smoke. Val was fairly certain that the couple were smuggling drugs, and he was not confident the boat would escape the attention of the customs service when they arrived at Bundaberg's marina. That was one of the reasons he needed to leave before they docked.

The gap in the southern breakwater was now almost abeam. It was time to go. He rolled over the edge of the decking between the two hulls and hung over the edge allowing his legs to trail in the water.

The muscles in his arms and chest screamed in protest.

Then he let go.

The luxury double-story house was one of many prestigious houses built on pontoons overlooking North Haven Marina. Val had been monitoring one of them for three days, ostensibly while fishing.

Today, however, he was dressed differently. He was wearing a lightweight bio-hazard suit, latex gloves, and a mask. On his back was a knapsack sprayer. There was nothing in its tank other than water.

A good deal less innocuous was the dark blue BMW parked a hundred meters down Gulf Point Drive. Val understood its menace all too well.

He busied himself, spraying water from his lance along the curbside, aiming it at the dandelions and capeweed.

His patience was rewarded when a Bentley Continental drove down the road and turned into a nearby driveway. As the electric garage door opened, Val divested himself of his spray unit.

A man got out of the car…and the garage door began to shut.

Val slipped into the garage and ducked down behind the car.

The driver, a portly man with a bullet-shaped head, began punching the keypad beside the doorway into the house. As the garage door clunked shut, Val stood up from behind the car and walked up to him. "Good afternoon, Mr. Stoddard."

The man spun round. "Who are you? What are you doing here? Get out, or I'll call the police." He pulled a mobile phone from his pocket.

Val reached over and took it from him.

Stoddard looked at his hands in apparent disbelief, then backed away from Val. "Who are you?"

"Let's go upstairs and talk about that, shall we."

Stoddard glanced at him fearfully as he let himself be shepherded up the stairs. When he reached the landing, he lunged toward an umbrella stand and grabbed at a walking stick.

Val stepped forward quickly and chopped him on the wrist with the edge of his hand.

Stoddard dropped the stick and backed away into the lounge room. "Who are you?" he demanded.

"I'm an old friend."

"Don't mess with me. I'm well connected with the police. Who are you?"

For a long while, Val said nothing. Then he pulled down his spray mask. "I am The Valkyrie."

Stoddard's mouth dropped open. "I…I heard you were dead."

Val shook his head. "You, of all people, should know that I don't die."

"But you were shot."

"And who, I wonder, told you that?"

Stoddard swallowed. "I have contacts."

Val nodded. "I bet the Saracens don't know you have a contact in their organization. A drug user, perhaps."

"Drugs! What are you talking about?"

Val made a show of looking around the luxury room.

"You have an expensive house and a luxury motorboat in the marina. How many millions would that be worth? And, of course, the Bentley. It's hard to imagine how you can afford all this on a pension after being a prison governor."

"I don't have to justify myself to you."

"No, but you do have to justify yourself to the dead: to those who have died because of you."

"You're talking rubbish. What could you possibly know?"

"I know more than you'd like, because I've been asking a lot of questions. Would you like to hear some of the things I've been pondering?"

Stoddard said nothing.

Val began ticking them off one by one on his fingers.

"Why were drugs so easily available in the prison while you were the governor?"

"Why did you tell me your daughter was in danger here in Adelaide when she was actually living with your estranged wife in the UK?"

"Why were the Saracens tipped off that I was hiding in the opal fields of South-West Queensland?"

Stoddard began edging away from Val.

Val followed him and continued to speak. "And I had to ask myself: Why would the Saracens want to kill David Albright? He held up a finger. "Shall I tell you what I think? I think you were running a highly lucrative drug cartel in the prison, and the Saracens were your competition." He paused. "So you used me to get rid of them. That was clever. But then you retired, and needed to tidy up loose ends. You needed to get rid of the only people not in your drug cartel who could be used to bring you to justice."

Stoddard said nothing.

"What? Nothing to say?"

Val felt the acid in his stomach begin to boil. He breathed in to keep his anger under control. In front of him was the man who had blighted his life for so long.

"By the way, the Saracens know about you. I told their club president what really happened." Val shook his head. "He's not very happy."

Stoddard looked at him aghast. "You did what!"

"The club president, Mr. Vossik—you may have heard of him. He's not a very forgiving sort."

Stoddard turned away and placed his hands on a sideboard. "No. No!"

Val pressed on. "They've been watching you, Stoddard. Did you know that? Have you seen the dark blue BMW that's been parked in your road off and on for the last few days?"

Stoddard shook his head, as if trying to wake himself up from a nightmare.

"Now you're the one being hunted." Val paused. "How does it feel?"

Stoddard pushed himself away from the sideboard, and began feeling his way backwards.

"And it's not just the Saracens hunting you Stoddard." Val kept pace with him. "I am hunting you, too."

"Y..., you?"

"Yes. I'm the Valkyrie—don't you remember?" He pointed at Stoddard. "And I have chosen you. It's now your time to die."

Stoddard screamed. "No!" Then he spun around, slid open the glass balcony door, and rushed to the balustrade on the far side. But there was no escape. He turned and faced Val, bracing himself on the rail behind him. "No!" he screamed again.

Then hell broke loose.

Stoddard's cries were cut short by the brutal stutter of a machine gun. Glass shattered around him, and the ceiling inside the unit became pockmarked with holes.

Stoddard jerked like a badly controlled marionette and collapsed on the floor.

Just as suddenly as it had started, the gunfire stopped. There was a screaming of tires…and then an eerie hush.

Plaster dust from the ruined ceiling hung in the air.

For a while, Val did not move.

Eventually, he picked himself up from the floor and stared at Stoddard.

His back was a bloodied mess. A dark-red puddle was forming rapidly around him.

Val pulled the breathing mask back over his face and walked downstairs.

He let himself out by the side door, picked up his spray unit and continued walking.

Pip glanced again at the vase on the coffee table. It contained six red roses. Sebastian had organized for a single rose to be delivered every day for the past six days. They'd been having lunch together when the first one was delivered. She'd smiled at the courier at the front door, and carried the rose back to the family room. Sebastian's response had simply been to get up from the breakfast bar, brush her hair to one side, and kiss the rose that was tattooed on the back of her neck.

The memory of it sent a shiver through her.

But Sebastian was not with her now. She was sitting with David, drinking hot chocolate in the family room. The two of them had just returned from the Starlight Restaurant at Windy Point where they'd shared a meal together. It had been a time to say the things that needed to be said—mostly without words.

She was to be married the very next day.

Pip glanced through the glass doors at the window above the garage. Sebastian was not back yet. Some of the young men from St. Georges had taken him out. She rather suspected that David had leaked the fact that Sebastian had no one he could call on to give him a stag night. The men of the church had risen to the challenge with a degree of enthusiasm that caused Pip to warn them of the direst consequences if Sebastian was not delivered to her next day in full possession of his faculties, and in one piece.

"And not too tired," she'd yelled after them. She was hungry to give full physical expression to her love—to explore, to delight, and to share.

Pip remembered the first time she'd seen Sebastian in this very room—his sun-tanned arms, the disturbing brown eyes—and his ridiculous whiskery face that looked like a half-sucked mango seed.

She smiled as she reached for her mug of chocolate. "Thanks for giving me Sebastian, Dad."

"Oh, I did little enough, darling. Sebastian was already seeking in his own way." He held his mug up in salute. "He found his way… and he found you."

She grinned and looked again at the room above the garage. When they returned from their three-day honeymoon in the Barossa Valley, she and Sebastian would be living there. They couldn't afford anywhere else. She reflected sadly on the loss of The Fire Stone, not least for the loss of its sheer beauty. But whilst she may have lost The Fire Stone, she'd found Sebastian.

Their wedding would take place in St. Georges, and the reception was to be in the hall beside the church. There was no wedding caterer. The church community was bringing the food. She smiled. *Just like Vanuatu.* David had dismissed any uncertainty she had with the arrangement saying, "People spend too much on weddings. I only wish they'd invest as much in their marriages. Let it be a community thing. It's more fun."

Mario from *Little Sister* had insisted on making the wedding cake. He'd kissed his fingers. "It will be *magnifico.*" Pip could well believe it. He'd always nursed the secret ambition of being a famous pâtissier.

Tiffany, of course, was scandalized. There was no grand ballroom; no waiters waiting on tables, and no rose arbor. "Pip, it will be so dreadfully…" she seemed to have trouble finding the right word: "earthy," she said.

Pip thought it a lovely compliment.

Her only real regret was that Val wouldn't witness her marriage to Sebastian.

It was still an odd feeling not having him around. She remembered, again how appalled she felt when David broke the news that Val had chosen to die to bring peace with the Saracens. Pip felt she had no right to the extraordinary gift he'd given, and had said so to her father.

"No one ever deserves the grace of another, Pip. That's why it's called grace."

She'd wept, of course. She'd wept for herself, and she'd wept for Sebastian.

Even now, as she reflected on it, a tear ran down her cheek.

Her father noticed it.

"Val?"

She nodded. "I wish he could be here to share..." She didn't finish the sentence.

David arched his back and stretched. "I think he's already had a good share in engineering everything that will happen tomorrow—perhaps more than you think."

"What do you mean?"

"Val, in his own way, did his best to organise a, er...bond between our two families."

"How? When?"

David said nothing.

"Tell me," she insisted.

"Ah, I rather suspect it began on the very first night you met him."

Pip shook her head. "No. I remember that night clearly. He only came to warn us."

"And I think he was entirely sincere about that. I just have a sneaking suspicion that he chose to take things to the next level very quickly."

Pip looked at him disbelievingly.

David shrugged.

She gave him a searching look, knowing as she did that David was very seldom wrong about such things.

"Why?" she demanded. "Tell me."

"I think he saw there was a chemistry between you and Sebastian from the very first, and decided it was a good thing—and potentially the saving of Sebastian."

Pip furrowed her brow. "But, I mean…we never said anything that would indicate…"

"No you didn't. But he saw it."

She sighed. "And I suppose you saw it as well."

Her father nodded.

Pip rolled her eyes. "I didn't stand a chance."

"Darling, it could have gone wrong in a thousand different ways —and Sebastian had a great deal of work to do in order to sort himself out. Nothing was certain." He smiled. "And you were responsible for steering things to their conclusion every bit as much as Val." David leaned forward and wiped the tear from her cheek. "You are very much your own girl, Pip. Never doubt that. And your mother would have been proud of you."

They were silent for a long time.

Finally, David rose from his seat and kissed the top of her head. "Goodnight, darling."

Pip hauled her thoughts back to the present. "Good night, Dad. Thanks for a wonderful evening."

David made his way out of the room, leaving her to her thoughts.

It was surreal. Tomorrow she would be married. Her wedding dress was hanging on the back of her bedroom door! She hugged herself with glee. The dress had a high belted waist, a sleeveless lace bodice, and a softly draping skirt. It was simple yet elegant.

Weariness started to creep over her. She yawned. It was time for bed—not that she was confident she would sleep.

Pip walked down the hallway to her bedroom.

The wedding dress brushed against the door as she opened it.

She glanced round the door to admire it one more time—and froze in shock.

Her mouth fell open.

There, looped around the neck of her dress, hung The Fire Stone.

She looked at it in disbelief.

She reached for it and turned it around in the light.

The fire inside it swirled and danced...

...and kept its secret.

Note from the author

Thank you for reading *The Fire Stone*. I hope you enjoyed it. Please consider leaving a review on Amazon for the benefit of other readers.

A lot of what you read was based on my personal experience of living in the Australian Mallee on the banks of the River Murray, and having the extraordinary privilege of spending a few weeks in the village of Lamap in Vanuatu—amongst the "happiest people on earth."

I'm pleased to be able to report that the "Stone Collection" of books is growing all the time. It includes:

The Atlantis Stone
The Peacock Stone

Four more are in the process of being made available.

To be kept up to date on new releases, sign up to my mailing list at www.author-nick.com. New subscribers will receive an exclusive bonus novelette, *The Mystic Stone*, a complete story, six chapters (15,500 words) in length. It is an adventure that takes place on Caldey Island off the rugged Pembrokeshire coast. I hope you like it.

Notes

Chapter 1

1. Vine blockies are vine growers.
2. 'Uppers' refers to drugs, specifically to stimulant drugs such as dexamphetamine ('dexies' for short).

Chapter 2

1. 'Ute' is the colloquial term for utility, i.e. a pickup truck.

Chapter 11

1. Gyprock is the Australian term for Sheetrock.

Chapter 15

1. A "bogan" is a derogatory Australian term for someone who is unrefined and unsophisticated.

Chapter 24

1. The American equivalent to Panadol is Tylenol.
2. Vegemite is a dark yeast spread that Australians paste onto their bread or toast.

About the Author

Nick Hawkes has lived in several countries of the world, and collected many an adventure. Along the way, he has earned degrees in both science and theology—and has written books on both. Since then, he has turned his hand to novels, writing romantic thrillers that feed the heart, mind, and soul.

His seven full-length novels are known as, 'The Stone Collection.'

His first novel, *The Celtic Stone,* won the Australian Caleb Award in 2014.

Also by Nick Hawkes

The Atlantis Stone

Benjamin is part Aborigine, but nightmares from the past cause him to disown his heritage. Unfortunately, he feels no more at home in the Western world and so struggles to know his identity. Benjamin seeks to hide from both worlds in his workshop where he ekes out a living as a wood-turner. However, an attempt on his life propels him into a mysterious affair surrounding the fabled "mahogany ship" sighted by early white settlers near Warrnambool in Australia.

Felicity, a historian, is seeking to rebuild her life in the nearby town of Port Fairy after a messy divorce. The discovery of the "Atlantis stone" whilst scuba diving results in her joining Benjamin in an adventure that takes them overseas to the ancient city of Cagliari in Sardinia.

An anthropologist dying of cancer and an ex-SAS soldier with post-traumatic stress, join Benjamin and Felicity in an adventure that centres on a medieval treaty, a hunger for gold… and, of course, the Atlantis stone.

More details at www.author-nick.com

(See next page for more)

Also by Nick Hawkes

The Peacock Stone

A young girl comes to live in the slums of New Delhi. It is a place of danger where street gangs rule. Through the initiative of a blind beggar, she is taken to work in the home of a rich businessman. There, she observes a world of education and privilege—a world that is out of her reach.

But danger still stalks.

A kidnap attempt forces her to flee to her childhood home in the tropical backwaters of Kerala—a land of wooden boats, fishing and elephants.

Violence, intrigue and love flourish.

Whether she survives will depend on her being able to understand the significance of the pendant given to her by the blind beggar—the peacock stone.

More details at www.author-nick.com

Made in the USA
Las Vegas, NV
08 September 2021